I0659786

BORROWED
TIME

BOOK 4 - GOLDEN STATE

Infinity Books

DÄNNA WILBERG

Ramirez & Clark
PUBLISHERS

Copyright © 2025 by Dänna Wilberg

All rights reserved.

No part of this book may be reproduced in any form or by any electronic or mechanical means, including information storage and retrieval systems, without written permission from the author, except for the use of brief quotations in a book review.

Cover Designer: Karen Phillips at PhillipsCovers.com.

Editors: Kirk Colvin and Beatrice Gregory

Formatted By: Terry Shepherd at TerryShepherd.com

Published by Ramirez and Clark Publishers LLC

ISBN Paperback: 978-1-955171-55-7

ISBN Hard Cover: 978-1-955171-56-4

This Book is Dedicated to Those Who Have Lost A Child or a Loved One to Drugs.

Evil succeeds when good men do nothing. – Edmund Burke

PROLOGUE

Dante Hernandez stepped in front of his wife and family, his body shaking. "Please, I beg you, not my family."

"Vamos!"

Dante herded his family close to his body. They moved from their plastic tented hovel toward a row of two-foot-high plants. Beyond the rows of plants lay a deep pit referred to as "patio de huesos" the "boneyard."

"Why you do this?"

"Cállate!"

"Please, not my family," he whimpered. "They do nothing."

The man replied to Dante's pleas with the butt of his AK47. "I said, shut up—or I kill you right here!"

Dante dropped to the ground, his wife, mother, father, sister, and children weeping. The man cocked the trigger demanding silence.

Dante struggled to his feet. Holding the torn flesh hanging from his face, he wobbled behind the others. When they reached the end of the boneyard, the man ordered Dante and his family to line up. The man's face filled with glee as his AK47 blasted the family with bullets, their riddled bodies gushing blood as they plummeted to the bottom of the pit.

CHAPTER ONE

Visitors

Death. Darkness. Voices crying in the night. Growling dogs. Rows and rows of greenery...Suzanne Cash winced and flailed in her sleep. Fear made her cry out. "Dear God, make them stop!"

She awoke, drenched in perspiration.

Sitting up at the edge of the bed, she collected herself, breathing in and out to slow her heartbeat. Being psychic took its toll on her, mind, body, and soul. Three months had gone by since her last encounter, but it seemed she had no sooner found reprieve from one situation, when another took its place. Dreams filled with horror, yet she couldn't pinpoint a reason for them. 3 A.M. The witching hour. She needed at least two more hours of sleep.

Her psychic friend Linda Schooler's remedy for times like these took the edge off: *Positive thoughts.* She and Sam were making plans to marry. *Life is good.* And yet burying herself under the covers couldn't get rid of the chill she felt in her bones. *Something bad is going to happen.*

As her body relaxed back into a dream state, she repeated a mantra in her head. *I am safe. I am loved. I am protected by the angels and spirit guides that surround me.* She eased into her alternate universe and began a new story...

It was December...the winds whipped into a frenzy. Drifts of snow collected along the Highway 50 corridor. *Late!* Sam was waiting. She glanced into her rearview mirror. "Mom, you look lovely—doesn't she, Dad?" *If only.* The emptiness she felt was enough to turn the car around and head back down the hill. "Life is but a dream," her mother sang.

The dream didn't last. Suzanne punched her pillow into a mound and wriggled into a comfortable position. She peeked at the glowing numbers taunting her from her nightstand. 3:18 A.M. "What's the use?" She slid out of bed, flipped on the bathroom light, and caught a glimpse of herself in the mirror. "Well, don't you look lovely?" Suddenly, her self-assessment came to a halt. She froze. Standing behind her was a dark-haired woman, her arms beckoning, her feet bare.

Suzanne spun around. "Who are you? And what are you doing in my bathroom in the middle of the night?"

"No sè."

Suzanne sighed. "I don't know either."

**

When Suzanne needed psychic advice, she called upon Linda for advice. "She was Mexican, or Spanish. What little Spanish I remembered from high school allowed me to move her toward the light."

Linda clicked her tongue on the roof of her mouth. "Interesting the visitation would present itself after your dream the dreams you've been having."

"That occurred to me too. She did seem unsettled, and what remained of her disheveled clothing gave me the impression she died under dreadful circumstances." Suzanne followed with a wisp of an idea. "I feel like she was running from something, or someone."

"Let it go, see what comes to you."

"Yeah. Hopefully I'll get some answers before bedtime—but hey—what do you say we have lunch tomorrow? I'd like to go through some bridal magazines with you."

"Oh gosh, I'd love to, but I've got an appointment at the Front Street Animal Shelter tomorrow. I think it's time for me to get another dog."

"Did you have one in mind?"

"I fell in love with a Brittney Spaniel pup. She's adorable."

"Sounds terrific. Another time then?"

"Sure. Why don't you come here? I'll fix lunch. You can meet my new dog."

"I'm warning you—my mother may tag along."

"I thought—"

"Yes. She's on the other side—but for some reason she's been hanging around. In my dreams, in my bedroom. It's kind of daunting. Especially when Sam is over."

"Woo! I can only imagine." Linda gave a whistle; her bird mimicked her in the background. "I hear your phone beeping—Sam, right?"

"You must be psychic! It is, I'll talk to you tomorrow." Suzanne clicked over to the other line. "Hi handsome."

"Hi Beautiful, I was wondering if you're available tonight. Short notice, but I'd love for you to come to my house, I—*we* were invited to a barbeque."

"Sounds fun, what time?"

"See you at 6."

Suzanne hung up, feeling elated. But when she went to

place her phone on the charger, she noticed a cold air pocket in the kitchen. She checked to see if she had left the freezer door open. *Nope.* She stood still, waiting to see if the feeling would manifest into an entity, and it did. Five of them.

**

Sam opened the passenger door for Suzanne, his eyes lingering on her bare legs. "You should wear shorts more often," he said.

She waited for him to get into the car before bestowing a light kiss on his lips. "You look pretty handsome yourself."

"Well, if nothing else, we'll dazzle everyone with our good looks," he replied with a laugh. "Seriously, though...I hope you're not bored. The barbeque is being hosted by one of the new guys. Probably be a lot of shop talk."

"I can hang—besides—if you're there, how can I be bored?"

Sam turned off at the last Camino exit. Half a mile down the road, he pulled onto a long winding drive lined with tall pines and parked diagonally next to a car he recognized. "Spence is here. You'll finally get to meet him."

"The cop with the bad temper?"

"He's doing better—right?"

She smiled, rubbing the tiny bumps surfacing on her arms. "Yes, I get the feeling he is, but—"

"But what?"

"Just a chill, I guess. Glad I brought a sweater." Sam took her hand and led her into the backyard.

"Sam!" Jake Walters called out. He grabbed a petite blonde by the waist and rushed toward Sam and Suzanne. "Hi—you must be Suzanne. I'm Jake, this is my wife, Brigette." Sam extended his hand to Jake's wife. "Come and meet everyone," he said, digging into a cooler and grabbing a couple of beers. "Sam?" He held out a bottle.

Sam declined. "No thanks. What about you, Suzanne?"

Suzanne shook her head. "Maybe a bottle of water later, but thanks." Sam steered her into the crowd, making introductions.

She didn't need an introduction to Spence. She picked up on his energy immediately. She hung back, listening to various conversations, none of which she could relate to until someone mentioned the drug cartels moving into the area. She felt another chill, and the faces she saw in her kitchen that afternoon came flooding back to her. Chestnut colored skin, and dark brown eyes appeared behind her own. "Excuse me," she said. "How many deaths are related to the cartels?"

"Which ones?" Spence stepped forward. "We have several coming up from Mendocino and Tulare County. We have the Sinaloa and Cartel Jalisco Nueva Generación, better known as CJNG—they've facilitated the distribution of billions of dollars' worth of drugs in California. And then you have the Norteño, Nuestra Familiá from Visalia..."

Sam interjected. "There was a massacre in Goshen earlier this year...rival gangs killed six people, including a baby—why do you ask?"

"Just curious," she said. "What smells so good?" She smiled, diverting their attention from her to the barbeque.

Jake picked up her cue. "Hungry? Grab some chicken or a burger—Brigette? Get Sam and Suzanne started on some grub, would'ja, hon?"

Sam walked over to the food table with Suzanne, his voice low, and inquisitive, "What's going on?"

"I had visitors this afternoon—five of them. Spanish speaking. Not sure of their origin, but from the way they were dressed they appeared to be migrant farm workers. I keep getting chills, like they've followed me here."

Sam slipped his arm around her. "We don't have to stay."

"No, I'm fine. I hope you don't mind me asking questions."

"Not at all. You are part of this department, even though you don't have a desk, or a badge." He nudged her. "Would you like a badge?"

"And who would pin it on?"

He lowered his gaze to her breasts. "I would be happy to volunteer."

She nudged him back. "Behave yourself."

As the evening progressed, Sam and Suzanne relaxed into party mode. A five-piece band set up like ninjas and had everyone in the yard rockin' in no time. The lead singer, Jenyn Darwell, was no stranger to the department. She worked in Social Services, and Sam had picked her brain on many occasions when he had juvenile repeat offenders. Mostly drug related. He had no idea Jenyn sang. "Wow, what a set of pipes," he said to Suzanne, but she wasn't listening to him, she was up on her feet, swaying to and fro, and shaking her tush to "Mustang Sally." Sam rose and joined her.

Spence stood close by watching the couple dance. When the music stopped, he took the opportunity to speak, "Why were you asking about the cartels?"

"Curious, that's all."

"Sam told me you have a gift—that you get premonitions or something like that."

"Something like that. Why?"

His mouth spread into a Cheshire grin. "Curious."

"I'd like to know more about the Goshen Massacre, but I'm sure Sam can fill me in."

Spence's pale blue eyes darkened. "If you ever need *me* to fill you in, all you need to do is give a holler."

Sam stepped up behind Spence. "You flirting with my fiancée?"

Spence's sly smile matched his inability to keep his balance.

"No sir. I wouldn't dream of it." He stumbled away, found a chair, and parked his load.

Sam grabbed Suzanne's hand. "Ready to go?"

"Did Spence get to you?"

"No—maybe."

"You don't have a jealous streak, do you, Sam?"

"Something about drunk guys hitting on women bothers me."

"I'm a big girl," she said, kissing him on the cheek. "One last dance? I love this band."

Sam twirled her toward the dance area. "We may have to do this more often." He held her close as they two-stepped to a "Sugarland" tune.

**

When they arrived back at Sam's apartment, he invited her inside. "Did you have fun?"

She threw her arms around his neck. "I did. I didn't realize you were such a good dancer."

"I didn't realize you liked spicy barbeque sauce on— *everything.*"

"Not *everything*," she said, her eyes mischievous.

He unlatched her arms from his neck, kissed her palms, and led her into the bedroom.

**

Morning sun crept across the room. Suzanne stretched across the bed. She heard Sam milling around in the kitchen. She inhaled the aroma of fresh brewed coffee and smiled. She bounced out of bed, wrapping herself in the bedsheet, but when she went into the kitchen, she clutched the sheet to her breast. "Sam?" No answer. *Am I dreaming?* She rushed over to the coffee pot and picked up the note propped up against a porcelain mug.

Suzanne,
Didn't want to wake you. Had a great time last night. Call you
later.
Love, Sam

Suzanne glanced at the clock. It was 10:10. She looked
around the room. *I know what I heard.* She felt someone
watching her. Her skin prickled. She turned around slowly.
The man standing before her bore holes in her soul. Half of his
face was missing, and what was left was filled with contempt.
She collapsed into a kitchen chair. "Why are you here?"

CHAPTER TWO

New Beginnings

Timarie and Paul Phillips met in college. Love at first sight manifested into a thirty-eight-year marriage, a house in La Jolla, California, two grown children and a grandchild on the way.

Paul, forced into early retirement when the garden supply company he worked for was bought out by a growing chain that rivaled Walmart, puttered around the house and worked in the garden. He meticulously reorganized every drawer in the kitchen and took long walks, contemplating the offer he took. The "adios" with a gentleman's shake, the chocolate cake with "Best of Luck" scrawled in blue letters, and the gift card to TOP GOLF. "Be glad you're not stuck here like the rest of us," one of the remaining employees said. But Paul didn't see it that way, he loved his job, and was sorry to go. Depression snuck in while he wasn't looking.

Timarie, tired of teaching fifth grade in a nearby public school, suggested they move. Paul's brow crunched with concern. "Move where? And do what?"

One morning, as if by divine intervention, an ad in the paper sparked her interest. "HORTICULTURISTS WANTED: Established cannabis farms looking for experienced persons to grow and maintain a variety of hybrid plants." She swept her long, wavy hair aside and whispered in her husband's ear. "Let's grow pot."

Paul's eyes widened. "You're kidding me, right?"

Timarie chuckled, "Nope."

"Tim, baby, I haven't grown weed since we were in college."

"It's like riding a bike...besides, this house is getting too big for us. We usually visit the kids on their turf in the Bay Area, so why spend our golden years maintaining," she swept her hand around the room, "all of *this*?"

"It's not cheap to get a grow license in California and it could take years—we'd be better off going to Oklahoma. They aren't as greedy."

"I don't want to be a billionaire, Paul, I just want to take control of our future, make our own way, forget about the principals and CEOs who've been pulling the strings for the last thirty-eight years. It's time we became our own boss, get a little business going, make our own hours, our own rules. We could move closer to the kids and the baby." She snaked her arm around his shoulders. "Isn't it time we put all the money we spent on college degrees to good use?"

"You're right, selling rototillers and chicken shit paid the bills, but maybe it was never meant to be my destiny."

"And teaching kids how to create a tornado in a bottle isn't mine."

Paul went to the kitchen window and gazed at the lush

garden they cultivated year after year. He turned, his mouth forming an upward curve, "Why not? Let's do it."

They spent the next couple of weeks strategizing. Timarie called Olivia, a young woman she met in her travels, who worked as a loan officer at Valor Lending in San Diego. "What are our options?"

"Unfortunately," Olivia said, "most investors will only fund permitted industrial property. Open land is too hard to protect. Finding a warehouse that is already set up as a grow house may be a challenge, but nothing is impossible. Let me see what I can do."

The couple were excited with their new prospects. They still had enough energy to start a business, and the knowledge to make their business successful. Paul shifted gears, spending every waking moment reading up on different varieties of cannabis plants. His master's degree in greenhouse and soil management, and education in plant cultivation, plant science, biology, botany, and horticultural economics, made assimilation a breeze. For the first time in thirty-eight years, he felt he was on his path. Timarie's superpowers included organics, horticulture science, mathematics, and chemistry. Had marijuana been legal thirty years ago, the world would've been their oyster. *Timing is everything.*

Days turned into weeks, weeks into months, with no prospects. Just when they were about to rethink their game plan, luck shifted their way.

"Break out your 'Grateful Dead' T-shirts," Olivia said, over the phone. "I found you just the right deal, but it's in Northern California, a town called Camino. Are you up for moving?"

Timarie and Paul exchanged excited looks. Paul cocked his head and raised his brow. Timarie grinned and nodded. "Yes," they exclaimed at once.

"Wonderful," Olivia said. "Can you come down to our San

Diego office? I'll introduce you to Valor's owner, Darrin Carlin, and we can discuss the terms."

The couple hung up the phone and hugged each other. Timarie's face lit up. "Can you believe it?"

"No, baby—I think you better pinch me." He picked her up and swung her around. "Camino, here we come!"

CHAPTER THREE

The Kenner Place

Suzanne put her call to Linda on speaker phone. "I sleep with one eye open," she said.

"I've never dealt with spirits wandering my bedroom at night," Linda replied. "Sounds like they're stuck."

"It's eerie. I don't know how to help them."

"They were drawn to your light for a reason, Suzanne. What does your intuition tell you?

"I sense something terrible happened—they want justice."

"What else?"

"I also feel they are here to warn me, but warn me of what, I'm not sure."

"I guess all you can do is gather the pieces of the puzzle and try to form the big picture. What does Sam say?"

"I haven't shared everything with him. He has enough on his plate. The catch and release laws are bogging him down.

Sam likes simplicity. Break the law, pay the consequences. Between the robberies, drug dealers, and who knows what else is slipping through the cracks, he's been pressed for time."

"How was the barbeque?"

"Fun—the band knocked it out of the park. I haven't danced in years."

"Sam too? Did he dance?"

"Yes, and he's quite good."

"Do you think your visitors have anything to do with Sam?"

"Funny you should mention Sam—one of the spirits showed up at his house, half of his face mangled."

"Enough to make you pee your pants, I'd say."

"He wasn't with the spirits I saw in my kitchen, but I got the feeling he may be part of the group."

"Car crash?"

Suzanne closed her eyes and let her mind wander, searching for clues. "No, I don't think so." Her heart beat a little faster. Her eyes welled with tears. A faded image of a family flashed by, leaving her with a sense of love, future, hope, *despair*. Suddenly, her body shook, sharp pains jabbed her midsection and the top of her head. A scream lodged in her throat. She felt herself *falling*.

**

Sam called an emergency staff meeting. "Three kids died from fentanyl last night—two, three, and fifteen. The scenario reads like this—the babysitter thought she'd get high while the kids were zoned out in front of the TV. She drops dead. The kids try to help, sampling the fentanyl in the process. We found what appeared to be candy laced with fentanyl on the coffee table."

Jeremy Grimes spoke up, "Is it possible the babysitter didn't know what she was taking?"

Sam sighed. "Yes, it's very possible—in which case we have a bigger problem than we thought."

Spencer held up his hand. "We've been staking out a couple of the new grow houses up the hill. Rumor has it the guys running these operations have moved up from Tulare County. The property is permitted to—" He glanced down at his paper, "Dan Fielding, but here's the deal. No one has seen Dan in months. One of his neighbors said he mentioned visiting his daughter, another said he was sick and in the hospital. We checked. Neither one is the truth."

Jake Walters chimed in, "Dan's up a few exits from me, on the other side of Highway 50—I noticed there's a for sale sign on the property east of his place. The Kenners lived there—went to school with Josh Kenner. They've been growing medical marijuana for years. I asked around, no one has seen the Kenners either. Not sure if there's any connection."

"Check with the county office, see if their permit is current, and find out when the property went up for sale. And check on the zoning, if I recall that area was rezoned as industrial after the last election."

Spence narrowed his eyes. "What are you sayin', Sam?"

"I'm saying two things—one—there aren't enough of us to go around so keep your ears and eyes open at all times, and two —I want to know who's responsible for killing those kids."

After his men dispersed, Sam picked up the phone and dialed the Planning and Building Department. "Let me talk to Russ in the Commercial Cannabis Department. Tell him it's Sam, he'll know who it is."

Moments later, "Sam—how's it goin', buddy?"

"Fuckin' peachy, Russ. We have three more dead kids. When is the FBI going to approve Live Scan so we can track these scumbags?"

"Why fix the wagon if it's not broken, Sam?"

"Not broken? You call fentanyl-coated candy not broken? Two, three, and fifteen, Russ! You call that not broken?"

"Simmer down, now. What makes you think our process of issuing permits has anything to do with those kids, and I'm sorry, by the way—I have grandkids that age—it's tragic. But you know yourself, the county needs the money the cannabis industry brings in, and it's your job to see that all the applicants are checked out once they finish with HdL."

"You know that's bullshit, Russ."

"We are screening the applicants, if they come in as legit—"

"Until the cartel runs them out of town and steals their business out from under them."

"And how is that our fault?"

"The cartel is like spurge, Russ, all it takes is one spore to take over the whole goddamn yard. Between our open borders, lack of law enforcement, and our incompetent protocol, we have one hell of an infestation. Who is following up on the permits—making sure they're complying?"

"You know we don't have that kind of manpower."

"Does that mean no one is checking on these clowns?"

"Take it up with the Governor, Sam."

"Yeah, right."

**

Sam's nature to investigate everything himself took him east on Highway 50 and north off Carson Road. He followed Spence's handwritten directions until he saw the real estate sign Spence mentioned in the meeting. Sam double-checked the description he was given of the property and eased down the gravel road. Barbed-wire fencing gave way to rock outcroppings, scrub oaks, sugar pines, manzanitas, and blackberry bushes. He imagined a person living a peaceful existence in the serene setting had it not been for a row of low cement structures spoiling the beauty.

He counted six, twelve-foot-high rectangular, windowless, concrete buildings. Pitched metal roofs covered in solar panels were the only features that gave the buildings character. The grow-houses Sam saw at lower altitudes had flat roofs, but he figured plants were grown year-round, and it would be easier to maintain an angled roof when it snowed.

Gravel crunching under the weight of a heavy vehicle warned Sam he had company. A man with a toothy grin rolled down his window.

"Help ya?"

"Are you the selling agent for this property?" Sam knew quite a few of the agents in town. This guy wasn't on his radar.

"Was—it sold last week—couple from SoCal bought it—why?"

"Just curious." Sam flashed his badge. The man's lips clamped tight. "Did you know the Kenners?"

"No, sir."

"Who hired you to sell the property?"

"The bank—property went into foreclosure—owner fell behind on his payments."

Sam nodded toward the padlock on the gate. "Mind if I have a look around?"

"Sorry. No can do—not without a warrant."

"If I was a buyer, would I need one?"

"Well, no—but—"

"And what if the buyers don't come through? Don't you usually have a back-up plan?"

"Why yes—but—"

Sam's eyes narrowed. "But what?"

"What is it you're looking for?"

"Oh," he said, jamming one hand in his pocket. "A place to retire one day. A place like—*this*." Sam knew growing cannabis required more water in low humidity areas such as this. "Is there a pond on the property? I love to fish."

The man's toothy grin returned. "Okay, I'll let you take a peek, but no photos."

"Cool." Sam stepped aside while the man unlocked the gate. "Love to build on a piece of land like this myself, one day."

"It's certainly beautiful. Where's the pond?"

"It's a hike."

"I'd love to see it."

The man checked his watch. "I need to be back in the office in an hour. If we hurry, we'll catch sight of it over the next rise."

The concrete buildings seemed ominous up close. Sam stopped, bending down to remove a stone from his shoe. The man seemed nervous.

"Like I said, I need to get back in the office."

Sam scanned the area while bent down with his back to the man. "Sorry, I detest the deep ridges in the soles on these shoes. The tiny stones drive me nuts."

"I hear ya." The man relaxed and continued his tour. "If this place were mine," he said, pointing to a lush thicket of bushes teaming with plump berries. "I'd be making me some blackberry jam. Look at those beauties!"

"Yeah, makes one wonder why people choose to grow marijuana in this area when there are so many other options."

The man gave Sam a side glance. "Simple. Money. And I would venture to say that some endeavors require privacy."

"A little too private if you ask me." He gestured to the openness. "Be easy to bump someone off, steal their crop."

Shocked, the man replied, "You think someone *killed* the Kenners?"

Sam chucked, "Just an observation, that's all." He cleared his throat. "What kind of fish are in the pond, any idea?"

**

Suzanne danced around the kitchen, Keener13 radio, turned up high. She sang, proud of herself when she stayed on key. Sam had invited himself to dinner, and she couldn't wait to see him, hold him, make love.

"Do You Believe in Magic" came on, making her smile. *Is magic what Sam and I have?* She wanted to believe it. "Mom?" She danced over to the refrigerator and pulled out items for a salad. "Mom? Can you hear me?" She listened. "I want you to know—if you want to go dress shopping with me next week, I would love to get your opinion." She lifted a metal bowl from the cabinet below her counter. "Linda is going too, which will be fun, but she's not you—you always picked out the prettiest dresses for me...homecoming...winter ball...prom. You always knew which dress would look best, even if it was still on the hanger."

She rinsed two handfuls of spring mix and patted it dry. "Do you remember when Jack and I went to winter ball? I wanted to wear a friend's dress, and you insisted on driving to San Francisco to the Jessica McClintock outlet store? And we had lunch at that Italian restaurant?" She sliced red grapes in half and set them aside. The olive oil went into the bowl first, followed by dehydrated onions. "Jack's jaw dropped when he saw me in the dress you picked out." She sighed. "I don't think I ever told you how much that day meant to me—or how right you were about the dress."

The universe had a way of tuning into her emotions when tears were about to spill. Jimi Hendrix sang "Angel." She listened carefully to the lyrics. "Yes, Mom, we were like the moon and the deep blue sea. How I miss you."

She wiped her eyes with the back of her hand. A chill gave way to a shiver. She looked for the source, expecting her mother to be standing in her kitchen. Instead, she saw a young woman, holding a child.

"Where did you come from?" Suzanne waited for an answer. Pictures formed in her brain. A truck circling a group of people, spraying dust in their tear-stained faces. The woman protected the baby as best she could, until the driver stuck his weapon out of the window and killed them all.

"I'm sorry," Suzanne said. Her heart filled with pain. "What do you want from me?" The air in the room grew colder as more spirits stepped forward. Spirits of various ages. Some maimed, some whole. The word "justicia" burned behind her third eye. "Justicia." *Justice.*

**

Sam arrived at seven-thirty. His clean-shaven appearance exited her. She touched his face, and kissed his lips. "I've missed you."

He circled her waist and drew her near. "Not half as much as I've missed you." His tongue slipped inside her mouth, and she welcomed him, pressing her body closer to his. "Dinner is ready, we should eat while it's hot," she said, gyrating her hips against his.

"Did I ever tell you how much I love cold food?"

She moaned. "I believe God made microwaves for moments like this." His hand cupped her breast, and her breath quickened with his arousal. "I think we should work up an appetite then—"

"You're not only beautiful, intelligent, and delicious—you are practical as well."

She took his hand and led him up the stairs. "I love when we agree."

Sam removed his clothes and pulled the blanket over them both. "What do you have the thermostat set on? It's freezing in here."

Suzanne wriggled out of her panties and tossed them on the floor. "It's not my air conditioning."

"No?" He nibbled on her shoulder, and his free hand roamed her body.

Suzanne responded to his touch, arching her back. His kisses knew no boundaries, and she wanted to enjoy every one, but—

"What's wrong? Relax."

"I can't."

He brought the blanket up further and tucked it under her chin. "Better?"

"That's not it—"

He propped himself up on one elbow. His pinched brow spoke volumes. "Tell me then—what's wrong?"

"You can't see them, but," she pointed to the wall across the room. "there's a group of dead people standing over there."

Sam's eyes grew large. "Holy shit!"

CHAPTER FOUR

Doubt

Sam's stare unnerved Suzanne. "What is it, Sam?"

"I should be used to it by now."

"IT? You mean *me?*"

"How can I blame you for something you can't control? I'm sure you didn't summon those spirits into the bedroom while we were making love! I mean–Geezus, there's a time and a place."

Suzanne didn't have an answer. Lifting her coffee cup to her lips, she returned his comment with a glare.

He reached across the table for her free hand. She moved it further away. "C'mon, Sweetheart. Don't be that way."

"And what way is *that*, Sam?"

Sam pushed away from the table. "I gotta go. We can talk later when you're not so confrontational."

"Confrontational? Now I'm confrontational."

"I'm sorry if I upset you." He kissed her forehead. "I'll call you later."

"Sure." She winced when the door slammed. *Dammit.* The cold spot in the kitchen spread across the room. She closed her eyes. "*What* do you *want?*" she snapped. A little girl stepped forward. Bullet holes dotted her small frame, her eyes, sad. Suzanne heard the name Trina in the recess of her mind.

"Trina?" The girl nodded. "Who did this to you?"

"A very bad man," the girl said telepathically. "There."

The girl pointed, and Suzanne saw her standing among the others at the edge of a pit. She heard their cries, saw the spray of bullets, and understood...the assassination was an act of *power.* A snake coiled around the image, reared its head, and rattled its tail. Black eyes loomed in her visual cortex. A man's reflection filled the obsidian orbs. Rattler skins circled the man's boots. An AK-47 rested in his arms like a baby, a smile plastered on his face.

"I see the man," Suzanne said, searching the room for the little spirit. Her voice sent another chill.

"He's coming for them."

"Who Trina? Coming for who?"

The girl was gone.

Suzanne lumbered up the stairs, her heart heavy. She turned on the shower and stripped out of a flimsy T-shirt and a pair of Sam's running shorts she had snatched on one of their trips. She lifted one long leg over the tub, then the other. The warm spray felt good against her weary skin. How was she supposed to make sense of it all? *Why come to me?*

The last thing she wanted to do was stress Sam out with more of her visions. He tried so hard to understand her, what she endured each time images flooded her third eye, each time she was helpless to make them stop. She soaped up a loofa sponge and began to scrub. Scrub away her angst. Scrub away her fear. Scrub away a gift that kept increasing, making her life a living hell. She threw the sponge at the wall and collapsed in the tub. Her tears blended with the water. Her shoulders shook. Her mother's face swam in front of hers. "C'mon, baby girl," she said. "You're stronger than this." Suzanne swatted at the air.

"I'm only human," she screamed.

CHAPTER FIVE

On the Road

"Is that it?" Timarie shoved a pillow on top of the cooler resting at the edge of the tailgate.

Paul nodded. "She's packed to the gills." He slipped his arm around his wife's petite waist. I'm going to miss this old place."

"Me too," she said, resting her head on his shoulder. "You ready?"

He swatted her backside. "You driving? Or me?"

"You go first. I want complete control of the radio." She smiled. "Wait until you hear the tunes I packed for when we lose reception."

His eyes grew large. "Did you rescue my Beatle collection from the garage sale?"

Her eyes twinkled. "You betcha!"

They both climbed inside their 2022 Ram ProMaster, the

vehicle they chose for its cargo features and retro CD player. No rear side windows gave them a feeling of security hauling their equipment, and the few prized possessions they were taking to their new home.

"I spoke with Olivia earlier," Timarie said. "She said a woman named Lucille will meet us in the morning with the key. She lives in Camino too, so she's flexible."

"Did you find a hotel for us to hang out in until we clean up the place?"

"I thought that's what you were doing on your laptop this morning while I was packing our toiletries?"

"Nope," he squeezed her knee. "I was finalizing the insurance and sending change of address notices to the bank and SSI." He rubbed her shoulder. "We want to make sure we get our checks in the mail, don't we hon?"

"Of course." She covered his hand with hers. "We can look for a place when we stop for dinner." Timarie watched the past thirty-five years of their life disappear in the side view mirror with a sudden feeling of foreboding. "I hope we're doing the right thing."

He glanced her way. "We haven't hit the highway yet, Tim—wait until we at least get to Barstow before you start having regrets."

～

CHAPTER SIX

Helpless

Sam sat behind his desk pouring over reports that had come in the last few days. Drugs. He had worked in Goldorado County for fifteen years. He watched kids grow up, the population rise exponentially, businesses come and go. For the most part, the vibe had stayed the same. Poverty reared its ugly head when the mill closed, putting hundreds of people out of work. Those who had owned property hung onto it like it was gold, doing what they could to make payments, even if it was something illegal. Those who couldn't cut it, lived on the streets, at least physically. Mentally, many of them had checked out long ago.

Jake Walters rapped on the door, breaking his reverie. "What is it, Jake?"

"We had another overdose last night—just wondered if you heard?"

"No." Sam steepled his hands on his desk. "Who was it?"

"You know Lefty Matthews—the owner of the gas station on Missouri Flat? His kid, Brian."

Sam bowed his head. "Sweet Jesus."

"Found him on Carson Road. Bare-naked, scrapes up and down his body. Looked like he got mauled by a bear, but the doc at Marshall said the wounds were self-inflicted." Jake shook his head. "We found an e-cigarette near the body. I sent it to the lab. "The doc said his heart stopped."

"Did you talk to Lefty? How's he doing?"

"Not good. He started howling like a coyote in heat. Spence hung out with him for a while. His sister showed up, said she was going to stay the night."

"Good. Any idea where he got the drugs?"

"Really Sam? There's shit everywhere! We've got dealers coming up from the border, setting up their little labs—grow houses—selling right out in the open. Like—what are we going to do to them? We make an arrest, they're out in twenty fuckin' minutes!"

"Settle down—I know. Unfortunately, I don't make the laws. I just try to enforce the ones we still have."

"It's bullshit, Sam—if we fart the wrong way there's an investigation—and yet we can't nail these guys for killin' our kids. Brian was fifteen, Sam—*fifteen*."

"I'll stop by Lefty's place later, offer my condolences. Maybe he can give us the names of Brian's friends. Meanwhile, check out the schools, see if anyone's heard anything about a party, or knows where Brian hung out."

Sam pounded his fist on the desk. Jake was right. He felt like they were in a chicken fight, a pillowcase over their heads, hands tied behind their backs...*the bad guys are winning*.

His mind took a detour. Suzanne. *She knows*. He thought about the ghosts, or spirits, or whatever the hell they were—

watching. Sometimes he wished he could communicate with them, establish a few rules. Number one: the bedroom is off limits—and the bathroom. Number two: No shenanigans during dinner, or when they had plans, or company. Number three: One appearance, none of this nightly stuff, or showing up in the morning while they were having coffee. He stabbed his pen into the ink blotter on his desk. *Get used to it buddy.*

He picked up his phone. "Hey sweetheart, hope you're having a great day. I have a stop to make on my way home. I'll give you a call afterwards. Miss your beautiful face. Bye."

Suzanne saw the light blinking on her phone. She knew it was Sam. She felt his energy. Saw his face behind her lids. Thought about his touch. *He'll be late.*

**

The convergence of the two psychic minds began over pomegranate spritzers served in Linda's sunny kitchen at a table set with quaint, colorful dishes and a bouquet of fresh flowers. Linda listened intently as Suzanne bared her soul.

"He was angry, I could tell."

Linda patted Suzanne's hand. "I can't imagine Sam being angry—he loves you too much, girl!"

"You're right, I'm being dramatic. It was the way he looked at me. Do you really think getting married is a good idea?"

"What?" Linda's eyes grew large. "Why—are you having second thoughts?"

"I love him, I truly do—that's why—oh, Linda, I don't want to make him crazy. I mean—dead people showing up out of the blue? It's unnerving enough for me—"

"Have you discussed your concerns with him?"

"Yes, many times, but each situation has been different—either someone is hijacking my mind, or showing me pictures, or—this is really the first time since Jack—"

"I can see your point. But Sam—Sam loves you. He knew what he was getting himself into—"

Linda rose and returned with two summer salads with roasted golden beets and fresh sliced strawberries, goat cheese, and pecans. The two women ate in silence, until...

Suzanne smiled. "You're right. We're a team."

Linda exhaled. "You had me worried."

"How do I establish house rules, Linda? How do I keep spirits from ruining my relationship with Sam?"

"You told me they want justice—perhaps if you and Sam work together—like you have in the past, you'll be able to give them what they want, and they'll leave you alone.

"I don't know where to start. I have no idea where they were murdered."

"Ask them."

"You really think it's that easy?"

"Haven't you done exactly that in the past?"

"It was different, the people I was looking for were alive."

"So were the people you're seeing—at one time. They won't rest until justice is served."

"You're right."

"I hope you saved room for pie."

**

Suzanne felt better after visiting with Linda. She was grateful for her advice and a delightful lunch. When she arrived back home, she put her purse down on the counter and closed her eyes. "Trina, if you're here, you need to show me where it happened. Show me where they took your life."

She waited. Nothing happened. And then suddenly, she was whisked away to a dark place...

She heard crickets. The heat of the night, cloying, suffocating...a woman sang softly in Spanish. The child in her arms, motionless. Sleeping? No. Images flashed through her mind.

The woman on her knees, pleading with a large man with a gun. "Please Senõr, I beg you. She's sick." Suzanne grabbed her head, feeling the blow.

"Trina, where did this happen? Show me where—"

Suzanne felt herself transported to a place deep in the woods. The thickness of the trees became dizzying as she searched for a landmark. An owl hooted and swooshed overhead. The sky, filled with stars. In the distance, she saw a campfire. There was music. Laughter. *Where are you?*

The phone rang.

"Hi Sweetheart, did you get my message?"

"I'm sorry, yes, but I didn't listen. I went to Linda's for lunch. I'm trying to figure out where my ghost buddies came from, so I can help them—and then, maybe, they'll go away."

"I really didn't mean to be so obtuse this morning—"

"I didn't need to react so harshly."

"I'm on my way to comfort a grieving father—can I call you later?"

"Of course. And Sam?"

"I hope you're going to tell me you love me—it's been a day."

"Now who's the psychic one?"

**

Sam rapped on a wooden screen door a few times before he heard a gruff voice telling him to enter. Lefty Matthews sat sprawled in a recliner, a beer in one hand, a pile of cigarettes burnt to ashes in the saucer balancing on the arm of the chair. His eyes, red rimmed, stared off into space.

"I can't begin to tell you how sorry I am, Lefty," Sam said.

"Fuck you are," Lefty grumbled. "He wouldn't be layin' in the goddamn morgue if you did your job."

"I wish I could take the blame—it would make it that much easier to correct the problem—and I would—in a heartbeat. But you and I both know things have changed around here, and try as we may, we have limited resources, and we can't keep an eye on every kid that goes out on Friday night. These kids are getting the drugs from somewhere—and I need your help to find out how Brian scored the drug that killed him."

Lefty squeezed tears from his eyes as his chin trembled, and his shoulders did a misery dance. "I told him to stay away from those kids—I knew they were trouble—their fuckin' pierced ears, that black shit around their eyes. Brian was a good kid—never gave me no grief—got good grades—" He lifted his gaze. "He got a job makin' pizzas—started savin' for a new snowboard."

Sam squatted down, placed a hand on Lefty's arm, "I won't quit until I find out who's behind this—you have my word."

CHAPTER SEVEN

Things that Go Bump in the Night

Timarie turned off Interstate 5 onto Highway 33 in Santa Nella. "I've been wanting to stop at Anderson's Pea Soup Restaurant since I was a kid," she said.

Paul chuckled. "I hate pea soup."

"Too bad. I'm sure they have something you do like—besides, it's all about the experience."

"Don't you wish we aged in reverse? I love this new spontaneity—even if it is over pea soup."

Timarie laid her hand in his lap. "Did you have something else in mind?"

He brought her hand to his lips. "You don't want me to have a heart attack before we start our new life, do you?"

"I packed your medicine—it's on the back seat, in the blue bag."

"Always looking out for me—that's what I love about you."

"And you go along with whatever it is I want to do—that's what I love about YOU."

Once they were seated in the restaurant, the couple marveled at the extensive menu and the Danish décor. "See, they have pork chops—you love pork chops," Timarie said. "Yum—mashed potatoes, gravy, all the things you shouldn't have."

Paul sighed. "The broiled salmon looks good. So do the shrimp skewers. What I'd really like is a juicy steak."

"You've been so disciplined, Paul. I don't think this once will hurt you."

"It's decided then." Paul gave the waitress both orders and said, "Now we just need to find a place to stay tonight."

Timarie opened her phone and began a search. "The Cary House sounds nice."

"Isn't that the place that's haunted?"

"Maybe. Is that a 'pass'?"

"What else is there?"

"Not much. Should I look for an Airbnb?"

"It's short notice," he said. "And we need long term."

"Let's stay at the Cary House until we can find something."

Paul agreed. "Hopefully we won't have an Ebenezer Scrooge experience."

"I've always considered myself an empath...you never know."

**

Before Paul and Timarie checked into the Cary House at 8:30 P.M., Paul checked the locks and engaged the special alarm they had installed on their new vehicle. The equipment they brought with them was fully insured, but some of it would be difficult to replace, and to him, the price of the alarm justified any inconvenience caused by someone's sticky fingers.

No one would be able to see the contents of the van by looking through the driver or passenger window, and the anti-theft mechanism he had installed made it difficult for someone to break in, never-the-less, nothing was full proof, and the right person with the right tools could abscond with thousands of dollars' worth of stuff.

The high-tech grow tent the Phillips' had purchased to get started accommodated four to eight plants. Before agreeing to trade their palatial home for a farm, he soaked the ten "skunk" seeds he had kept in a film canister in a wooden box since college to see if they would grow. To his delight, five females flowered, and three males were viable. The variety originally bred by Dutch Passion in 1978, had been crossed with Mexican, Afghani, Columbian and a secret blend he and his roommates cultivated in the closet in their dorm room. Skunk, being 65% Indica, a strain that produced a voluptuous plant, easier to grow, with a THC content of 16-22%, and a CBC/CBN of 1% made the product more marketable.

Paul climbed into bed next to Timarie, who had her nose in the "Cannabis Grow Bible." He knew she was already planning a crop layout, and adding up the dollars it would cost to implement their ideas. "We have so many choices, Paul—if this doesn't work out, we can grow grapes."

"We've sunk a lot of money into this farm, I'm betting on us making a killing with Betty and Joe."

"You've named the plants?"

Paul gestured toward the small terrarium in the corner of the room. "Betty, Joe, and the gang."

"Sounds like a rock band."

He draped an arm around her middle. "Tomorrow—our future unfolds."

She kissed him lightly, closed her book, and clicked off the light. "Are you nervous?"

"No, should I be?"

"Trepidation is a natural response to uprooting your life to start a pot farm, I guess." She snuggled closer to Paul. "They sure do keep it cold in here."

**

At first, Timarie thought she was dreaming. She rubbed her eyes, blinked a few times. The figure remained, floating to the left of the doorway. She grabbed Paul's arm and shook him. "Paul," she hissed, "Paul. Wake up!"

Paul groaned. "What?"

"There's someone in the room."

Paul rolled over and sat up. "Where?" He reached for the switch on the table lamp. "I don't see anything."

"There—by the door."

"Tim, you must've been dreaming, hon. There's no one there."

"I can see him—he's—he's full of bullet holes."

Paul squinted, trying to appease his wife. "Sorry, my darling. I don't see anyone."

"He's standing right there for fuck sake!"

Paul pulled Timarie into his arms. "There's no one there, honey." He squeezed her in his embrace and kissed her temple. "Try and go back to sleep, hon. We have a big day tomorrow."

Timarie shivered. The man turned and disappeared through the wall.

**

The next morning, the couple walked down the block to Sweetie Pies. The restaurant was filled with patrons. After a fifteen-minute wait, they were shown to a table. Later, when their food arrived, they dug in, slathering butter on thick slices of cinnamon walnut toast.

"What if it's an omen?" Timarie stabbed at her ham and cheese omelet.

Paul sipped his coffee, concern creasing his brow. "I'm sure what you saw was a combination of your imagination kicking in after reading all the reviews for the hotel and being exhausted."

"Never saw a ghost before—perhaps you're right."

"This bread tastes homemade—try the olallieberry jam."

"Is that your way of saying you don't want to discuss what I saw?"

"Not at all—I'm serious—this may be the best goddamn toast I've ever tasted."

Timarie scooped a spoonful of jam onto her buttered toast. "When we were kids, my friends and I tried to summon Mary Worth."

Paul stopped mid bite. "And—"

"Nothing happened, really, except a couple of the girls freaked out and called their moms to come and get them. I, however, will swear to this day that someone or something touched my hair."

"You're not really sorry we did this, are you?"

"No—it was my idea. And I'm not losing my mind—I know what I saw."

"I believe you, Tim. And you did warn me that you're the empathetic one."

She reached for his hand. "This is why I love you. You never doubt me."

He smiled. "Never will."

CHAPTER EIGHT

Sleepless Nights

A sleepless night didn't help Sam's mood. He left Lefty's place later than he anticipated the night before. His heart hurt listening to the man cry over his son. Sam remembered when Brian was ten, how he said he wanted to be a police officer. "Catch bad guys." *Like me.* Lefty lost his wife to cancer and had been raising Brian on his own. The loss of his wife was a punch to the gut. Losing Brian was a kick in the balls. No one deserved to lose a child. *No one.*

By the time Sam had arrived home, it was late. He called Suzanne as promised, but she sounded sleepy, so he didn't keep her on the phone. He tossed and turned most of the night unable to get her off his mind. The haunted look in her eyes that morning when the entities appeared in the kitchen...He hated seeing her like that—vulnerable and burdened by the weight of her psychic abilities. He wanted so badly to carry her load—but there was nothing he could do. The visions were an integral part of her, like her beauty and intelligence. All he could do was listen, be supportive. *Believe.*

He bunched up a pillow and held it to his chest, imagining her soft skin against his, the smell of her hair. Sometime after 3A.M. he fell asleep.

**

The next morning, Jake tossed a folder on Sam's desk. "Here's the names of the couple that bought the Kenner place. They're scheduled to pick up keys today."

"Thanks. I took a ride out there. Looks like a nice place."

"Yeah, the Kenners seemed happy there—until they disappeared."

"We don't know that, Jake."

"They vanished, Sam."

"There was activity on their credit cards..."

"So?"

"Jake—we have other issues that need our attention. Kids are dying at an alarming rate—let's focus on them for now." Sam flipped through the folder Jake brought in. "Another cannabis grow business—great." He slammed the folder closed. "Any luck at the high school?"

"Talked to a couple of punks. They had amnesia of course—"

"Keep trying. I want to know where Brian Matthews scored those drugs."

The phone rang. Sam nodded at Jake. Their meeting ended when Sam picked up the phone.

"Hey Sam, Curt here from the coroner's office—got a minute?"

"Hi Curt, yeah, what'cha got?"

"Brian Matthews tested positive for alpha-pyrrolidinopentiophenone—Flakka."

"Bath salts?"

"Yeah, Flakka is one of the newer psychoactive synthetic cathinones. Also referred to as the Zombie drug."

"That would explain the self-harm the ER doc assessed on arrival."

"Yeah, self-harm, delusions, violence, aggression—Flakka prevents the reuptake of norepinephrine and dopamine in the brain—increases heart rate—which is what ultimately killed the kid."

"Heart attack?"

"Yep."

"How many of these cases are coming in, Curt?"

"Bath salts? Dozens—first for Flakka. Bath salts are cheap—five bucks a hit. People think we have a meth and fentanyl problem—this stuff is just as bad or worse because it's affordable."

"Thanks for calling me directly, Curt, I appreciate it. Send me the report."

"I don't envy you, Sam."

"It's a shit-show, alright. The drug dealers are making the stuff here now—every time we get one formula on the illegal substance list, another one pops up."

"I'll let you know if any more Zombies come in—good luck."

Sam carefully replaced the phone on its cradle. He pulled out his cell and keyed a group text to Spence, Jake, and Jeremy. IN MY OFFICE NOW.

**

Relieved and well rested, Suzanne busied herself with laundry and yard work. A load in the wash, one in the dryer gave her time to tend to her roses. It had been a week or two since her mother made an appearance, she thought maybe getting outside would ground her, raise her vibration.

Suzanne grabbed a ball cap and her shears. The temperature was perfect. She took a deep breath and exhaled. Something brushed her shoulder, and she spun around. "Steven! Why do you insist on scaring the crap out of me?"

"I rang the bell—"

"How am I supposed to hear it if I'm outside?"

"Communing with nature?"

"Yes...and you? Why are you here?"

"I was in the neighborhood—Karen went to her mom's—she fell—broke her hip."

"Sorry to hear that—want some coffee?"

"Sure. Can we sit out here? I love this yard."

"Remember when we used to climb that tree?"

"I do—and you were scared shitless—climbing up *and* climbing down."

"Want cream?"

"Please."

Suzanne slipped inside, checked her laundry, and poured two cups of coffee. Once they were fixed to their liking she returned to the patio. "I haven't seen mom in a while—is she hanging out at your house?"

"Don't be ridiculous, Suz."

"Why are you *really* here?"

"Do you think Karen's cheating on me?"

"Why would you think such a thing?"

"Just a feeling. Thought maybe you could turn on your superpowers and tune into her head or something."

Suzanne snipped a dead blossom off her rose bush. "What I *can* tell you is that if you are half the jerk with her that you are with me, I'd leave your ass in a heartbeat."

"I'm serious, Suz. She said her mom broke her hip, but I think she had this trip planned way before it happened."

"I'm listening—"

"I figured I'd clear some of the icons off the desktop while she was gone, you know, that tedious shit some people don't make time for?"

"And?"

"I thought I'd clear out the cookies, the history, defrag the disc, give her more room."

"I need to do that, too."

"While I was scrolling through the history, I saw she had been checking out flights weeks ago."

"Maybe visiting her mother was on her mind before the fall?"

"That's not all—I stalked her Facebook page. Guess what I found?"

Suzanne put the shears down and sat by her brother's side. "I have no idea."

"Tage Betterman, a guy she dated in college was all over her page."

"All over? What does that mean?"

"They were majorly flirting—with their fucking little hearts and emoji's."

"So, you think she's with him and not her mother—"

"He lives a block away from her mom's house. She packed her best underwear!"

"Oh Steven, Karen's not like that—"

"She's changed, Suz. We used to have the same tastes in food, TV shows, movies, books—now we can't agree on anything." He shook his head. "Don't even get me started on our sex life."

"Thanks. I appreciate the omission."

"What do you think? Anything coming to you?"

"Steven, it doesn't work like that. Why don't you ask her?"

"And if I'm wrong? My suspicions will drive another wedge between us."

"Pay a surprise visit to her mother's. It might help if she sees you as a compassionate husband rather than a jealous idiot."

"My cup is empty, dear sister." He handed her his cup.

"I need to get my laundry out of the dryer."

"I can wait."

Suzanne knew what it was like to have doubts. She felt bad for Steven, and yet she couldn't imagine being married to someone like him. *Filterless. Controlling.* She also knew Steven could be sweet and charming when he wanted to be. She burst through the back door.

"You want my honest opinion?"

Steven scrambled to his feet. "Are you getting something?"

She placed two fingers in the middle of her forehead and closed her eyes. "Yes, I'm getting something alright—I see a man—he can be a buffoon, rude, inconsiderate, and egotistical—"

"Does he have blonde hair? 6'2?"

"I see a woman who is patient, kind, loving—what I don't see is them together much longer—" she opened her eyes. "If he is going to continue being a horse's ass!"

"You're kidding me, right?"

"Steven, offer her a rose, not a cactus. If she's soaking up some love from this guy it's because she's not getting it from you." She held up one hand. "Trust me."

Steven collapsed in the chair. His shoulders slumped. "Why do you always have to be right?"

"Because I love you, and I want what's best for you."

Steven jumped up and kissed her forehead. She laughed and hugged him tight. "Mom's here. She's giving me a thumbs up."

**

Once Steven departed, Suzanne showered, dressed in a

grey romper, and headed out. She decided to do some research on communicating with spirits by going to a metaphysical store and perusing their selections.

Linda had recommended Planet Earth Rising as a source for materials, meditation tools, crystals, and books. When Suzanne arrived, she was overwhelmed with the selection the store offered.

"Can I help you?" Suzanne spun around, coming face to face with a handsome gentleman with long golden hair banded at the nape of his neck, and amber-colored eyes.

"I'm just looking—a friend recommended I come here for a book on spirits."

"Ah—are we talking communication, manifesting, dealing with a death experience?"

"I'm new to this, so I thought I'd browse a bit."

"Let me show you what we have." Electricity zinged through her body as he touched her elbow and guided her forward. "This way."

His touch made her woozy. The images dancing in her head were unsettling, haunting, erotic. She saw herself in his arms, their bodies tangled in heated pursuit of fulfilment. Breathing in unison, fingers entwined, the image came forward, revealing intent...the braided gold bands on their fingers matched.

He reached out to grab her, his smile genuine, concerned, "Are you all right?" His gaze fixed on hers. A knowing of something yet to be discovered came and went in a flash. "So much energy in here—if you're sensitive, it can be quite daunting."

"Yes," was all that squeaked out from her lips.

She followed him to a large bookshelf sectioned by category. He pulled a copy of "The Complete Idiot's Guide to Communicating with Spirits" from the shelf and held it up in front of him. "This is our most popular—many find it helpful."

"Really—may I?" She took the book and flipped through the pages, read the blurb, and handed it back. "I think I'm a little more advanced...What else?"

"Feel free to peruse. I know the right one will find its way into your capable hands."

"And what makes you so sure I'm capable?" She felt her cheeks flush.

"I knew from the moment you walked in the door that you are one special lady." He chuckled. "That's not a come on—I feel things."

"Interesting..." She turned back to the books. His eyes were on her. She pulled another title from the mix. "What about this one?" His fingers brushed hers, sending a thrilling sensation down to her toes.

"The Spirit World in Plain English." He glanced up at her, his lashes dark, and long. "Plain English, how can one go wrong?"

"You sold me—I'll start with this one." She handed the book back to him and followed him to the cash register.

"Anything else I can interest you in?" His gaze dropped to her lips. She just about choked.

"No—no, that's all I—" She caught herself swooning over the angelic being before her. "Do you see spirit?"

"Yes—since I can remember. How about you?"

"Since my near-death-experience."

"Sounds intriguing. I'd love to hear more." He opened the cash register drawer and lowered his voice. "Are you free for dinner?"

Extracting her wallet from her purse, she glanced at her phone. A missed message from Sam. She placed two twenties on the counter. "Dinner no, but perhaps a cup of coffee?"

"I get off at three. There's a coffee shop down the street. Will you meet me there?"

"Yes. I'd like that."

Suzanne clutched the packaged book to her heart. "I'll see you in a bit." She turned on her heel, feeling light, and airy. She couldn't hold back a smile as she exited the store. *What is wrong with you?* She felt giddy inside. She clicked on Sam's message. "Hey, sweetheart. I was looking forward to dinner tonight, but something came up—I'll call you when I'm free." Guilt seeped in. Why was she relieved with their change of plans?

**

The atmosphere in the coffee shop felt surreal. The rich aroma of freshly roasted beans filled the air. From behind the granite counter, the hissing of expresso machines and the whir of blenders mixed with the murmur of distant voices, created an almost otherworldly symphony. However, her focus was on the man walking in the door.

"I never introduced myself—Garian Dodge," he said, taking the seat across from Suzanne.

"Suzanne Cash," she replied. "I've already breezed through a chapter in *The Spirit World in Plain English*. Interesting information. Have you read it?"

"To be honest, I've only thumbed through it. I'm not much of a reader, and although my gift didn't come with instructions, I've learned how to deal with it in a practical sense."

"What's your secret?"

"I treat spirits as I would if they were alive."

"Do they come to you at all hours of the day and night? Show up in your bedroom, kitchen, wherever they please?"

"Nope. Don't allow it."

"How do you keep them in line?"

"When I was little, they would come into my room at night and scare the crap out of me. Of course, my parents didn't understand why I was screaming my lungs out—but I was fortunate enough to have a babysitter who was clairvoyant. She saw them too and taught me how to talk to them."

"I can't imagine getting used to this—this—"

"Phenomenon?"

"Is that what you call it?"

"Why don't you explain to me what's happening—perhaps I can help."

Suzanne waited until he returned with a cup of coffee to begin her tale. When she finished, he reached for her hand across the table. His expression sympathetic, warm. "How awful for you," he said. Even the sound of his voice affected her.

"This may sound crazy," she said, "but I think we've had a previous life together."

"Is that why I'm feeling so comfortable around you?"

"I don't know much about past lives, but I do know I keep getting flashes of us together."

"And I am rejoicing in the synchronicity of our meeting. Today was my day off. My friend asked me to cover her shift at the last minute...otherwise, our paths may never have crossed."

Suzanne smiled. "I came out on a whim."

He nodded toward her engagement ring. "I see you're spoken for."

Suzanne slipped her hand beneath the table. "Yes. We're recently engaged."

"Lucky guy."

His eyes fastened to hers. She could hardly breathe. "What about you?" As he stared into her eyes, warmth spread to a place reserved for another. Why did he affect her so? She wanted him. Plain and simple. But betraying Sam was not an option. She needed to know, "Who are you really?"

CHAPTER NINE

Paradise

Timarie and Paul pulled up to the gate in front of their new property. A stout woman greeted them with gusto. "I'm Lucille," she said, her Irish lilt adding a touch of warm to her words. "Welcome to Camino."

The couple rolled out of their van wide-eyed and slack jawed. "It's breathtaking," Timarie exclaimed.

Lucille nodded. "Yes, lovely piece of land, indeed. I'm sure you'll be very happy here." She pushed open the gate. "Drive down to the house. I'll meet you there."

Paul and Timarie hopped back into the van. "I can't believe we're doing this," Paul said. He started the engine and eased through the gate. When they reached the house, he killed the motor and helped Timarie out of the passenger side. As they stood in front of a large two-story with a slate tile roof, Paul took Timarie's hand. "This is it, hon."

"The house looks larger in person, doesn't it?" Timarie went into animation mode. "I love the brick walkway and the porch. We can have coffee out here in the morning."

Paul shaded his eyes from the afternoon sun. "The grow house looks pretty ominous—I'm more used to greenhouses for growing things, not artificial light."

I'm sure Betty, Joe and the gang won't know the difference once they're settled in."

Lucille parked beside the van and lumbered to the door. Timarie didn't envy the woman's swollen ankles. "I guess we'll have to get used to this terrain, coming from concrete and blacktop." She twirled around. "This is heavenly—the crisp air —the smell of the pines."

"You can expect a little snow now and then too. There's plenty of wood left over from the previous owner—which is a stroke of luck—we've been getting colder winters lately. I'm sure you'll enjoy the peace and quiet. No one around for miles." Lucille inserted the key in the door and waited for the couple to enter. "Needs some airing out—but we checked out the appliances, they all work—and the furniture the previous owner relinquished is in decent condition—we didn't find any rodent droppings anywhere."

"Hallelujah," Paul said.

"I know this place was a steal—but is there anything we should be made aware of? I mean—the previous owner isn't going to come back to claim his property, is he?"

"The Kenners disappeared. Vanished. No one has heard a peep from them in years. We were surprised the property was left in such good condition—I mean my company cleaned up trash and—" The woman flicked her hand. "You made a good choice. I'm sure you'll be very happy here."

Lucille continued with the walk-thru, focusing on the home's positive features. She pointed to the wooden beams flanking thirty-foot ceilings, stainless steel appliances, the farmhouse kitchen sink, and the rustic tile floors. "A little elbow grease, and I'm sure you can bring back the shine."

The bedrooms were large, the bathrooms small, and dated. "I know what I'll be doing for the next few months," Paul said, giving Timarie a wink.

"Paul knows I require plenty of room in the bath."

Lucille chuckled politely. "Shall we take a look at the outbuildings?"

**

Sam studied the photo of himself hanging on the wall in his office. His uniform crisp, his future promising, his ideals as high as the sky. He never dreamed a county so rich in history and culture could house so many monsters. The jail was filled with undesirables. But nothing pissed him off more than people who hurt the elderly, women, and children. He would fight to the death to seek justice on their behalf.

He waited for Spence, Jake, and Jeremy to enter his office before closing the door. "We have a problem here, gentlemen—and we need to take every action possible before we lose another child. Tell me what you've got. Who's moved in, and what are they peddling?"

Spence spoke up. "Sinaloa and Cártel Jalisco Nueva Generación have taken over the marijuana market in the Mendocino, Humboldt, and Siskiyou Counties—drugs, guns, human trafficking—the whole enchilada. They're coming in from Minnesota."

Sam shrugged. "CJNG and the Sinaloa are definitely encroaching on Northern California. Tell me what I don't know. Seen anyone peculiar in town, hanging around the schools?"

Jake chuckled. "Seriously, Sam?"

"Is this funny to you?"

"No sir—it's just—"

Sam glared at the officer. "I know this is a diverse community, but I want ears open, eyes in the back of your head. I want to know who's dealing, and I want them stopped."

Once Sam dismissed his men, he checked his phone. Suzanne hadn't responded to his text. He checked the time. *Where is she?*

**

The coffee shop was filling up. The rise and fall of the din became more apparent as the hours ticked by. "I hold a class on Thursday evenings, I take meditation to a deeper level," Garian said. "I would love for you to join us."

"I haven't begun to tap into this so-called 'gift'," she said, using air quotes. "I never know what to expect."

"I may be able to help if you like. Seeing spirit can be very daunting."

"I'm so happy to be sharing my thoughts with someone who understands," she said. "I did go to the Psychic Institute in Raleigh, North Carolina, but I only lasted a day." Her phone vibrated in her purse, sending another wave of guilt her way, and yet she couldn't relinquish the feeling that she was where she wanted to be, and with whom. It was as if she were under a spell. *He understands.*

"In your case, I would say you've been called. Thrown into a situation for a purpose. I feel my clairvoyance was predestined. I've had time to adjust."

"Do you ever get scared?"

"I did as a child. As I said, my parents believed I was having night terrors..."

"I saw my deceased fiancé from the beginning...he would show me things, which eventually led to tracking a serial killer."

"That's intense."

"It was." She imagined having this conversation under the covers. Another place, another time. "Where are you from?"

"Chicago, originally. We moved to Cali when I was ten. Broke my heart. No more snow."

"Strange, my family is from there also."

"Small world." His smile was infectious. Dimples appeared above a square jaw. His eyes sparkled, now more green, than gold. He reminded her of a Viking God, an anointed knight, his broad shoulders capable of carrying a heavy load, his full mouth exuding confidence with every word he spoke.

"I really should be going," she said. Heat rose to her cheeks. "Sam has been trying to get a hold of me, I'm sure he's wondering where I am."

"If you were my girl, I'd feel the same. What about my class? Will you come?" He raised one brow. His eyes focused on her lips.

"What time?"

**

Timarie kept quiet as Paul and Lucille discussed the outbuildings' electrical potential. "I plan to use LED grow lights to keep the cost down, but—" He gestured toward the expanse of the room, "it will still cost a bundle once we populate the space."

Lucille agreed. "You can always get yourself some solar panels—they're not cheap, but in the long run—"

"What did the previous owner use? Do you know?"

"The Kenners really didn't discuss their business with anyone that I know of. They kept to themselves."

Paul nodded and flashed a glance at Timarie as if he sensed something was bothering her. "What do you think, hon?"

"I think we have a substantial space to fill. Betty, Joe, and the gang better get busy."

"That's my girl." Paul threw his arm around her shoulders and gave her a peck on the cheek. "I think champagne is in order."

She snuggled against him. "I think you're right."

**

Sam laid his gun on Suzanne's entry table. "How was your day?" she asked, drawing him into her arms for a sensuous embrace. His mouth felt warm on her neck. His nibbling sent chills down her spine, and she moaned. "I suggest we stay here —make love—order take-out."

He devoured her mouth, his hands kneading her buttocks. "I missed you today—you didn't pick up when I called."

Guilt washed over Suzanne, making it difficult to look Sam in the eye. Her kisses stopped. "I was out. I didn't hear my phone."

"Where were you?" he asked, his breath hot in her ear.

She removed his hands from her body. A razor-sharp tone cut through what she perceived as a controlling question. "I was shopping." She turned away. Images of Garian Dodge rushed through her mind like a brush fire.

Sam kissed her shoulder. "Hey, it was just a question."

How could she explain meeting a lover from a past life? "I went to a metaphysical shop—to find a book on ghosts."

He wrapped his arms around her waist, pulling her close to *his* fire. "And what did you find?"

"I met a man."

Sam's arms dropped to his sides. "I see."

"He invited me to his workshop," she replied, attempting to sound nonchalant.

"Good. I'm glad you're pursuing answers—what happened to Linda?" His tone had a bite to it. Suzanne crossed her arms.

"Linda doesn't have bullet-ridden ghosts showing up out of nowhere."

"And this—what's his name?"

"Garian. Garian Dodge"

"And this guy *Garian* does?"

"Yes. He sees spirit all the time." Suzanne shook her head. "I can see you're not keen on the idea."

"No—I think it's great."

"Then why are you behaving like a jealous boyfriend?"

Sam shoved his hands in his pockets. "I didn't realize that's what I was doing. I just asked a simple question." Silence between them lingered. He patted his stomach. His words came out hostile. "I skipped lunch today—mind if we decide what to order?"

Suzanne stepped back. "I'm not really hungry. Perhaps we should do this another time."

Sam returned a perfunctory smile. "Yeah, sometimes it's better to call it a night than risk a battle." He rubbed her shoulder and kissed her cheek. "Let's pick it up tomorrow."

She watched the door close behind him.

**

That night, Suzanne writhed in her sleep. "Don't go," she cried, tugging at the man's woolen coat sleeve. He released her hold with a rough hand, pulling on his leather boots. Her hand dropped to her lace décolletage, and she wept. Outside the wind howled. Waves crashed against the rocky sea wall.

"I'll come back to you, I promise," he said, closing a heavy wooden door behind him. Suzanne scratched at the door like a she-devil, her chest heaving.

"No, you won't," she sobbed. "No, you won't."

Suzanne sat up, gasping for air. Her dream felt so real. *Garian.* In her heart she knew she had loved him. She laid back down, closed her eyes, and let her imagination flow like water. Soon, she saw how they met in a meadow behind the king's stable, their first kiss, the first time they made love...the birth of each of their seven children...she wondered if Garian had an inkling of their life together? All she knew was that she had to see him again.

CHAPTER TEN

Guilty Pleasures

"You're engaged to be married, girl," Linda said, throwing her hands up in the air. "Meeting this guy doesn't cancel out the love you have for Sam—" Her eyes grew wide. "Or does it?"

"No—of course not," Suzanne replied. "However, I do want to take his classes. He gets me."

"When do you plan to see him again?"

"Tonight. His class starts at seven."

Linda tapped her fingers on the table. "Ever think about getting your astral chart done?"

"Why?"

"We really do come with instructions...our birth date, along with other specifics dictates our path. That doesn't mean we don't have free will—it's more of a guide—a manifest, so to speak."

"I thought when Jack led me to Sam, I was put on my path. I don't understand why Garian is upsetting my applecart."

"It's like writing a book. Key characters move the story along. It's your job to figure out what to put on the next page."

The image that came to Suzanne's mind was a heart. *Breaking in two.*

**

At 6:50 PM, Suzanne entered Planet Earth Rising, a notebook in one hand, a latté in the other. The latté was spontaneous, not a drink she normally ordered, but for some reason, a sudden craving took control. She eased into a chair in the back row, removed her denim jacket and crossed one leg over the other. When she looked up, she felt Garian staring at her from across the room. Chills zipped up her spine, and she was flung into another time, another place...

"Once we marry," he said, his posture cocky and sure, "I forbid you to see him again." Suzanne peered through the eyes of a woman in love. She nodded, her face feeling as warm as the burning candles surrounding their love nest.

"And you, my lord, will curb your appetite for the ladies?"

"That is of a different matter," he said, removing his surcoat. The gold cross embroidered on his tunic shimmered as he pulled it over his head. His bare skin against her breast stoked the flame below, his touch set her on fire. His lips closed on hers. His tongue probed and teased...

"Welcome, Suzanne." A burst of laughter broke her reverie. She looked around her, all of the seats were filled.

"Thank you," she sputtered. Heat exploded in her cheeks. She wanted to bolt out of the room. A woman sitting next to her smiled, extended her hand.

"Hi, I'm Barbara Ybarra, I'm an astrologist—Garian's classes *are* stimulating. Welcome."

Astrologist? Linda suggested she see an astrologist. *Maybe there are no coincidences.* "Thanks, I'm Suzanne," she said. "Happy to be here."

**

When the class took a brief break, Barbara handed Suzanne one of her business cards. "I know it's not the same as seeing ghosts," she said, "but I think I can at least construct a chart that will provide some answers for you. Especially if your gift has come to you in what you perceive as a random act."

"It was random, all right." Suzanne reached for a butter cookie and placed it on a napkin. "What do you need from me to get started?"

"Birth date, time of birth, where you were born..."

"I think I have my birth certificate stashed in a box in my closet. I'll find it and give you a call."

Barbara nodded and flitted over to another attendee leaving Suzanne wide open for Garian's attention. "What do you think so far?" he asked.

"The cookie's delicious—would I be a glutton if I took another?"

"Help yourself," he countered. "Excuse me." He moved on, leaving her with a mouth full of cookie.

Good. I don't need any complications in my life. I'm happy with Sam. But when she bent over to retrieve the napkin she dropped, he stepped forward, and her eyes grazed over his crotch. The zing that traveled into her nether land was unexpected. Her eyes rose to meet his.

"I enjoyed our chat the other day—perhaps we can do it again?"

She swiped cookie crumbs from her mouth and smiled. "Sure."

**

Sam slid behind the wheel after a long day at work. He didn't want to go home, not yet. He hadn't seen Suzanne in two days, and the brief conversation he had with her the day after their misunderstanding was less than satisfying. They agreed to dinner on Friday. He googled "Planet Earth Rising." *Don't do it, buddy.* But by the time he had put the gearshift into drive, he had lost the battle.

Twice he was tempted to turn the car around and head for home, but the thought of spending another night without Suzanne's voice whispering sweet nothings in his ear was unbearable. He knew she wasn't his possession. Which is why he hadn't pressured her to set a date for their wedding. Was she going to turn to this Garian guy when she needed someone to understand what was happening to her, all because he made a terrible blunder? How he wished he could go back. All he wanted to do was kiss her sweet lips, make up for any hurt he had caused and fall asleep in her arms.

He drove by her house. It was dark. He pulled into the driveway and waited. And waited. *Planet Earth Rising closed at nine.* At twenty past midnight he gave up and drove home.

**

"Last call," The waitress announced. Garian gave her a nod.

"One more for the road?"

Suzanne was vehement. "No—no thank you. I should be going."

Garian checked his watch. "Time flies—but I'm glad we got the chance to talk again outside of class."

"I'm looking forward to the next one. I feel I have a better understanding of the entities that are seeking my help."

"You can always call me, day or night—3am if need be."

"Thank you, I appreciate—" He grabbed her hand. His eyes glistened like golden goblets in the low lighting.

"I know we have a connection. I feel it, and I know you do too...the question is...what do we intend to do about it?"

He brought her hand to his lips. She could feel his hot breath on her fingers and wanted to feel his lips on hers. The temptation, maddening. "I—I'm engaged—I can't—I wouldn't—couldn't—"

"I don't believe we were *all* created to be monogamous. We've been reborn into soul groups where we have shared many lifetimes together. It's only natural to share the love we felt for each other when we meet again—whether we were child and parent, brother and sister, husband and wife, or *lovers.*"

"I understand the concept—but I believe we reap what we sow. I would be hurt if Sam were to share his love with another." An image of Garian in the arms of another flashed though her mind and crushed her. "Our relationship must remain platonic."

"In that case," he said, grabbing the check, "You better get yourself home." Suzanne rose, he blocked her advancement. "Do friends hug?"

"Sure," she said, regretting the agreement the moment she stepped into his arms.

"See you next week," he said, his warm breath brushing her ear.

**

The drive home felt surreal. Suzanne replayed her conversation with Garian, noting where she had let her guard down, and where she may have encouraged his attention.

As she pulled onto her street, she noticed a car backing out of her driveway. "Sam?" She froze at the stop sign, unable to move forward. Guilt bubbled inside her chest. Adrenaline pumped through every nerve ending. *What was he doing here this late?*

~

CHAPTER ELEVEN

Visitors

A t 4am, Suzanne was awakened by a chill in the room. She bunched the covers beneath her chin and tucked them around her body. She couldn't get warm. As her eyes adjusted to the darkness, the reason gave her a start. A group of people stood by the doorway, covered in blood and dirt. Suzanne sat up.

"Who are you?" She softened her tone. "How can I help?"

The man stepped forward. His muddy clothes hung loose on his thin frame. "Trabajamos y no nos pagan. De todos modos nos matan.

Susanne's Spanish was so rusty, she could barely piece together what the man was saying. "You worked for no pay? But they killed you? Who are *they*?"

"El jefe, el que tiene la marca en la cara."

"Where was this boss man with the mark on his face?"

"La granja."

The farm. "What can I do to help you cross over—go to God?"

"Encuentra el hombre, tiene que pagar. La justicia nos hará libres."

Suzanne struggled with the interpretation. She got *find, man, pay, justice will free us.* "Can you tell me where the farm is?"

"En las sierras, donde los pinos crecen altos."

"In the Sierras, pine trees?" *That could be anywhere.*

Suzanne brought her knees to her chest. She could barely make out their expressions, but she could feel their pain. "I'll do what I can, as soon as I can figure out where to start."

**

Sam tossed his blankets on the floor and pounded his fist on the mattress. He sat on the edge of the bed and raked his hands through his hair. He glanced at the sobriety coin on his night-stand. It was the first thing he added to his pocket in the morning, the last thing he removed from his pocket at night. The coin was a constant reminder that he had a choice. At the moment, he felt weakened by love. The thought of losing Suzanne to another hadn't crossed his mind. Why was he torturing himself now? Maybe it was natural to feel a little jealous...After all, Suzanne was a beautiful woman, smart, charismatic, and sweet...who wouldn't fall for her? But who was this guy? Sam Googled his name. If he was the same Garian Dodge that appeared in his search, he was stiff competition. Handsome, younger...like one of those guys on the bachelorette show his dispatcher Kelly fawned over. But Suzanne wasn't one to be swayed by a pretty face any more than he was. *Then why are you feeling like a dinner mint when she can have cake?*

Sam went into the bathroom, opened the medicine chest, and shook two melatonin tablets into his palm. He needed to sleep. The stress at work was taking its toll. He didn't have time to mope. He had bad guys to catch.

He climbed back into bed. Right before he placed the melatonin under his tongue, his phone lit up. The text made his heart happy. *Trying to communicate with the dead makes me wish you were here with me. I miss you.*

He left the two melatonin tablets on his nightstand, threw on a pair of jeans, splashed water on his face, brushed his teeth, and texted back: *Leave the back door open. I'm on my way.*

**

Timarie couldn't close her eyes. Although the Carey House oozed with charm, she found hotel beds lacked the comfort of home. Her head swam with conflict and determination. She visualized replacing the floral sofa in the family room with a rustic brown western style leather sofa, with bump texture trim, and matching wing-backed chairs. There was enough light in the room to pull it off...but then she'd have to reconsider the wall texture...and everything on the walls would have to go. The light fixtures changed for sure...maybe add a light shag rug...so many choices. The other thing that prevented her from getting some shut eye was the figure that appeared and disappeared several times since Paul began snoring.

Are you real? She didn't expect an answer. Nor did she have the energy to try and converse. They would begin the clean-up in the morning, and she needed a good night's sleep. She placed her hand atop of her husband's, willed herself to let go of her thoughts and step into dreamland. Suddenly a disturbance stole the moment. Timarie went to the window.

**

Outside the hotel, a teenage girl stumbled past Timarie's window, babbling about dildos growing in her mother's flower garden. She stopped in front of Foundation Plaza, clutched her heart, gave her soul to God, and did a faceplant in the middle of Main Street.

**

Sam eased Suzanne's door closed behind him and twisted the lock. His phone buzzed in his pocket. He glanced upstairs, the bedroom light was on, but he wasn't sure if she was still awake. He took the call in the kitchen.

"Metzger." He could hear sirens in the background.

"Grime's here. Sorry to bother you, boss, but I thought you'd want to know—someone reported seeing sixteen-year-old Carissa Jones collapse on Main Street. She's dead. By the looks of her, I would venture to say she OD'd."

Suzanne appeared at the top of the stairs. "Sam? Is that you?"

He stepped into view. "Yeah—be right up." He walked back into the kitchen to finish his call. "Have you notified the parents?"

"Just the mom. Dad's out of the picture. Mom's on her way to identify the body. I happen to know Carissa. She used to babysit our—she—she was a good kid, Sam."

"I'm in Sacramento—I'll be there as soon as I can." Sam hung up. He bounded the stairs like a man late for church. When he entered the room, Suzanne was stretched across the bed, wearing only a scrap of fabric. He went to her, finding her lips and caressing her body. "I can't stay," he said between kisses.

She held him close. "Why? What happened?"

"Another dead kid." He released her and cupped her face in his hands. "I hate to go." His kiss was gentle. "I love you so much."

Suzanne kneeled on the bed and wrapped her arms around his neck. "I'm here if you need me."

He rose to his feet, regretting the timing. "We need to find out where these kids are getting the drugs from."

"The cartels are killing more than kids."

Sam cocked his head. "You know something I don't?"

Suzanne slipped into a bathrobe and tied the sash. "They're killing their workers. They're bringing them across the border, working them like dogs, then assassinating them."

"How—" Sam stopped himself. "Your ghosts?"

"Yes. They can be very chatty when they want to be."

Sam looked around the room. The questioning expression on his face made her laugh.

"No, they're not here—not now."

"I wish I could wrap this up and come back—your bed is so inviting."

"I'll be here—" She reached into her nightstand, pulled out an object and pressed it into Sam's hand.

"What's this?"

"A house key." She placed her hands on his shoulders, pivoted his body toward the door. "Go—come back to me when you finish—I'll be waiting.

CHAPTER TWELVE

An Encounter

The room seemed too bright. Suzanne rolled over, acknowledging the empty space beside her. *No Sam.* She took a deep breath and exhaled. "I miss you already," she confessed to the void in the room. No Sam, no spirits. "Mom?" No answer. She dragged herself downstairs.

A cup of coffee and a piece of toast were a constant in her morning ritual. She searched Sam's cabinets for a loaf of bread. *The freezer.* She checked there. *Bingo.* Of course, that made sense. Sam was hardly ever home. *No one likes stale bread, do they?* She found a half of a stick of butter in the fridge, still in the wrapper. All she needed was a toaster.

Once she had finished a light breakfast, she cleaned up her mess, and washed the few dishes Sam left in the sink. *Now what?*

She dug in her purse for Barbara Ybarra's card. No sense

wasting her day. She had questions about her past, present, and future. She hoped Barbara could provide some answers. *Am I ready to commit to Sam for the rest of my life?* Waking up alone hadn't bother her before...now she had a choice to make. And if she moved into Sam's place, would she feel lonelier than she felt at this moment?

She picked up the phone and dialed Barbara.

"I'm so glad you called," Barbara said. "I've been thinking about you since we met at the class the other night."

"Ditto! I'm anxious to get a reading."

"Do you have the information I need to get started?"

"Yes. I was born on August 30th, at 12:42 p.m."

"Great, and where were you born?"

"I was born in Tustin, California. My parents lived in Chicago but wanted to take my brother to Disneyland. I came two weeks early.

"You're a Virgo. You have a mind of your own," Barbara chuckled. "I don't need to draw up your chart to impart that much information—the rest will take me a day or two."

"Is being a Virgo a good or a bad thing?"

"All signs are good...I'll know more once I plug in your numbers. Every chart is different. Every person is different... your natal chart is like a blueprint of your life's journey. It's not like reading your horoscope in the newspaper...it's tailored to you, and your soul's purpose."

"I have so many questions—"

"Well let's see if I can provide some answers for you—will you be at the next class?"

"I planned on being there, yes."

"Let's meet an hour before the class starts—there's a coffee shop down the street."

Suzanne flashed on the handsome face she sat across from

at the very same coffee shop. "I know the place—I'll see you there.

She hung up feeling jubilant. Losing her parents at such a young age deprived her of asking questions about her childhood. Her mother hadn't been visiting lately, and she missed her. She hoped Barbara would be able to fill in some of the blanks...reveal her life's purpose...maybe give her some insight into her chance meeting with Garian.

She turned on the faucet in the shower and stripped out of her robe. When the water felt right, she stepped inside, and under the spray. Suddenly, she stilled, listening. *Footsteps.* She frantically searched the shower for a weapon, grabbing a backbrush. Would a poke in the eye buy her time to escape? She gripped the handle, ready to strike.

That's when she saw the silhouette of a man and held back a scream. *Is he undressing?* It suddenly occurred to her that she had given Sam a key, and she peeked through the door. When she was sure it was him, she opened the door wider, striking a pose. His expression was a mixture of bewilderment and mirth.

"Were you planning on beating me to a pulp with that thing?" he said, pointing to the back brush.

"Actually, I was going to ask you to scrub my back."

Sam yanked off his socks, dropped his pants, underwear, and stepped into her arms. "I would be happy to scrub your back," he said, between kisses. He ducked under the spray, pinning Suzanne against the tiled wall.

Suzanne pumped a dollop of body wash into her palm and began smearing it on Sam's midsection. Lathering him a little lower ignited his kisses. "I want to be inside you—*need* to be inside you." He felt for her readiness and groaned.

"I want nothing more," she said, her chest heaving against his. He lifted her waist high and lowered her down until they connected in bliss. As he rocked his body against hers, she tightened her legs around his waist and moved her hips in tight circles. She felt her soul soar as waves of pleasure reached new heights and she cried out. Sam thrust himself deep inside, joining her in ecstasy.

Once they both caught their breath, Suzanne eased herself down. "Now that we got that out of the way—" she said, suppressing a giggle, "What are you doing here? It's—" He silenced her with a kiss.

"I had to see you."

Suzanne's playful demeanor flipped to a serious tone. "Another death—"

His eyes held her gaze. "Yes. A sixteen-year-old girl. She used to babysit one of my deputy's kids. He had arrived first on the scene." Sam wrapped a towel around Suzanne. Standing behind her, he spoke softly. "Hungry? We haven't gone to breakfast in a while." She stiffened. He spun her around. "You were showering—I interrupted—you have plans."

"No—I—I was going to read. I just wanted to freshen up before I got dressed."

He lifted her chin. "You can tell me *no*."

"I confess, I did have toast and coffee, but an omelet sounds good."

"Excellent. I'm starving." He tucked her wet hair behind her ears. "Besides—it will give us time to discuss our wedding plans without interruption."

**

"I'm having my astral chart read," Suzanne said, reaching for Sam's hand across the table. Morning Toast was emptying out, leaving them one of only a few tables occupied. The waitress brought water and coffee, took their order, and was off elsewhere, giving them their privacy. "I'm rather excited. It was Linda's idea, and as fate would have it, I met this amazing woman at the class I went to the other night."

"What are you hoping to find out? I mean—how does that work?"

"I gave her my birthdate, time of birth, and where I was born—"

"Did you give her your social security number too?"

"No—why would you—" Suzanne's ire rose.

"Just teasing. It seems like something a charlatan would ask, that's all."

"Barbara is NOT a charlatan, and how dare you even think that?"

"I said I was kidding."

"What I heard is that you don't trust my judgement for one —and two—you are not interested in—"

"You're right. I'm being an ass. I guess it bothered me when you didn't come home the other night."

Suzanne's face pinched into a scowl. "That *was* you—you were at my house."

"I wanted to surprise you. I didn't expect you to be out so late."

"The class ended at—"

"Nine."

"Were you spying on me?"

"No. I checked the store hours—to gauge when I could expect you home."

"I went out for a bite to eat afterwards. I had no idea you'd be—*waiting.*"

"I must've dozed. I left shortly after midnight—you weren't home."

"Why didn't you tell me?"

"I didn't get the chance."

"I was with Garian. We met up at B.J.'s—I had a glass of wine and a street taco—I left at 11:50—it took me twenty-two minutes to drive home."

"C'mon, Suzanne. I didn't ask—"

"You didn't have to. I offered. I don't want you to feel as though I'm not being up front about my relationship with Garian."

"Relationship? I thought you just met the guy?"

"I did...but it feels like I've known him forever."

"I see." Sam sipped his coffee and diverted his attention to the waitress across the room. "You'd think the service would be better with less people in here."

"You're not jealous, are you?"

"Should I be?"

"Absolutely not."

"You can honestly tell me you feel no attraction to this guy?"

Suzanne sat back in the booth, lost for words. Sam's intense gaze made her search for something to say. "There's a connection—past life. I keep getting flashes of us together—I can't tell what time period it is, other than it was way before electricity. We had seven children together—"

"Seven children? That's quite a connection."

"I know—can you imagine?"

"No, I can't. Nor do I want to imagine you with some other guy—regardless of when it was." Sam dug his fingernails into his palms, his jaw clenched. "Do you have feelings for him?"

"I—I don't think so, Sam. I love *you*. I am just as perplexed by all of this as you are. Spirits, past lives—this is all new to me." She leaned forward. "All I know is that right now I have no say over what comes to me. Spirits or past lives —I'm trying to understand—and I need to know if you're willing to help? Or if I need to figure this shit out on my own?"

The food couldn't have arrived at a better time. Sam collected his thoughts. "You're right. I don't understand—I want to—believe me, I try. It seems like the deeper you get into this gift of yours, the further you get from me."

"That's not true. I'm trying to get a grip on it FOR you."

"For *me*?" Sam stabbed a potato with his fork.

"I have so much to learn from Garian—it's a mystery."

"Until you can figure it out, I guess there's no sense discussing a wedding date then, is there?"

Suzanne held back tears and pushed her plate away. "No. I guess not."

**

Paul carried a box filled with lighting equipment and thermometers into the concrete structure. Timarie followed in his wake toting Betty, Joe, and the gang. "I have an icky feeling, babe. That girl—dead in the street like that—it's not a good omen."

"We're not used to seeing kids OD in the streets because we lived a prestigious, sheltered life, Tim. That kind of stuff happens all the time."

"I saw that ghost again," she said, placing the plants on a concrete shelf bordering the far wall. "I didn't see his whole body, but I'm pretty sure it was the same ghost I saw the other night."

"The Cary House is haunted—what else is there to say?"

"I'm not sorry we are doing this, hon, I just want to be cautious—we need a good alarm system, and motion detection lights. I've seen them advertised on Amazon."

"If that will make you feel better..."

"I believe it will."

"Ok, let me finish unloading the van and we'll take a peek at what they have."

Timarie shivered. "Is it cold in here? Or is it just me?"

CHAPTER THIRTEEN

The Space Between

J ake slid the coroner's report across Sam's desk. "Fuckers are using Carfentanil now, as if we don't have enough problems with fentanyl.

Sam sighed. "Get Grimes in here. I need to know if Carissa Jones was a drug user." He scooted his chair away from his desk and crossed one leg over the other. "Carfentanil is a pain killer administered to large animals. If they're adding it to heroin, or selling it as such, we have a huge problem. It's got a rapid onset, lasts longer than fentanyl, it's less expensive, easier to obtain, and easier to manufacture than heroin."

Jake nodded. "And obviously very deadly."

"Brian Mathews OD'd on Flakka, Carissa Jones OD'd on Carfentinil—do we know if they went to the same high school?"

Jake shrugged. "Not sure, I'll check it out."

"Thanks. I'm going to take a ride out to the Kenner place,

welcome the new owners. Just so happens they are the ones that made the call about Carissa Jones. Get back as soon as you get something."

"Do you still want to talk to Grimes?"

"Yes. Have him call me."

Sam checked his missed calls. None were from Suzanne. His heart sank.

**

Suzanne sat in her Adirondack chair, her legs tucked beneath her, a cup of herbal tea in her grasp. She felt numb. She set her tea on the side table and closed her eyes. She didn't expect a vision, but one came to her, clear as a bell. A teenage boy. *Raphael.* But that's not what his friends called him, they called him Caramelo. *Candy?* He was handsome, charming. *Thirteen.* She saw him in a crowd, shoving his way past the Border Patrol, his hands covered in blood. She shook off the image, but the feeling of dread lingered. *Now, who are you?* She wondered. And what did he have to do with the migrant workers murdered by the man with the scarred face?

Her first reaction was to call Linda, but then she would ask about Sam, and Suzanne didn't want to lie. Things were not right between them. She and Sam should be working together, not drifting apart. It was more than her gift causing the wedge between them. Garian's face loomed behind her third eye.

**

"Sam, it's Grimes. Jake said you wanted to talk to me?"

"What do you know about Carissa Jones?"

"It's been a couple of years since I saw her, but at that time, I liked her because she was smart, studious, and had goals."

"Any idea if she would've been one to experiment with drugs?"

"Two years ago, I would've said, a big hell no—but kids change, Sam."

"See what you can find out for me, will you? Two dead kids with goals seems coincidental...my theory may not hold water, but I'm wondering if someone is trying to solicit unsuspecting customers."

"Gotcha—that would make more sense. We checked out Brian Mathews' friends...none of them seemed like tweakers."

**

Sam drove up the hill. The beauty surrounding him contradicting the darkness brewing in his soul. He'd been getting a weird vibe from Suzanne lately, a vibe he couldn't define. He went down the list of probable causes:

Working too much. Slacking off in the bedroom. Not calling enough. Not making her feel special. Not taking her places.

The list came as a result of a relationship he'd had with a woman years ago. *Dysfunctional*, totally his fault but he blamed his drinking. She accused him of being selfish, indifferent, uninvested in their relationship. *In anything.* When he got sober, he avoided getting serious...*until Suzanne.*

He never considered himself insecure...or the jealous type, but things had changed since she met that guy at Planet Earth Rising. The detective part of him wanted to investigate the situation—find out who this guy was...

Deep in thought, time evaporated. He had reached his destination and turned up the lane leading to the gate. The gate was open. He drove down to the house and parked beside the Ram ProMaster.

"Mornin'." Sam extended his hand. "I'm Sam Metzger, from the Sheriff's Department." Sam flipped open his wallet, displaying his badge.

"Hi there, I'm Paul." Paul glanced at the badge and shook hands. "Is this about what happened over by the Cary House? Or did I manage to break the law already?"

Sam returned his wallet and shoved both hands in his pockets. "I stopped by here before you moved in...I was curious about the family who owned the property before it was sold."

"Looks like they just up and left—furniture, linens, kitchenware—we thought maybe they were planning to rent it out. Turn it into one of those Airbnb's. Make a beautiful retreat, don't you think?"

Sam absorbed as much as he could with his peripheral vision as he nodded in agreement.

"C'mon in, meet the wife." Paul set down the box he was holding. "Tim? We have company," he yelled through the open front door.

A slender woman with silver hair appeared on the porch, her smile, warm and genuine. "Hello. You're our first visitor. Welcome."

"My wife, Timarie," Paul said, brimming with pride.

Sam smiled cordially. "Sam Metzger." He extended a hand. "Pleased to meet you."

"He's from the Sheriff's Department," Paul said.

Timarie's body language changed in an instant. "Did she die?"

"Yes, Ma'am, I'm afraid so. I just have some questions—and I was hoping to take a look around the property."

Paul rested a hand on Timarie's shoulder. "Don't you need a search warrant?"

"I was hoping I wouldn't—this has nothing to do with you folks."

The couple concurred. "All right then, where would you like to start?" Paul nodded toward the grow house. "I take it you checked out our grow license?"

"Yes. I fully support legal grow businesses. The previous owners were growers too, did you know that?"

"Yes, but I heard they skipped town."

"I hope you're right." Sam shaded his eyes. "Did you see anyone else on the street last night, Mrs. Phillips?"

"No. I was headed to dreamland when her shouting drew me to the window." Timarie shook her head. "She was yelling all this nonsense, then suddenly she clutched her chest—looked to the sky—threw her hands in the air and fell forward." Timarie's eye twitched. "I called 911." She lowered her gaze. "I feel so sorry for her folks. What a tragedy."

Sam nodded. "Yes. Tragic indeed."

Paul wrapped an arm around his wife. "What else can we help you with?"

"Mind if I take a look around?"

Paul narrowed his eyes. "No problem—it's not like we're hiding any dead bodies—"

Timarie moved Paul aside. "Want to start in the house? We haven't changed a thing yet. The realtor had someone come in and tidy up a bit before we got here, though."

Sam's line of sight went directly to the vaulted ceiling. "Wow, that's a lot of wood."

Paul smiled. "Beautiful, isn't it? The place is in really good condition—quality workmanship for sure. I can't imagine someone ditching a place like this."

"Our good fortune—right, hon?" Timarie opened the wooden slats on the windows to let in more light. "Don't mind the dust. When I mentioned someone tidied up a *bit*, I meant very little."

Sam walked from room to room, searching for clues that explained the Kenner's exit. Nothing seemed unusual until he reached the back of the house. He bent down to examine a gouge in one of the dressers in the bedroom. "May I?"

Paul nodded. "Need a hand?" Together, the two men moved the dresser away from the wall. "Is that what I think it is?" Paul squatted down to Sam's level.

"Appears to be a bullet hole." Sam shined a penlight in the hole. "Looks like it came out the other side of this wall."

"There's another bedroom next to this one," Paul said. "Let's see if you're right."

The threesome huddled in the next room, sliding a wardrobe closet out of the way. Sam stuck his finger in the hole, then lifted the rug that had butted up against the cabinet. His suspicion confirmed, he dropped the edge of the rug. "Looks like I'm going to have to bring in a forensic specialist."

"Blood?" Timarie's face paled. Paul cradled her in his arms.

"I'm sorry. I'll have my team in and out as quickly as possible."

"Why has this taken so long to investigate? I mean—the owners have been gone for over two years."

"It's a long story—and a very strange one—there may be ghosts involved."

Timarie gasped. "I saw a ghost at the Cary House—he looked like he'd been shot."

"Interesting. When was this?"

"Last night—and the night before."

Sam placed his hands on his hips. "You might check into getting yourself some good security cameras."

Timarie nudged Paul. "See? What did I tell you?" She turned to Sam. "I've had this awful feeling..." She clasped her hands in front of her. "You don't need to hear an old lady ramble—we will cooperate in any way we can, right Paul?"

"Of course. Let me give you our cell phone numbers."

"Thank you, that would be great. Mind if I take a look down by the pond?"

Timarie shuddered. "Help yourself."

**

Sam and Paul walked down to the spring-fed lake in

silence. Sam stood on the edge of the bank surveying the area. He pointed to an area up the hill. "Have you been up there?"

"No. Tim and I bought this place sight unseen, well that's not true—we had photos, and a video. There was drone footage of the place, and well, it looked too good to pass up. What closed the deal was the grow house. The wife and I are horti-culturists."

"Cannabis is a profitable business." Sam signaled he was moving on with a wave of his hand. The two men climbed up the bank.

Sam walked toward a clearing. He squatted down, pinched a bit of soil and sniffed the sample. He stood and moved the dirt around with the tip of his boot.

"What is it?" Paul stepped gingerly toward him.

"Smells like an old burn pit." Sam alternated looks between the clearing and the lake. He snapped a dead branch off a nearby bush. "We had a lot of rain last year. I imagine this area was pretty dried up before then."

Paul followed in Sam's wake. "The pictures we received from the realtor must've been taken after the rain."

Sam contemplated the lake once more. "We may have to drag the lake—any objections?"

"Not if you think it's necessary—but may I ask why? What are you looking for?"

"Once I have that bloodstain analyzed, I may be looking for a dead body—or two."

CHAPTER FOURTEEN

Written in the Stars

S uzanne arrived ten minutes early for her appointment with Barbara Ybarra. She ordered an iced tea and instructed the barista to put Barbara's order on her card.

When Barbara arrived, Suzanne stood and gave the astrologer a hug. "I'm so excited," she said, "but first, order a drink—I'll wait."

Suzanne stared at the manila envelope Barbara placed on the table, as if the words on the documents inside could speak. Her mother's face flashed across her mind's eye, and she smiled. When Barbara returned with her drink, Suzanne was eager to get started.

Barbara withdrew the contents of the envelope and grabbed her laptop out of her bag.

Suzanne viewed the charts before her with interest.

Barbara donned a pair of blue metallic reading glasses and began, "I'm so glad you decided to have a reading with me. It's an interactive experience, and I will be sharing with you what is suggested at this time, and some of the core themes as suggested in your natal horoscope."

Suzanne set her elbows on the table and propped her chin on her laced fingers. "Okay, sounds good..."

Barbara presented one of the documents containing a circular diagram, her birth date, time of birth, and a set of coordinates pertaining to her place of birth. Pointing to various sections on the pie chart, she said, "The greatest emphasis in your chart is on your mind and how to offer the gift of that to the world. You've already told me of your psychic abilities, and I believe that it relates back to the mother figure in your early home—" Barbara paused, "—And perhaps it was inherited from mother line, or at least from her love and protection for you that steered you to be so perceptive and eventually open up to these abilities." Barbara took a sip of her coffee.

Suzanne leaned back in her chair, processing what was said. Her mother's face loomed in her mind, snippets of moments they shared supporting the information. "Steven, my brother, and I always thought my mom had eyes in the back of her head. She always seemed to know what we were up to—or when we were about to get into trouble."

Barbara smiled. "The father figure is also strong...but perhaps he was so involved with his work that he wasn't truly present for you."

"Yeah, Dad worked hard...but he made time for me and Steven when he could."

Barbara continued. "Yes, the Sun in the chart represents the father figure in the home, even if it is the mother taking that role, and how we are able to stand up for ourselves in life. When the father is not truly present, the mother will often save the day."

Suzanne fondly remembered the day her mom helped her ride her bicycle without training wheels. "My mom definitely did double duty when she had to—"

"There are also unique parts of your chart that suggest a vulnerability with sexual intimacy...a tenderness that wants to engage but might fear opening up readily..."

Suzanne shifted in her seat recalling sex in the shower with Sam.

"And really, because there is also a sense of danger present in your life, that would be a sensible reaction."

"Danger?" Suzanne's eyes grew large. "That's in my birth chart?"

"Not so much literally. More of a—" she said, using air quotes, "sense of its presence."

"Can you elaborate?"

Barbara held up Suzanne's natal chart and pointed to one of the symbols. "This is Pluto near your Ascendant. The Ascendant represents how you project yourself out into this world. It's complex, but I think it goes with your psychic mind. You feel that someone or something might be lurking at times."

Suzanne nodded. Barbara couldn't have been more right.

"Mercury in your chart is in an exact square to Pluto in Scorpio." Barbara chuckled. "Professionally—you can enter hidden areas of the minds of others, and sometimes the general spirit world."

"Yes—spirits are showing up that I don't know. First there was my dead fiancé, then my mom—"

"Were you able to see spirit before your near-death-experience?"

Suzanne tilted her head. "Maybe—when I was a little girl, ten, maybe eleven, I remember being sick—chicken pox I think—I had a high fever, my mom was worried. I remember waking up soaked, my fever broke, and my grandma was sitting on the edge of my bed."

"Right now, you have a transit of a planet that is pinging the area of your chart that pulls people around you *and* spirits from the other side to the Mercury and Pluto area in your chart."

"That's incredible."

"The experience will get stronger and stronger as time goes on for the next couple of years—and it may attract some unworthy experiences, so you might need to learn how to manage it."

"I'm speechless."

Barbara tucked the chart back into the envelope. "Are you in a relationship?"

Suzanne turned the diamond on her ring finger with her thumb. "I'm engaged to a wonderful man, but—"

"But?"

"Sam tries so hard to understand my—" she paused, struggling for the right word, "*gift*? If that's what you want to call it—but I've been having these enlightening conversations with Garian and—and all of a sudden everything feels complicated. Messy. I've had flashes of a previous life with him—and it's all so new to me. I love Sam—and yet..."

Barbara nodded sympathetically. "Yes. I can see that. And it may get even more complex." Barbara tapped on the manilla envelope. "Your chart suggests a new person in your life—someone you can talk to—a teacher figure. It could be Garian... or someone else. But what shows in your chart is some pretty hot romance. I compared it with Garian's chart, which I did a year ago. You two have a synastry between you—but there will be something that puts a damper on it. There will be some confusion in the relationship—perhaps because you will need to make a decision about it at some point."

"How could you know—"

"It's all here, Suzanne." Barbara pushed the envelope toward Suzanne. "It's called destiny."

"I wasn't expecting—"

"No one ever does. We are in control of our lives *to a point*. Rest assured, there are no coincidences."

"Is it possible that what you're seeing is my recollection of a past life with Garian?"

"Anything is possible. If you want, I can give you the name of an excellent past life regressionist. You may find your answers there." Barbara patted Suzanne's hand. "Don't look so glum. The total solar eclipse this year in the United States will hit the ruler of your 6th house of work, exactly, so you will be tied up with work. It also hits the ruler of your 7th house, which signifies your partner in life, so it is putting focus on both of those areas."

Suzanne pressed her lips together, preventing *holy shit* from leaving her mouth. She never mentioned that she and Sam worked together. "This is going to take time to process."

"Yes—and most important, you need to take care of yourself, so you don't wear yourself out. Any questions?"

"I'm sure once I digest this information I will. For now, the bottom line is that I have unwanted spirits and a past with a man that I hardly know."

"Life is about lessons. Both issues are about your ability to stand up for yourself—and to learn what it is you want out of life, not just what draws your attention and what *feels* like love."

"Ouch."

Barbara chuckled again. "Funny you should say that. Your

birth chart suggests your permanent wound, and we *all* have one, is feeling completely demolished by the risk of intimacy. Even when it does work out, and long before you know it, it's exhausting for you."

Tears threatened to spill. Deep inside, Suzanne knew Barbara had nailed it.

CHAPTER FIFTEEN

Home Sweet Home

Dove Johnson, Goldorado's forensic expert, extracted a shallow plug from the Phillips bedroom floor. "We'll do a DNA test and get back to you, Sam."

Sam agreed with the plan and walked Dove to the door. "I may need you again."

"Sure, no problem. You doing okay, Buddy? You look beat."

"Yeah, fine," Sam said. "A lot on my mind, that's all."

"How's that gorgeous fiancée of yours?"

"Suzanne's great. I'll tell her you asked about her."

"Thanks—set a date yet?"

The question caught Sam off guard, and he scowled. "Been too busy tracking down the scumbags dealing to our kids to think about it. Suzanne's been busy as well..."

"Oh really? What's she up to?"

Sam switched to his game face. "She's taking classes—psychic stuff."

"Cool. Give her my love."

"Sure." Sam retraced his steps back to the bedroom.

Paul stood akimbo, staring at the hole in the floor. "I think I can find a wooden dowel to fix the hole."

"I can recommend someone—"

"Don't worry about it, Detective Metzger. I'm pretty handy."

"Okay then, if you insist." Sam swiped his face. He needed a shave. He needed sleep. *I need Suzanne.* The polite phone messages they had left each other over the last couple of days gave a clear indication that there was a problem, and yet neither of them tried to resolve the chasm growing between them. His dad gave his mom a wide berth when there were issues. *This too shall pass,* his favorite line when things went south. Not being a relationship expert Sam did what came naturally—he followed in his father's footsteps. *I hope it passes soon.*

Timarie entered the room, yanking him from his pity party. "Can I get you something cool to drink, Detective?"

"Thanks, but I was about to take a walk down to the lake, if you don't mind."

"Not at all. Haven't been down there yet myself—mind if I join you?"

"If you have the time, that would be great."

Timarie followed Sam past the grow house. She waved to Paul. "I'm heading down to the lake with Sam—be careful in there, please—and don't hang up those lights until I return."

"Yes, ma'am," Paul said.

Sam slowed his pace, waiting for Timarie to catch up. "How long have you two been married?"

"Thirty-eight bliss-filled years," she replied.

"That's nice to hear."

"What about you? Are you married?"

"Engaged."

"Wonderful. When's the big day?"

Sam glanced at her. "We haven't set a date yet."

"There's no hurry, I guess. Love doesn't have an expiration date."

Sam glanced at her again, appreciating her wisdom and refinement. In some ways Timarie reminded him of his mom. Classy, intelligent, sweet. He felt compelled to share. "Suzanne is a gifted psychic. Sometimes I don't understand—I want to—I guess the detective in me needs everything to be in black and white."

"Paul doesn't get it either. I know I saw a spirit at the Cary House—he could care less. Maybe it's a guy thing."

"I wish I could see what she sees, but I don't. Makes it hard."

Timarie's eyes gravitated toward the clearing. "Good place for a bonfire."

"I was looking at that the other day. Seems the previous owners had the same idea."

Timarie encompassed the view with a sweep of her hand. "It's beautiful," she exclaimed. "The photos don't do it justice."

"You definitely bought yourself a piece of paradise. I'm sorry we have to disturb it."

"Disturb it? How?"

"Paul didn't tell you? I have my men coming out to drag the lake."

Timarie's hand covered her mouth.

"I'm sorry—I guess he didn't tell you."

"No. Why? Why drag the lake?"

"To make sure there is nothing lurking down there beside the fishes."

**

Suzanne opened her book and began to read. After a moment, she checked her watch. It would be dark soon. No Sam. He left a voice message the day before and another the day before that. *Call him.* Her pride wouldn't allow it. Barbara's words haunted her. *Permanent wound.* She thought back, wracking her brain for clues that would support why intimacy was a problem for her. Jack died. Did his death leave a permanent scar? Ben's abuse? She shouldn't have married on the rebound. Their relationship was doomed from the beginning. And what about Sam? They got off to a rocky start. She didn't exactly consider tracking a serial killer dating.

She closed the book. How could she concentrate with so many questions looming over her like a dark cloud? She enjoyed the time she had spent with Garian the night before. Stimulating conversation, good wine and laughter. Intoxicating. But her heart hurt knowing that Sam hadn't made an effort to see her. *Can't have it both ways.* The ring on her finger sparkled in the sun's last kiss. She needed answers.

"Linda! It's been too long—how are you?"

"I was just thinking about you," she said. "What'cha up to, girlie, girl?"

"Linda–have you ever heard of Diane Potter?"

"Has anyone NOT heard of Diane Potter?"

"I had my astral chart done as you suggested...pretty interesting. Barbara recommended a past life regression with Diane Potter."

"What are you going after?"

"I need answers about that guy I met at Planet Earth Rising."

Linda sniggled, "He's rattled your cage, has he?"

"He's fascinating..."

"I'm sure he is."

Suzanne exhaled, her words spilling out, "I think it was charted that we meet."

"Too bad you can't clone yourself."

"I don't think that's necessary...I mean I have no intentions of—Sam and I are—"

"How 'bout we discuss this over pie?"

"Can I bring anything?"

"No, no. Unless you have some old shoes you don't want. My Brittney Spaniel has a shoe fetish."

**

Suzanne gathered several pairs of shoes she hadn't worn in years. One pair drew her attention. Black leather, with a latchet buckle. She wore them when she and Steven went to a Renaissance Faire at Casa de Fruta in Hollister years ago. She held one shoe in her hand and closed her eyes...

The vision came immediately...

He held her close, her bare breasts pressed against his muscular chest. The bell sleeves of her dress hung loose at her sides. His kisses felt hot on her flesh. He released her hair, letting it fall past her shoulders, and grazed each of her nipples with his teeth. His eyes searched her face. "Do you love me, Émilie du Châtelet?"

"As much as I love conceptualized energy, my dearest Voltaire?"

"You are too bold with your thoughts, Mademoiselle." He grabbed her hand and pressed it against his erection. "Perhaps this is the energy you crave?"

A soft groan escaped her lips, and she lifted her skirts, welcoming his proposal. "Can your lightning be contained?"

He undid his breeches and lifted her skirts higher. Émilie wrapped one leg around his waist and guided him inside of her. The latchet buckle on her shoe shimmered in the candlelight as their bodies rocked back and forth.

Suzanne held her breath as the sensation shot through her like a jolt of electricity, and she dropped the shoe. "Geezus!" she cried. "What the hell was that?"

The wetness between her thighs confirmed—how could a memory feel so real? *Or feel so good?* Curious as to who the couple may be, she scribbled the two names on a pad of paper she kept by her nightstand. Was she Émilie? And the man she referred to as Voltaire, was he Garian? How many past-lives had they shared together? She looked forward to Linda's insight.

**

When Suzanne pulled up the drive, Linda greeted her at the front door, wiping her hands on her colorful apron. "Come, come—I'm taking out the last pie. Strawberry rhubarb."

"My favorite. Where's your puppy?" A brown and white face peeked around the corner and issued a soft woof. "You're beautiful," Suzanne said, petting the dog's head with her free hand.

Linda was beaming. "She's a sweetie pie too, aren't you Daphne?"

Daphne's tail wagged so hard Suzanne wondered how it stayed attached to the animal's body. "I brought you lots of shoes to chew up—but I'm warning you, Daphne—if you have strange visions, I am *not* responsible."

"This I want to hear—have a seat. Do you want ice cream on your pie?"

"Absolutely." Suzanne took a seat and began her story about the shoe and the couple who appeared to be her and Garian, but had different names. "It was nuts, Linda. I could feel what they were feeling—and I must say, if I could bottle the experience, I would be rich."

"My—a past life that strong cannot be denied. You should

Google the names, see what you come up with." Linda set her fork down on her plate. "What about Sam?"

"I love Sam."

"But?"

"I can't explain the passion I experienced with this man—we have some serious history." Suzanne took another bite of her pie. "I am hoping to figure it out by having a past life regression with Diane Potter."

Linda nodded. "Damn tootin'. You can never go wrong with another lightworker on your team."

Suzanne laughed. It was just like her psychic friend to say something to lighten the load. "Thanks."

"What's going on with your ghosties with the mosties?"

"Garian suggested I talk to them as if they were alive. I was able to get more information, but I still don't see how I can help. A man with a scar on his face in the Sierra pines doesn't give me much to go on."

"Meditation?"

"When I close my eyes and relax, I get thrown into a past life."

"Interesting."

"My chart indicated that what's going on in my life right now was written in the stars. Isn't that crazy?"

"Funny how that works. Somebody got the memo—I mean whose idea was it to name the stars and make charts based on a person's birthdate, time of birth, and location?"

Suzanne pushed her empty plate aside. "He gets me, Linda. Garian gets me. Sam struggles to understand, and although he believes what I share with him, he doesn't feel it. Garian feels it. We speak the same language."

"Are you attracted to Garian?"

"Sam asked me the same thing." She sighed. "I'm attracted to the freedom of baring my soul without judgement, or scrutiny. And the couples I've seen in my visions are clearly attracted to each other." Suzanne stood, gathered the dishes and brought them to the sink. "I haven't discussed any of my visions with Sam. When I tried to tell him about the spirits, mentioned they were riddled with bullet holes...I swear I saw him cringe."

"I'm sure things will play out as God intended."

"I want to believe that, Linda. But according to my chart—I have a decision to make.

CHAPTER SIXTEEN

Reach Out in the Darkness

S am sat in front of his TV, an In 'n Out burger and fries congealing on the tray table before him. His focus was on the news.

The reporter delivered the information in a disconnected voice, telling the viewers about the drug cartels trafficking migrants, forcing them to work on illegal marijuana farms...how the black-market farms were producing toxin-tainted crops, making, and distributing drugs laced with fentanyl, threatening California's clean water supply.

The reporter went on to say, "The migrants pouring across the border are ending up in Humboldt County, fueling the illicit growing operations staffed by undocumented workers."

Next, Humboldt County's Sheriff appeared on air telling the CBN journalist, people coming here in hopes of a better life ended up getting a rude awakening. "Modern slavery is happening right here in Northern California. Labor trafficking is a major deal in the Golden State when it comes to marijuana. Not to mention illegal drugs and sex trafficking—"

"Why is it getting out of hand?"

"Defunding the police—not enough manpower to be effective. We're outnumbered. We have no money for resources."

"What is the governor doing to assist with this problem?"

"He won't take our phone calls or respond to our emails."

Sam pounded his fist on the table and switched the channel. The story of Carissa Jones, the girl who died days before, was being featured on another news station. Sam turned up the volume, and leaned in closer, canvasing the screen for anyone who looked suspicious at the girl's memorial service. Listening to testimony from family and friends was heartbreaking. They all agreed Carissa was a happy, good person, who participated in school activities, and was loved by all. *So, what happened?* Sam's phone buzzed. It was Jake.

"Jake—anything on Carissa Jones?" Sam lowered the volume on the TV. "Just watched a clip from her memorial service. She didn't appear to be the kind of girl to get wasted."

"Same consensus here, Sam. I'm stumped. Brian Mathews —nothing on him either."

"Great—what's up?"

"We got a kid in ICU over at Marshall."

"I'm listening..."

"He ran his car off the road. CHP took the call...the kid didn't know his ass from a teakettle...CHP did a sobriety test... the kid was wasted. All they could find on his person was a container of breath mints."

"What are your thoughts?"

"I'm sending the mints to the lab."

"Good call—is the kid going to be okay?"

"I hope so—I'm going back in there. I'll keep you posted."

**

Suzanne fixed herself a salad, ate half and put the rest in the fridge. She stared at her phone, willing Sam to call.

She caught a glimpse of what appeared to be a woman with a small child in her arms. She couldn't see the woman's face, but in her head, she could hear the woman weeping and had to ask, "Why are you here?"

The weeping stopped. The spirit vanished. Suzanne thought about her reading with Barbara, her reference to the idea that something or someone is lurking at times. *So true.* She dialed Sam.

Sam's greeting seemed warm, but unease gnawed at her. *Is it him? Or is it me?* "I haven't heard from you—everything all right?"

"Yeah. Sorry I haven't called...super busy with work, that's all."

"You sound tired."

"I am...and frustrated."

"With me?"

"No, Suzanne, not you. You are my—I know it may not always seem that way, but you're my happy place."

Suzanne bit her lip. His admission invoked her guilt. "Sam —I'm not sure how the universe works—not completely—but I do know that this journey was charted from birth. Written in the stars...and this craziness is part of the plot." She took a breath. "I had my chart read. The bottom line is, everything that is happening is meant to happen...including meeting Garian."

"Oh, Suzanne—please honey—if you're breaking up with me, let's do it in person."

"I—no Sam. I'm not breaking up with you—but I do think a little space would do us both some good."

"What is it, Suzanne? Just tell me."

"I don't *know* what it is...I'm looking for answers, can you try and understand?"

"Sure—yeah. Take all the time you need."

**

Sam hung up the phone feeling gut punched. In the past, he would have turned to alcohol. Right now, he needed a friend. Someone who would understand a person like Suzanne. He dialed Timarie Phillips.

"Mrs. Phillips—hope I'm not calling too late—it's Sam Metzger."

"Hello Sam. Paul's out in the grow house with Betty and Joe."

"You have company—perhaps another time."

"Betty and Joe are our cannabis plants."

"Oh." Sam chuckled. "It's really you I wanted to speak to, do you have a minute?"

"Sure—what can I do for you?"

"You said you saw a ghost at the Cary House—did that scare you?"

"Yes. At first."

"Do you see ghosts a lot?"

"No—hasn't happened since I was in college." Timarie hesitated. "Why?"

"My fiancée sees ghosts too."

"Yes, you mentioned that—do you think there's some connection?"

"I—no, I wasn't suggesting—but wouldn't that be interesting?"

"Sure would. I doubt it though. I'm pretty sure my ghost came with the room."

"Does Paul—"

"Oh hell, Sam. Paul thinks I'm bonkers half the time. He tells me he needs facts, not fiction."

"Does that bother you?"

"I'd be lying if I said 'no'—but we've been married so long, I accept that he's not comfortable with my experience. After all, what can he do about it? Can't sock a ghost in the eye, or beat 'em with a stick. In other words, he can't rescue me. That part is harder for him to process I think than the idea that there's an afterlife."

"I knew I called the right person."

Timarie snickered. "It's taken us many, many years to understand each other. Patience is key."

Sam ended the call on a serious note. "Thanks for the ear. Just wanted to remind you we will be out to drag the lake in the morning."

Timarie chuckled. "Sure you did."

CHAPTER SEVENTEEN

Discovery

As promised, Sam arrived at the Phillips' the next morning at 8 o'clock sharp. "Not what I expected." Paul said, removing his hat and scratching his head. "I pictured heavy equipment, nets, and divers."

Sam let out a soft laugh. "Yeah, we should update the terminology now that we have all this modern equipment." He nodded toward the diver and the man launching a small craft into the water. "If there's anything down there, Larry and Cliff will find it."

The two men launched the boat off the bank and motored slowly to the middle of the lake. Sam and Paul looked on as the men checked their communication devices and powered up the AquaEye, a handheld underwater sonar scanner.

Sam pointed to the site. "Cliff operates the sonar device.

He'll give Larry a heads up if he sees something and together, they'll hone in and document the discovery."

"That's really cool—what happens if they find a body?"

"The coroner will examine it, determine time of death, check dental records, DNA...it's a process."

"Saw a movie once where a bloated body covered in slime popped out of the water–nearly peed my pants."

"I can't guarantee what the condition of the bodies will be in...it takes a few weeks to a few years for skeletonization to occur. So many factors are involved. Oxygen levels, temperature, humidity, insects, fish..."

Paul shuffled his feet. "And you're thinking if they do find a body, or bodies, that it could be the previous owners?"

"We'll need DNA testing to draw that conclusion."

"Then why—"

"A wise woman once told me to go with my gut."

Paul burst into laughter. "Sounds like something my wife would say."

Both men turned a while later when they heard Cliff shout. "Hells bells, Nell!" Larry stalled the motor. He leaned over Cliff's shoulder to have a look, and then turned to Sam on shore.

"Sam, we're gonna need some help on this one—there's a whole graveyard down here!"

**

One by one, the remains were carefully brought to shore. Bits of shredded material that presumably clothed the victims, clung to their muddy bones. A rusted chain welded to a rusted anvil was extracted from the water. The shackles were empty, but still engaged.

"Seventeen so far, various sizes," Sam told the mayor over the phone. "We've barely scratched the surface."

"When will you have them ID'd?"

Sam put his phone on speaker and walked over to where forensic examiner, Dove Johnson squatted over a pile of tiny bones. When Dove turned, Sam saw tears in his eyes. He turned the tiny skill, with one gloved hand revealing metal fragments. "What is it Sam? I'm kinda busy here."

"The mayor is asking how long to ID the bodies."

Dove rose, his face twisted in rage, but his response seemed calm. "He'll get a copy of the report when it's finished."

Sam ended the call and returned to Dove's side. "Shrapnel?"

Dove nodded. "Looks like a couple of the bullets are still intact in some of the larger skulls. Off the cuff, I'd estimate the time of death between one and a half to two years. I'll be able to give you a better timeline once I test the proteins in the bones.

"I'll get a couple of divers to collect as many bullets as they can."

"I don't know how long it's going to take to find out who these people were, but my wild guess is that there are at least three families here, including children and elders."

Sam clenched his teeth. "This was a goddamn massacre."

Dove patted Sam's arm. "I can at least get you a ballistics report ASAP."

"Thanks, buddy. We can start there."

Sam stopped by the residence before returning to the station. Suzanne's ghosts haunted his soul. What was the connection? He rapped on the door. Timarie answered. "Come in," she said, her tone laden with sadness and worry.

"I'm sorry this is happening, you two are such nice folks," he said.

"It's unfortunate, yes, but once you're finished, we can resume our business as planned?"

"Yes, I don't see why not. Your permits are in order and the property belongs to you now. We appreciate you allowing us to invade your space."

"Who knows how long those bodies would have remained undiscovered if it hadn't been for you."

Paul appeared in the room. "Never saw anything like it."

"Yes, I was telling your wife how sorry I am to involve you folks in the mix."

Paul cleared his throat. "Had we known we were buying—"

Timarie cut him off. "It's going to be fine, Paul. We can handle this."

Paul slid his arm around her waist and kissed her temple. "I married an optimist," he said.

Sam managed a weak smile. "I need to get back to my office —thanks again for your cooperation."

Sam drove back to Placerville, the weight of the day settling in his shoulder muscles and in the back of head. He dialed Suzanne. His call went to voicemail.

**

"For today's class, we're going to do a meditation exercise, at which time, I'd like you to focus on seeing spirit. Let's get started." Garian slowly paced in front of his students, his hands clasped in front of him. "While taking deep breaths, I want you to think about someone who has passed on...perhaps you didn't get to say goodbye...or maybe there's a question you didn't get to ask before they left the earth plane...or maybe you just want to find them, bask in the love you once felt. Father, mother, grandfather, grandma...a dear friend...close your eyes...picture them there...what do you want to say to them? Deep breath..."

Suzanne closed her eyes, concentrating on her breathing. Garian's voice settled in her mind, directing her to a place where time disappeared, and her ethereal body was one with space. He claimed that "beyond nothingness lay the answers to the quest." She was transported to a place she'd never been. A small village...then a hovel made from cardboard and sheets of tin. Smiling faces greeted each other in love.

Where am I? Garian's voice bled through the haze. "Look around. What do you see?" She knew those faces, but not their smiles. A small girl danced around the room, her shabby skirt twirling. "We're going to America," she sang. *Trina?*

Suzanne became the observer as the universe imparted scenario after scenario. Long days under a blistering sun picking strawberries, tomatoes, avocados, baling hay, eating flour tortillas, drinking rationed water. *San Martin Peras, Oaxaca.* The words formed behind her third eye.

A young woman joined the little girl, holding her large belly as she danced. "America," she cried victoriously. "Este es nuestro nuevo hogar!"

The scene shifted to a desolate area, where the young woman's screams echoed in the night. The cry of a baby followed. *She gave birth in transit.*

Next came the assault on her olfactory senses, the stench of urine, feces and sweat. She heard menacing voices, whimpering, grunting, sobbing...she saw snippets of rape, brutal beatings. *Murder.* Suzanne moaned.

Another voice intruded on the horror. "Suzanne? Come back to the room. Suzanne?"

When Suzanne broke free from her vision, all eyes were on her. "I'm sorry—I saw—it was terrifying."

Garian bent down and took her hand. "You okay?"

"I saw them. I saw them when they were alive."

"Who?"

"The spirits—in my house."

CHAPTER EIGHTEEN

What Lies Below

The Phillips were up early, sipping coffee on the porch. Paul raised his face to the morning sun, eyes closed. Sam and his team, who had doubled in size overnight, began milling around at 7 A.M.

"Like a swarm of bees," Timarie said. "I had no idea it would come to this, Paul, did you?"

"Nope."

"What are we going to do?"

"Let them finish their investigation, finish unpacking our things and move forward."

"You're okay with bullet holes in the wall, blood on the bedroom floor, and dead bodies in the lake?"

Paul gave his wife a side-glance. "Not one bit—but we made a decision to grow pot, and watch the sun set each day, together, without the stress we've been under for the last forty-five years."

"Hmph. Like this isn't stressful," she mumbled. "It's creepy, if you ask me."

Paul resumed soaking up sun. "It'll be over soon. Hopefully, justice will be served. That's all we can ask for. If we hadn't bought this property, they may never have found those bodies—or what was left of them."

"Sam's a good guy," she said, switching gears. "I'd love to meet his fiancée—the psychic—have her come here, see if anyone is hanging around."

Paul shifted his weight, his eyes remained closed. "Have you felt anything?"

"No, but we've only been in the house a few days. Once everyone clears out—when it's just you and me—"

Paul reached for Timarie's hand. "Everything is going to be fine—I promise."

Sam watched the couple from a distance, observing the love between them. He wondered if he would know such love. Suzanne hadn't returned his calls. He promised himself that he would give her space, let her figure things out without his interference, but his heart ached, and it was hard focusing on the problem at hand.

Although Dove hadn't finished his report on the bodies found at the bottom of the lake, it was obvious a massacre had taken place...bullets lodged in bone, partially shattered skulls... and then there was the bullet hole and the blood stain in the house. He suspected the Kenners were killed in their home. He had no idea who the others were. He had heard from Sheriffs in other counties that his crime scene was typical of cartel activity. "The cartels are ruthless," one of them had said. Sam agreed. *Children, babies.* Ruthless, indeed.

Sam approached Timarie and Paul. "Sorry about the invasion—we should finish up by the end of the day. The divers pulled up the last of the bodies..."

Timarie squinted against the sun. "They found more?"

"Yes, Ma'am. Two more human skeletons were discovered about a hundred yards from where we found the others, and what appeared to be canine bones."

Timarie clutched her throat. "Did the people who lived here have dogs?"

"I'm not sure." Sam shoved his hands in his pockets. "I hope once this is all over, you two will find the peace you deserve."

Paul nodded. "That would be nice."

"My men are still collecting evidence. I'm heading back to the station. If you need me for anything, please don't hesitate to call—and again, I appreciate your cooperation."

"There is one thing—" Timarie rose from her chair.

Sam's expression, now quizzical. "What's that?"

Timarie smiled. "You said your fiancée sees spirits?"

Sam shied away from the question for a moment. "Yes, she does."

"Do you think she'd come here...take a look around?"

Paul stepped forward, his stature grabbing Sam's full attention. "We have been itching to fire up the barbeque. We planned on going into town, picking up some steaks...we'd love for you and your fiancée to join us."

Sam hesitated.

Timarie placed her hands on her hips. "I can't read minds," she said, "but I can tell you're conjuring up an excuse not to accept our invitation."

"It's just that—"

"Nonsense! A man's gotta eat."

"I thought you said you couldn't read minds?" Sam raised one brow. "I'll have to check with Suzanne. What time?"

"Six. Don't be late."

Sam nodded. "Yes ma'am."

**

After much deliberation, Sam dialed Suzanne. His heart won out and did a double flip when she picked up.

"Hi Sam, everything okay?"

"Yeah...how about yourself?"

"Fine. I was about to vacuum."

"Do you have dinner plans?"

"No—I—"

"I'm doing an investigation up in Camino...the couple that owns the place invited me—us—for dinner tonight. They insisted I bring you. It *is* work related and—to be honest—I could use your help."

"I'm listening..."

"We found nineteen decomposed bodies in the lake on their property, and I believe a murder occurred inside the house...I could use your take on the situation."

"Sam, I don't know. I have my plate full with—"

"Of course—but I hoped—Timarie said they'd love to meet you—what was I supposed to say?"

After a beat of silence, she responded. "What time?"

Sam exhaled. "Six. We can meet at my place, say, five-thirty, and ride together."

"I'll see you then."

"Great. Thanks." His words lingered. "It will be great to see you."

"Same here."

He hung up feeling disjointed. Torn between elation and dread.

**

Suzanne stared into her bathroom mirror. "Who are you?" She focused on her eyes, looking for any hint of deceit. "You love him, don't you?" *Truth.* "Then what are you doing, playing with his heart?"

She couldn't get past the tingling sensation she felt when Garian was near. Visions of their past taunted her. She had never felt so helpless in someone's embrace. Whatever they had shared, it was powerful.

At 4 P.M. she dressed in a pair of white capris, a Monet print chiffon top, and pulled her hair into a ponytail. Sam said it was a BBQ. He liked her in shorts, tight jeans and dresses. A little cleavage drove him wild. She wanted to look nice for him, without projecting any sexual innuendos. She knew if she didn't control the situation, she would lose herself and give up pursuing the answers she was seeking. For the time being, sex with Sam was off limits. *It's only fair.*

But when she arrived at Sam's apartment, it was all she could do to restrain from running into his arms. She gave him a quick peck on the lips and made an excuse to recheck the locks on her car. By the time she finished going through the motions of testing her door handle, he was waiting for her in his car.

"You're going to love this couple," he said, beaming.

"I'm surprised you accepted their invitation if you're investigating them."

"Not them. The house. The crime was committed long before they moved in. I won't go into detail. But something you said made me wonder about the place."

She eyed him suspiciously. "Now I'm really curious."

"I'm sorry I haven't shown you more support."

"What do you mean? You've always—"

"The ghosts—"

"Oh Sam, I'm having a hard time processing it myself."

"Exactly. I should've been helping you find answers."

She patted his hand. "I'll be fine with Gar—I'm learning."

"You can talk to me, Suzanne. You can always talk to me about anything—including ghosts—you don't need—"

"Sam—please. Don't."

"You're right. Let's just have a good time. Timarie and Paul are delightful. I'm sure they will love you as much as I do."

She smiled. "I can't wait to meet them."

**

Timarie was the first on the front porch when Sam and Suzanne arrived. Paul followed, his chef's apron askew, a pair of barbeque tongs in one hand, a bottle of beer in the other.

"Six o'clock on the dot—thanks for being prompt."

Timarie assessed her guests discreetly. "My—Sam didn't tell us how beautiful you are...love your top...very artsy."

"Thank you—I'm Suzanne."

"Timarie—and this handsome guy is my husband, Paul."

Chills ran up and down Suzanne's body and she shivered. She glanced at Sam who was watching her closely. "Sam mentioned—" She stopped herself and reconsidered her thoughts. "He said you're new in town."

Paul stepped forward, extending his hand. "It's been a wild ride so far, but it's nice meeting new friends. Hope you're hungry."

Suzanne turned to Sam. "Sam also mentioned barbeque—sounds delish." She looked around taking in the scenery. "It's lovely out here."

Timarie and Paul exchanged glances. "We're hoping for the best."

Sam cleared his throat. "We have more to process—Paul and Timarie have been very accommodating."

Suzanne's focus was drawn to the lake. She saw them there —her ghosts, and she gasped. She didn't wait for anyone's approval. She ran toward them. "Is this where it happened?" she called as she got closer. But by the time she reached the spot where they stood, they were gone. Sam caught up.

"What is it, Suzanne? Who were you yelling at?"

She turned to him, her face pale. "The same spirits I saw in my house."

"How many were there?"

"I didn't count—" She took a cleansing breath and gave Sam's question some thought. "Three families. Five children. Two elders. One baby. A young mother. Several men and women..." she closed her eyes, then opened them. "Seventeen in all."

"Do you know their names? Or where they came from?"

Timarie and Paul walked up and stood on either side of Sam. Their expressions reflected their concern. "What is it?" Paul asked.

Suzanne turned away. She closed her eyes trying to visualize the group in her mind's eye. *Trina.* She recognized the little girl. Her mind began to swirl with visions. It was dark. Crying. Bullets sprayed back and forth like a fire hose. Suzanne blocked her face with her hands. She didn't want to witness the bodies fall into the pit. *The lake—it wasn't there.* She pivoted toward the threesome. "This lake is new."

Paul shrugged. "It was here when we looked at the property. The realtor said it's fed by a spring that runs from the sierras."

"The little girl is showing me a dam."

Sam spoke up. "I can get topography reports from the building department. I'm sure the lake has filled up considerably in the last two years." Paul and Timarie clung to each other as if the revelation would knock them over if they didn't hold tight.

Suzanne shaded her eyes from the waters glare. "I got something the other day, but it was all jumbled. The language I'm sure was Spanish. I saw a boy, a desolate town. I don't know if there is a connection."

Sam brightened. "Anything you can give me is helpful. Anything."

**

After dinner, Timarie gave Suzanne a tour of the house. Suzanne immediately picked up on the murder that took place in the bedroom. However, she didn't think it was the owners. She heard men arguing in Spanish. "Diablo—" she said. "One man called the other Diablo. The other man didn't respond well to the insult—he shot him."

"He could be one of the victims we pulled from the lake."

Suzanne pictured a frenzy of growling animals and snapping jaws. "No." She shuddered. "The man, Diablo, fed him to the dogs."

CHAPTER NINETEEN

Man With the Snakeskin Boots

Raphael hung outside the fence of Miller's Hill Middle School, waiting for the bell to ring. The stack of books he carried in his backpack were for show. Raphael never made it past fifth grade. Where he came from, the only education he received came from experience—his survival, formative. San Martin was becoming a ghost town. Open borders into the U.S. made it possible for his people to dream.

Raphael thought he was safe when he broke free from his fellow travelers and made it across the border unscathed...until a man cut him off at the pass, nearly running him over with his truck. Down on all fours in the dirt, the boy slowly raised his gaze from the man's dusty boots trimmed in snakeskin, to the jagged scar etched on his menacing face. With the barrel of an AK-47 butted up to his forehead, Raphael knew he was defeated and pleaded for his life.

The man picked him up by the scruff of his neck and tossed

him into the bed of his truck like a ragdoll. The teen curled into a fetal position, protecting his face and his organs from the gnashing teeth of a canine sentinel lying two feet away. He knew if he tried to flee, the dog would rip him to shreds.

The boy was taken to an underground facility in the desert where he was stripped naked, sprayed with a high-pressure hose until his skin was raw, but clean. Three men licked their chops like he was a steak dinner. He better understood their hunger when they bent him over a bale of hay and carried out their intentions.

When the brutal attack was over, Raphael could barely stand, let alone walk. "Welcome to California," one of the men said, and the other two broke into laughter.

Weeks passed with regular beatings and sexual assaults before Raphael was given his first assignment. Fear, being a great motivator, Raphael grew aware of what was in store if he failed. His job was to pass out the *candy*, get the kids to come back for more. "Culo de caramelo," the men called him. *Candy ass.* Raphael perceived his new nickname as more of a threat than one of endearment, the consequences for underper-forming severe.

Raphael was clever, cute, charismatic. He had no problem blending in. Business was picking up at the high schools. And even though there were a couple of casualties, Raphael was able to convince his customers that the victims were *estúpida*. He claimed they must've had a death wish and took too much of his candy, or they mixed something dangerous with the drug. Raphael claimed he had given explicit instructions on how to throw a party without overdoing it. What he neglected to say was that the drugs were made by amateurs inducted into the program by default, or that the potency of candy varied from batch to batch.

Once a week, the scar-faced man, known only as *jefe* or

boss, drove him to different locations to pick up his allotment. Each night, one of the other men collected the money. Raphael learned fast that his till better be on the dime. Any shortages resulted in excruciating consequences, death, or both. The boss wasn't concerned about quality control. The life expectancy of his workforce was limited, depending on whether they were making carfentanil, fentanyl, flakka, bath salts, or meth. The deadly chemicals that went into making the drugs were used in unsafe conditions, with little or no ventilation.

Most of the chemicals came from China. The pill pressing machines were imported from Germany, India, Italy, China, and even Missouri. Single punch tablet candy presses were used in making fentanyl-laced goodies for the younger crowd. The idea was to get kids addicted, so they moved on to bigger things. But again, quality control didn't exist. Kids died. But that wasn't Raphael's concern. He was hombre de caramelo. *The candy man.*

The workers were handpicked at the border. It was jefe's assumption those making it past fifth grade could follow instructions, and they were brought to the labs. Men who appeared strong were commandeered as guards. The others were put out in the cannabis fields to harvest. The immigrants were gathered under the pretense that they would be paid a handsome wage, but the truth was, they were all dispensable. Raphael was no fool. He knew his days were numbered, and he looked for a way out.

**

Sam studied the report he received from Dove. Just as he predicted. Two of the remains identified belonged to the Kenners. The others came back unidentified, and therefore unclaimed. Bullet fragments extracted from the bones and found in the lake were logged in as 7.62x39mm rounds, used in AK47s, and 7.62x35mm, used in AR15s. Both types of ammunition were found in the victims, suggesting more than one shooter. Dove commented, due to the similar entry pattern, he believed the bodies had been lined up and shot. More testing was required to accurately pinpoint when death occurred.

Sam tossed the report in his drawer and leaned back in his chair. He pinched the bridge of his nose, relieving some of the pressure building up his head. The call he received from Jeremy Grimes at six that morning left him reeling. "Daniel Arroyo died a few minutes ago."

Daniel Arroyo, the teen found unconscious at the scene of a car crash turned seventeen last July. The breath mints found in his car were heavily coated in fentanyl. "Mother fuckers," Sam seethed. He called Jake into the office and lit into him.

Jake crossed his arms across his chest. "What the fuck, Sam. You know we've been busting our asses out there—cut us some slack."

"I want a man assigned to surveillance at each of the schools."

"And what about the rest of the county? We just let it go to shit?"

Sam slammed his hand on his desk. "Do whatever you have to do to be resourceful, dammit! These kids are getting this shit from someone, somewhere—I want to know who, and I want to know NOW."

Jake nodded. "All right. I'll get on it." He pivoted on his heel and left the room.

Sam picked up the phone keyed in a number and waited for his cue to leave his message. "Suzanne, we need to talk."

CHAPTER TWENTY

Past Lives

The hypnotherapist's words melted from her lips like warm caramel on a sundae. "I want you to close your eyes and surround yourself with protective white light and take a nice deep breath. This will send a signal to your mind and body to slow down."

As Suzanne's ethereal body sank deeper into the leather recliner in Diane Potter's office, she felt a pang of trepidation, weighing what she had to gain from her past life regression versus what she could lose. And although she had done nothing to be ashamed of with Garian, she still felt as though she were betraying Sam by revisiting their love from the past. *Did you love him then more than you love Sam now?* The inquisitive voice inside her head sounded like her mother's.

"Mom?" Suzanne mumbled. Her long lashes fluttered like butterflies.

Diane interjected. "Sometimes we have people who butt in, it's common but let me know...if you want to talk with your mother, we can go there...but this is your time..."

Suzanne's eyes volleyed back and forth behind her lids. Her mother blew her a kiss and disappeared. "She's gone."

Diane spoke. "Okay. Let's continue taking care of you...

Suzanne sighed relief, her stress ebbing away. Sam's face loomed behind her closed lids as she listened to Diane's soothing meditation.

"While you're breathing in protective white light, I want you to feel a warm, relaxing energy coming up through your toes, the ball of your feet, your heels... This feeling of relaxing energy is now moving up through your ankles, through your calves, into your knees, up through your thighs...you can feel your thighs resting against the chair, feeling very heavy and very relaxed."

Sam's face dissolved into a vision of rolling hills. Suzanne could hear the clippity-clop of a horse's hoofs as Diane's voice lingered in the distance...

"Now, this wonderful calming energy is traveling up into your lower back, your upper back, and up through your shoulders. Your shoulders are very heavy now and feel very relaxed as do your upper arms, your lower arms, wrists, hands, and fingers. In fact, your fingers almost have a tingly sensation about them. I want this feeling of calming energy to travel through your face, your nose, your cheeks, your forehead. Right up through the top of your head..."

Exhilaration traveled through Suzanne's body as the horse's hooves pounded into the earth...

"With each continued deep breath, you will breathe in this protective energy. And as you breathe out, you will release anything of a negative nature, stresses or pains, any worries or concerns... As you continue to breathe in this white light, realize that you're filling your body with positive energy and that there's no room for anything less than positive to remain. This will continue throughout this session without any effort on your part..."

Suzanne's body tingled with excitement. *He's there. Waiting.*

"Continue to concentrate on your breathing, breathing somewhat deeper, assimilating the breathing pattern of when you're asleep, signaling to your mind that you would like to relax further. You'd like to go into a deeper state of relaxation, a higher state of consciousness. Nothing will distract you or disturb you in any way. In fact, any outside noises will help you to go deeper."

Her horse came to a halt. Suzanne gathered her skirts, hopped down, and navigated her course...Deeper into the woods she went. Her pace quickened from a clip to a trot, then to a run...

"And now, as I count down from 10 to 1, with each descending number, you will find yourself relaxing that much deeper, still... 10, 9, 8, relaxing deeper, 7, 6,

5, going deeper, 4, 3, 2, almost there, 1, deeper still...Where are you?"

"In the woods. He's there, I can feel my excitement mounting..." In her vision Suzanne glanced over her shoulder, listening to Diane's words.

"The air is filled with the rich, woodsy scent of evergreen trees, tall grasses, and the fragrance of flowers. As you move closer, you notice that around the base of this mountain is a pathway made of flat, smooth stones... You're drawn to follow it and as you begin to walk down this path, you notice the little white flowers peeking out of the deep green foliage that edge the pathway. This lends a quaint, yet mystical sense to your surroundings...you find yourself in a meadow filled with sweet grass and wildflowers in hues of extraordinary colors. The meadow is spacious and extends out to the base of a beautiful mountain. These surroundings feel good, safe, and peaceful..."

Suzanne emerged from the grove of trees into the meadow of which the hypnotherapist described. Her heart was about to burst with anticipation.

"The path seems to wind around to the other side of the mountain where you've never been before... and you feel drawn to follow it...to see where it leads you..."

Suzanne's breath quickened. She could feel the corners of her mouth lift into a smile. *Almost there.*

"Feeling very safe and protected you walk along the path... and it begins to curve around the base of this mountain...and you didn't notice it when you first started out, but you now begin to hear the familiar sound of cascading water...and you pick up your pace a bit, and before you know it, you have arrived at the other side of the mountain. The pathway has led you to a magnificent waterfall..."

Tearing at her bodice, she released her bosom from its prison of silk and whalebone. Next came her skirts, her pantaloons...she was naked.

"As you stand before it, you can feel the light, refreshing mist on your skin. You observe how the water descends creating a mist in the air as it fills the round rock pool below. Even though this pool is very wide, it's shallow enough—so, you feel comfortable wading in it. And the temperature of the water is perfect..."

She moved gracefully toward the edge of the water...Diane's melodic words guiding her forward...

"Without hesitation, you step into the gentle pool of water and feel the instant calming effect it has upon your entire being. You step forward allowing the cascading waters to descend over you. The water feels refreshing, cleansing and completely soothing..."

Suzanne's body felt buoyant, *free*...

"Relaxing even deeper now, you realize this is the time and place to let go of any worry or fear you may have been carrying around in your mind. And you include any other unconstructive emotions, or mindsets that have been intruding on your positive nature..."

She laid back in the water, floating like a cork on the sea. Rainbows glistening in the mist doused her until it was as if she were made of diamond dust.

"Allow the waterfall now to rinse away any and all vestiges of negativity... rinsing it all away under the cascading waters...feel the release, the letting go...the relief and the lifting of any heaviness that was once there. Feeling so deeply relaxed and light of spirit..."

A butterfly landed on her hand, and she welcomed the creature in her mind... Suzanne dipped underwater, as the butterfly flitted above her...when she surfaced... "Voltaire—my love. You came."

"How could I not, my dearest Émilie?" Voltaire stripped out of his waistcoat, shirt, breeches, and dove into the water. When he reached her, he gathered her in his arms in a tight embrace. Suzanne felt as though she were watching a video of two lovers, with one exception, her heart was attached to the story. As she tossed and turned in the chair, Diane's voice wafted through the air...

"And now it's almost time to leave the waterfall, so you step back for a moment standing in the gentle pool of water, taking a fully nourishing deep breath...and as you do, you realize how much lighter you feel and how very centered you are. Standing before the waterfall you feel strong, refreshed, and renewed...

Locked in an embrace, they bobbed in the water, kissing, playing, loving, fulfilling each other's needs.

"And as you turn to leave, you become aware of the sun's rays beaming down upon your body with its nourishing warmth like a comforting blanket. And the golden energetic glow of the sun acknowledges your heart's strength and vitality. And the glow illuminates the love you hold within your heart that is a healer unto itself..."

She waded toward the shore, about to leave, but when she turned, another man had taken Voltaire's place...a man she recognized but could not place. His essence, strong, powerful. The hypnotherapist's voice urged her to move forward.

"Gather the information you need from this moment... realize, from the peaceful surroundings of this waterfall, this is the perfect place in time to retrieve answers that will help you in your healing and discovery."

"—you came," Suzanne mumbled, as if in a deep sleep.

"Being very balanced in mind and body and under your own control at all times, as I count down from 5 to 1, upon reaching the number 1, I want you to step out into a life that has a direct correlation to an issue you are having in your current life. This information has always been there, and now is the perfect time to retrieve it..."

"I am with child," she cried.

"My heart is yours, and forever will be," he said.

"5, 4, 3, 2 - 1 Stepping out now..."

Suzanne reached the shore, grabbing her clothing as she ran.

Diane's words became the pulse coursing through her body.

"Now, knowing its time to return... you begin your journey

along the stone pathway, bringing yourself all the way back...all the way back up to here and now feeling strong, resilient and refreshed."

Suzanne mounted her steed, and let the wind carry her home.

"Go ahead and open your eyes..."

Suzanne sat up and wrapped her arms around her body. "It was him."

Diane made a note. "Who? And what was your connection?"

"There were two men. I called one Voltaire, the other was so familiar, my feelings for him deep, undeniable. Voltaire called me Émilie. I saw Voltaire and Émilie the other day in a vision when I held a leather shoe I had worn to a Renaissance Fair." She shivered. "I find it bizarre how clear these visions are."

"Could you tell what period of time you were visiting?"

"By the way they were dressed, I'd say somewhere in the mid seventeen to eighteen hundreds."

"Any idea where you were?"

"Sam and I visited Paris last spring. The skies and the countryside reminded me of France."

"What else do you remember?"

"I was in love with them both, but I think one broke my heart—I couldn't quite make the connection. I felt as if I knew him, but nothing came to me. My emotions for them both were so strong."

Diane nodded. "It's all there, all we have to do is go get it." She turned off her recorder. "Go home, look up the names you got, see if there is any significance to what you are dealing with now. Chances are, there is a strong correlation. We can do another regression when you're ready."

**

When Suzanne arrived home, she took the hypnotherapist's advice and fired up her commuter. She typed in Voltaire and Émilie. What came up in her search blew her mind. She dialed Linda.

"You're not going to believe this," she blurted into the phone before Linda could speak.

"Well, Missy. I gather it's pretty darn exciting—you sound like you're about to levitate."

"I had a past-life regression with Diane Potter today. The two people I've been seeing in my visions really existed—"

"Remind me of the names—"

"Voltaire and Émilie du Châtelet."

"Wasn't he a writer or a poet?"

"Yes. Writer, poet, philosopher... Émilie was a brilliant mathematician...and although she was married, she and Voltaire had a passionate love affair for over fifteen years."

"So, you think you were Émilie, and this guy, Garian, was Voltaire?"

"Quite possibly. According to history, Émilie broke Voltaire's heart when she took up with a younger man, the Marquis de Saint-Lambert, another poet. She ended up getting pregnant with his child at the age of forty-four and died after giving birth. Voltaire was devastated."

"Interesting. A love triangle. Kind of what's going on in this lifetime, wouldn't you say?"

"No—I'm not—Sam is—"

"I'm not saying you're having a thing with Garian, but if history *is* repeating itself, it would be interesting to know why? What is there to learn from the experience?"

"Émilie and Voltaire made great strides during the Age of Enlightenment according to the article I read, perhaps my relationship with Garian is supposed to be one of enlightenment, and nothing more?" Even as her words escaped her lips

Suzanne imagined the passion between the couple, invoking once again a sense of betrayal. Or *guilty pleasure?*

Suzanne ended her conversation with Linda and scrolled through her messages. Two missed calls from Sam and a voice message. The urgency in his voice made her bubbly mood go flat.

"What's up Sam?"

"I need your help."

"More dead bodies at the Phillips' place?"

"Not this time. We have another dead kid."

**

Suzanne wound her way through the lobby, signed in, and was escorted to Sam's office.

"Why didn't you text—I would have met you?"

"It's okay. I'm a big girl. I can find my way."

Sam took a moment to access her attitude. "I appreciate you coming all the way down here."

"No need to thank me. I'm on the payroll."

"Everything okay? I sense—"

"I'm fine." The smile on her face didn't reach her eyes. "Why don't you fill me in?"

"Someone is distributing deadly drugs at the schools. The latest death was a seventeen-year-old who ingested a breath mint laced with fentanyl. He ran his car into a tree. He's the fifth victim in the last two weeks. We haven't been able to get a bead on where the drugs are coming from."

Suzanne closed her eyes. She saw children playing in the street, their clothes tattered and filthy. Animals roamed freely, their bones protruding from their emaciated hides. The scene segued to another...immigrants huddled in groups, trying to stay warm as they navigated their way towards the U.S. border. Suzanne pressed the universe to reveal more. Suddenly, a man with a gun turned and looked her in the eye. His scarred face had appeared to her once before, when he fed one of his men to the savage beast trained to keep his workers in line. This time it wasn't a dog she saw tethered to the heavy chain...it was a boy. *Raphael.*

**

The sketch artist listened as Suzanne described the boy's face. "Dark hair, brown eyes...long lashes. Full lips, small nose... yes, like that, but the face is slender, almost feminine. He's beautiful."

Sam peered over Suzanne's shoulder. "How old do you think he is?"

"Thirteen."

"You sure?"

"Yes. The number popped up with his name. Raphael."

"You knew the kid's name? Why didn't you—"

"I didn't connect the dots."

Sam moved away, creating a chasm between them. She watched as he stood in front of the window, his hands shoved in his pocket, one hand clutching his sobriety coin, she surmised.

"The boy has a dimple in his chin," she said to the artist, her eyes still fixed on Sam. "Make his hair longer." She stepped away from the artist. "Sam?"

He withdrew his hands from his pockets but didn't budge. "Thirteen," he muttered. "Geezus."

Suzanne placed her hand on his shoulder. "He comes from nothing."

"Am I supposed to feel sorry for him? And what about the kids who overdosed on the poison he's peddling?"

"It's not what you think."

He sighed and swiped his face with his hand. "I'm sure you're right. Thanks for doing this. As soon as you finish with the sketch, I can get my men to pick him up."

"I'd like to be here when you bring him in."

He nodded. "Of course."

Suzanne watched him go, her heart feeling as though it were being squeezed. She loved him, but she was seeing sides of him that made her second guess her feelings about marriage. The juxtaposition between Sam and Garian gave her reasons to question her future. Sam was intense. Garian was calm, *sensitive*.

"Suzanne?" The artist's voice broke her from her reverie. "How's this?"

Suzanne studied the drawing. "Yes. That's him. That's Raphael." ***

CHAPTER TWENTY-ONE

Making Up is Hard to Do

Steven was parked outside of Suzanne's house when she arrived home. She was in no mood to spar with her brother. She had had enough attitude from Sam. In all fairness, she may have caused the riff between them. Ever since she met Garian, things had changed. She was hungry for the knowledge that brought them together, she wanted to understand why she craved knowing more about the past they had shared. Her desire to be with Sam waned; it was as if Garian held her under his spell, one she didn't want to break free from. Their conversations were stimulating, and deep, something she didn't have with Sam. Was that the attraction?

Steven stepped out of his car. "Hey Suz."

"What's the occasion?"

"I was in the neighborhood."

"You were waiting..."

"Okay, yeah, I've been here a while."

Suzanne eyed him suspiciously. "What's up?"

"Can we talk?"

"Sure," she nodded. "Have you eaten? Let's go get a burger."

"Nah, can't. Karen's started cooking already..."

"Excellent. Then she hasn't ditched you for her college crush."

"Nope. You were right about that."

Once inside, Suzanne poured herself a glass of wine. She offered one to Steven, but he refused. "So, tell me—what's on your mind?"

"You don't know?"

"Steven—I'm not a mind reader."

"You were right about Karen. She told me everything, and it was like you said—she liked the attention she was getting from her old crush."

Suzanne wondered if she had the same issue with Sam. Perhaps she liked Garian's attention. It seemed as though the flame between them went out when the entities showed up. "Nothing psychic about it, Steven. I used common sense, that's all." Suzanne grabbed Steven's face. "Are you going to tell me what happened? Or do I have to squeeze it out of you?"

Steven brought her hands to his mouth as if to take a bite.

"Don't you dare!" she cried. "Now tell me why you waited, God knows how long, to talk to me?"

"I need to know how to make things right with Karen. How do I show her how much she means to me?"

"Quit being an ass for one. I mean—your snarkiness is funny to a point, but I'm sure it gets old. Try having conversations that aren't about you. And for God's sake, take her somewhere nicer than Dairy Queen."

"She loves Dairy Queen."

"No, Steven—*you* love Dairy Queen—she's just along for the ride."

"She told you that?"

"It's the tone in which she mentions Dairy Queen when I ask her where you two have been lately."

"Oh."

"Yeah—oh. When's the last time you did something spontaneous?" Her late-night rendezvous with Sam came to mind. *Lemon pie. Stargazing.* She missed those times.

"I thought married couples were supposed to be comfortable with their lifestyle. We can count on one another—we finish each other's sentences."

"What about passion?"

"We had that."

"Passion isn't something you had, it's something you have."

"Do you think Tage Betterman is more passionate than me?"

"I think you should stop worrying about Tage Betterman and start being the man she needs *you* to be. He's a distraction for—" Suzanne words struck a chord. She wasn't referring to Karen. She too needed attention. "Take her on a cruise. Or a late-night picnic. Remind her why she fell in love with *you*." *Before it's too late.*

Steven slumped into a kitchen chair, deep in thought. Suzanne's brain buzzed, rehashing her own words. Images of a young woman running through a field, fistfuls of teal colored silk bunched in her hands, tears streaming down her face flitted through her mind like an elusive butterfly. *Did he break my heart? Or did I break his?*

"I better go. Karen hates when I'm late." Steven rose, his arms stretched before him. "You're all right, kiddo. Mom and Dad would've been proud."

Suzanne pulled out from his embrace. "Funny, Mom said the same thing about you."

Steven pivoted around in a circle, "You're kidding me—she's here?"

Suzanne smiled and pointed toward the doorway. "Yep—right over there."

**

Suzanne wasn't expecting Sam's call. It was late, she was dressed for bed, a facial mask in place, and a book on spirits propped on her bent knee. "Hey," she said.

"Sorry I didn't get a chance to thank you for coming down today. The sketch was very helpful. Some of the kids at the high school recognized him. Candy man is what he calls himself."

"Excellent." She paused, suddenly feeling awkward.

"I know I've been acting like a horse's ass lately—how can I make it up to you?"

"We've both been occupied, Sam. No one is at fault."

"I miss you. I miss holding you, kissing you, feeling your heart beat against mine..."

"I love hearing you say that Sam but—"

"I'm listening..."

"I need time to figure things out."

"Take all the time you need. I'm not going anywhere."

"Good to know. Did you find the boy?"

"Not yet. Which reminds me, I need to call Timarie and Paul, follow up on the carpenters I recommended to repair their floor." He paused. "How about if I give you a ring when we find the boy?"

Suzanne sensed the sadness in his voic and wanted to cry. The vision of the woman running through the field reappeared in her third eye. *Why is she running away?*

**

Sam's heart sank. He knew she wanted her space, and he saw no other choice than to give her what she wanted, but damn it hurt. He believed she loved him, and that everything would be all right...however, in that moment the ache in his heart made him feel like a liar.

He dialed the Phillips' residence. No one answered.

CHAPTER TWENTY-TWO

Home Invasion

Timarie heard the noise first and called to her snoozing husband. "Paul," she hissed. "Paul—wake up! There's something outside."

"What—what?" He eased himself upright, rubbing sleep from his eyes. "Must've dozed off."

"There's something outside—shhh...listen."

They both remained quiet for a moment, assessing the noise outside. The sound of breaking glass caused them both alarm. "I shut the door to the grow house, didn't I?" Paul asked.

"I thought so."

Paul leapt to his feet. Timarie followed him to the window. A face appeared in the window, startling them both. The bang on the front door was followed by a spray of bullets. Paul pulled Timarie to the floor, shielding her trembling body with his six-foot frame. They both flinched when the door flew open and heavy boots came toward them.

"What have we here?" The thick accent made the couple shake even more.

"What do you want? Money?" Paul stammered. He sat up, his jaw set as he spoke. "You can take my plants—they'll bring you a fortune—please let us—" The butt of an AK-47 knocked the words out of his mouth and loosened his front teeth. Blood pooling on his tongue prevented him from saying more.

"Please," Timarie begged. "Don't kill us—we're botanical engineers—scientists—we can help you."

The man's scar rippled as one side of his mouth lifted into a snarl. Just then two men came up behind him. One of the men held a plant in his hand. "Aye hombre! Que bueno es esto."

The scar face man examined the plant, his gun aimed at Paul's head. His sinister scowl vanished. More inquisitive now, he asked, "You grow this?"

Paul swallowed hard. "Yes, my wife and I—"

The man withdrew the AK-47 as he barked orders to his men. "Amarralos."

Once the couple was bound, gagged and blindfolded, they were shoved into the back of their own van.

Timarie reached for Paul's hand in the darkness. Laughter erupted when another man's hand intervened. Despite her resistance, he guided her hand into his mouth and sucked on her fingers. Timarie shrieked, prompting another bought of laughter. Hands tied; her only defense was to kick. Big mistake. A fist came out of nowhere. She saw stars.

**

"Go away!" Suzanne sat straight up in bed. Her wet hair clung to her face. Her nightgown clung to her skin. Chills ran up and down her body. Her pulse raced to keep up. She took deep breaths, willing the stampede in her chest to slow down. *Just a dream.*

The spirits across the room didn't concur.

"What do you want?" *Silly question.* She knew the answer. They wanted justice.

In her dream she saw a man and a woman. They were vaguely familiar, but she couldn't recall where she knew them from...they knelt before the scar-faced man, their heads bowed, as if in prayer. *No, not prayer. They were pleading for their lives.* She scooted back down and pulled the covers to her chin to quell her shivering. *Why am I so cold?* Her legs began to cramp, a sharp pain shot through her temple. She saw stars. Her body felt as though it were detaching from her brain. *I'm falling. No. Losing consciousness.* She struggled to stay alert, but it was no use. She blacked out.

**

Timarie awoke, her head splitting with pain. She felt for the lump throbbing near her temple. She reached for Paul, came away with sticky fingers and groaned. The rag in her mouth muffled her cries. Paul didn't respond. The sound of heavy footsteps silenced her.

"Cuidenlos. Si causan problemas, mátalos."

She couldn't see who was speaking, but she recognized his voice. It was the scar-faced man. His deep voice, as memorable as his cold eyes. She remained still. Whoever the man was leaving in charge was given the order to kill her and Paul if they caused trouble. Her bladder was full, and she was on the verge of passing out again.

Small hands reached for her blindfold and lifted it slightly. She could barely make out the boy's face. "Ah, Americano," he said. He clicked the roof of his mouth with his tongue. "Poor lady."

**

Sam put an APB out for the boy as soon as the sketch was finished, but the boy was nowhere to be found. He had every man available casing the schools, convenient stores, fast food joints, and anywhere a kid might hang out. No luck. He thought about calling Suzanne to see if she felt anything, but thought better of it. He decided to call Timarie and Paul instead. When he didn't get an answer, he left a message.

"Hello, this is Sam Metzger calling from the Goldorado Sheriff's Department. I was checking to see if the carpenter I recommended came through for you...I appreciated your cooperation, the least I could do was make sure we cleaned up after ourselves. Give me a call at your earliest convenience, please. Bye now."

He had a bad feeling about the Phillips. Maybe Suzanne was rubbing off on him or he was disappointed neither of them picked up. Granted, calling them was a diversion of sorts, only because he liked them, and wanted them to be happy living in the county he was sworn to protect. Or maybe it was because Timarie reminded him of his mom, and right now he needed someone to confide in. He was miserable without Suzanne. And he didn't know what to do.

＊＊

Suzanne awoke close to noon. She looked around the room. She was alone. The dream had drained her energy, but blacking out? That concerned her. Her head still hurt close to her temple, and she felt for a lump. *Nothing there.* She recalled seeing the boy again, but couldn't remember where, or when. She got up to take a shower, in hopes that the foggy feeling would go away.

She turned on the faucet and checked her phone. She half-expected to see a message from Sam. *You're pushing him away.* She read the text she received from Garian.

Will you have time to hang out after class on Thursday?

Butterflies filled her stomach. She replied:

Perhaps...what did you have in mind?

She waited for his reply. After a few minutes, she gave up and stepped into the shower.

Suddenly, she felt thirsty. Her wrists ached. Raphael's image flashed like a strobe behind her closed lids. She changed the shower head setting and let hot water pummel her shoulder muscles. Why am I so sore? Suddenly she was bombarded by snippets of information at a dizzying rate. She wanted to stamp her feet to make it stop, but she knew the information was important. Pay attention.

She saw the lake by the Phillips' place, the dead bodies, the scarred-face man, the little girl, and Raphael. She heard the cries of the victims as guns riddled their bodies with bullets. She saw Raphael running...her head began to throb...she felt dirty. Ashamed. Violated.

She rinsed, dried, and picked up her phone. "Sam? Sam—what happened?"

**

Sam, startled by Suzanne's call, didn't connect the dots. "What are you talking about?"

"Something's wrong. I'm seeing the boy, the Phillips' place. Is there a connection? Did you find him? Was he there? At the lake or something?"

"Slow down." Sam closed his office door. "Tell me again, what did you see?"

"It all came so fast. I saw Raphael, the Phillips' place, the migrants who were killed—and that man."

"What man?"

"He has a long scar on his face."

**

Sam opened his laptop and keyed in cartel members. He scrolled through page after page of mugshots. After the third page he stopped. "I'm sending you a mugshot of one of the Sinaloa Cartel members, Carlos García.

Silence lingered between them for a moment, and then, "Okay, the photo came through—but it's not him. The man I keep seeing has a broader face—meaner eyes."

Sam resumed scrolling through his inventory of thugs. "Is it possible the scar is recent?"

"I don't know—anything is possible."

"It would be very helpful if you could come down to the station and go through this list with me."

Suzanne checked the time. If she got home by 4 P.M., she'd have time to freshen up before class. "I can be there in an hour, but I have a hard stop at three."

"Fair enough. See you soon."

Sam viewed a couple more pages to occupy his mind. Hard stop at three? It was Thursday. Suzanne had class on Thursday nights. *Some things are more important.*

Acid burned in the pit of his stomach. Stay busy. Don't think about her. Them. He had an hour to kill. He decided to take a ride up the hill, pay a visit to the Phillips.

When he drove up the drive, he noticed their vehicle was gone. Perhaps one or both went to town. As he pulled up closer to the house, he took a double take. A buck stood in their doorway munching away on a piece of bread, the plastic wrapper dangling from one antler. Sam's blood ran cold. This can't be good.

He hopped out of his SUV, scaring the buck away. Luckily in the buck's haste to get away, the wrapper took flight as well.

Sam drew his weapon and proceeded with caution. He didn't get too far into the foyer before he spotted blood on the floor. "Jake—it's Sam. Send a team up to Phillips' place—I got a bad feeling."

**

Suzanne waited in the lobby for Sam to return to his office. The least he could've done was text her, let her know when he planned on returning, but she had the feeling something was very wrong. She appealed to the desk sergeant. "Can you call Sam? Ask him which mugshots I'm supposed to be looking at? I don't need him to be here for that, do I? Aren't they in a database?"

The desk sergeant obliged. "I sent him another message—let him know you're still waiting."

Suddenly, her phone rang in her hand. "Hey—sorry, I'm at the Phillips' home trying to figure out what happened. When I arrived, their car was gone, the front door was wide open, and there's blood on the floor."

"Maybe one of them got hurt—did you call Marshall Hospital?"

"Yes. They're not at Marshall or Folsom."

"Of course—"

"Do you know something?"

"The dream I had last night—there was a woman and a man—they seemed familiar, but I couldn't place them."

"Stay put. I'll be there in ten."

**

"Take your time. Let me know if any of these guys look like the man in your dream."

Suzanne stared at the screen, trying to visualize the scar-faced man as she scrolled through the photos. Some looked similar, the hatred in their eyes a reflection of what lay beneath the surface and in their souls. Time passed quickly, but the data was overwhelming, and sitting hunched over a computer, taxing. She leaned back to stretch. She felt the heat of Sam's body behind her.

"It's 3:02. You said you had a hard stop at three."

"This is more important."

"Thanks," he said, and gently squeezed her shoulder. Their eyes held for what seemed like eternity. Sam broke away first. "I better check in with my men."

"Sure," she said, and turned her attention back to the screen.

He paced the room, talking, texting, stealing glances her way. He wanted to take her in his arms, kiss her into the night. Make love to her until dawn. He had to have faith that she'd come around in her own time. It was 3:30. Baby steps.

"None of these men match the man in my visions. What shall I do now?"

"There are several cartels moving into this area, the Sinaloa, La Linea, and CJNG are the biggest. I could keep you here for days...maybe when you have more time..."

"Those people are missing, Sam, I will do whatever it takes..."

"Great. Let me grab a couple of coffees, be right back."

Sam dialed Jake. "Anything?"

"The blood belongs to Paul Phillips. We matched the blood on the floor with the DNA sample he gave us before we dragged the lake. Wasn't much of a scuffle."

"Did you check the grow house yet?"

"Sure did. It's a mess. Mostly broken glass, bulbs and such..."

"Are the plants still there?"

"Negative. We didn't find any plants."

"Either someone got lucky, or someone knew what they were growing. Those plants aren't your ordinary variety."

"Hard to believe anyone would kidnap someone over a few pot plants."

"The Phillips are horticulture engineers. Those weren't just any plants."

"That gives us a place to start."

"Excellent. Keep me posted."
**

At 8P.M. Suzanne received a text from Garian.
Change your mind?
She smiled. Something came up. Sorry.
Right.
Right? She shook her head. What was that supposed to mean? Why would he have any reason to doubt her?
I'm working. Missing persons.
No response. She tossed her phone back into her purse. Deep inside, she wasn't surprised by his actions, or lack of. Unlike Sam, Garian demanded attention...when he wanted it... when it suited him. He had a tendency to pout when he didn't get his way.

"I got us a couple of sandwiches. I feel guilty keeping you so late."

"It's fine. In all honesty, I'd love to find out who this guy is myself. He gives me the creeps."

"I never realized how many criminals had scarred faces."

"It almost seems like their battle scars are a rite of passage, like tattoos."

"Two steps forward, three steps back. We catch these guys, send them back to Mexico and they show up a week or two later. They've dug tunnels from Mexico to the U.S., there's no stopping them."

"The good thing is the couple in my dream were still alive." She paused. "I know you think Raphael is a punk that needs to be put behind bars, but I see a kid who is trying to survive."

"I can't determine that until we find him."

"I believe when you find him, you'll find the couple and visa-versa."
**

Suzanne got home later than expected. She was exhausted

and immediately readied herself for bed. The house was quiet, free of drafts, cold spots and entities. She looked forward to a good night's sleep. She purposely left her phone downstairs. She didn't want to keep checking to see if Garian left a message. She felt disappointed at his reaction to her absence. *Life happens.* It wasn't long before she drifted off to sleep.

In her dream she leaned out of the window, the neckline of her gown slouched around her bare shoulders, her bosom in full swell. She held a locket in her hand, sliding it back and forth across the mirror link chain circling her neck. Where is he? The sun would be setting soon...too late for an outdoor picnic...her heart no longer light, but laden. He's not coming. The life inside her moved...regret consumed her soul...she wanted to die.

The scene morphed into another. Sam, waiting at the altar, while she and Garian made love on her living room floor. "No," she murmured in her sleep. "I can't—" But there was no use protesting, Garian slipped inside her, and they became one.

At 3 A.M., she awoke, feeling as though she had run a marathon. Her skin and hair, damp. Her heart, stampeding in her chest. She opened her eyes and screamed.

CHAPTER TWENTY-THREE

Survival of the Fittest

Timarie tried to scream, but the gag in her mouth muffled the sound. Her eyes darted around, trying to make sense of her surroundings. Dirty concrete walls. Earthen floor. She hadn't a clue.

The man with the scarred face loomed over her, the barrel of the AK47 pointed between her eyes. She glanced at Paul. His eyes were bugged out, his face beet red. Her first thought was, *He's having a heart attack.* Her eyes pleaded with her captor. *Please don't kill us.*

Miguel Guzman, better known as Diablo, had no patience for mewling. His mission was clear: deliver the goods, no excuses. Being tipped off that the Sheriff's Department was dragging the lake was a stroke of luck; discovering the new occupants were horticulturists an added bonus. If he could leverage his position by producing quality cannabis, he might climb the ranks, retire in style, like the men who employed him. A Beatles song echoed in his mind. Baby You're a Rich Man, Baby You're a Rich Man, Baby You're a Rich Man too. He understood the gringo's language, everything came with a price.

He slung his gun over his shoulder and deftly pulled a switchblade from his boot. His deep voice rumbled with mirth as he saw the terror etched on Timarie's face. With one swift motion, he sliced her gag in two. She gasped for air, but remained silent.

"Your husband—he can be trusted not to be foolish?"

"Yes."

Miguel eyed Paul with suspicion. "I will kill him—"

Timarie shivered. "We won't cause you any trouble. I promise."

"Very well, then." He cut the fabric from Paul's face, nicking his cheek. The sight of blood made him laugh. "Oops," he said, laughing harder.

Raphael stood close by. He didn't flinch.

"Get them food and drink," Miguel demanded. "Then bring them to me."

Raphael obeyed.

**

Back at the station, Suzanne hit the return key on Sam's computer, bringing up another page of photos. Her eyes scanned back and forth, while she secretly prayed for the scarred face to appear on the screen. Sam placed a cup of coffee on the desk, along with a chocolate croissant on a napkin.

"Anything?" he asked.

"Not yet. Are all of these men in prison?"

"I wish. A good percentage were deported, but chances are they've crossed the open border and are walking our streets." Sam noticed she had been rubbing her wrists. "You okay?" He nodded toward her hands.

"Yeah. No. I'm fine...I guess."

"I'm listening." Her expression softened, and he saw a spark of emotion...maybe gratitude.

"I woke up screaming last night. I was so terrified." Tears filled her eyes, and Sam rushed to comfort her.

"Aw baby, I should've been there with you." He massaged her shoulders. She stiffened.

"I'm okay. It was scary, that's all...an empathetic reaction... nothing to worry about."

"I think you being terrified is a lot to worry about."

"I didn't bring it up for you to—" She stopped, mid-sentence. "Oh Sam, I don't want to hurt you."

Hands up, Sam surrendered. "No—I'm good—really." He checked his watch. "I'll be right back—I told Kelly I'd touch base with her before she left today." He didn't wait for Suzanne to respond. He turned and left the room.

Suzanne scrolled through another page;dignitaries her thoughts focused on the pain she just caused the man she loved instead of the faces before her. She almost missed the one she'd been looking for. Miguel Guzman. "There you are."

**

Miguel studied the small plants. "You say these are how old?"

Paul explored his teeth with his tongue. The sips of water he was given didn't wash away the grit from the rag that had been stuffed in his mouth. "Forty years," he said. "I germinated them in college."

"Tell me what to do."

Paul glanced at Timarie, then directed his answer to

Miguel. "I started with skunk seeds...I soaked them for a while...waited to see if they would sink or not. Healthy seeds sink, indicating their potential for sprouting." He shook his head. "You don't want to bother with the floaters—it means they're non-viable—you're wasting your time. I can help you identify the best candidates for cultivation—but first—let my wife go free."

Timarie screamed when Paul's demand was met with the butt of Miguel's gun.

**

Miguel wasn't pleased when one of his men reported that Raphael's description went out on an APB, but when he got word that his was too, he exploded. "Poli puercos!" They both would have to lie low for a while. He had a mind to kill the kid, but then he'd have to find another pretty face to keep his men happy. Fortunately, he recalled a conversation he once had with his boss.

"Few people know about the underground facility in Omo Ranch," the man said, in a cocky, hushed, *you know what I mean* voice. "It was once a logging and mining town. It's a rural area, everyone lives on their own accord. Some grow grapes, some have small fruit farms, some you don't ask."

"Albert Cody has a place there. He likes to stay on my good side. He's a convicted pedophile–served his time, but he still has an itch for kiddie porn. He'll do *anything* to stay off the radar."

**

The plan was solid. Miguel knew alerting the police to his invasion would draw attention. Albert didn't need anyone nosing around his property asking questions. He packed up his tent, fishing gear, his laptop, a stack of magazines and let Miguel have the run of his place. "Live and Let Live," his motto.

Miguel put extra watch around the perimeter of the ranch, sent another *rata de borde* to peddle the goods at the schools. Border rats were useful, expendable. He left Raphael to play host to the gringo couple, who in turn would elevate his status... in time. It would all work out. Eventually.

He, himself, had been a border rat. He worked for a farmer picking tomatoes for three years before the cousin of a drug cartel member took notice. Ricardo Garcia, a Sinaloa member, groomed Miguel for success once he proved himself by killing a rival gang member.

Ricardo had connections and took Miguel under his wing. Miguel attended parties with beautiful women and wealthy men. Men who didn't like to get their hands dirty. Political figures, Hollywood moguls, foreign dignitaries, and such. Drugs were big business. Everyone wanted part of the action, but it was guys like Miguel that kept the money flowing, and the open border made his job that much easier. One gringo called the immigrants minions. They were loaded onto buses and shipped all over the U.S. to be sold into drug trafficking, sex trafficking, domestic slavery. Miguel considered himself fortunate to take his pick of the border rats before the others, but life could be better...

When Miguel was sixteen, one of the drug lord's *putas* lusted after him. She was barely sixteen herself. Javier was the drug lord's name, he was at least thirty, and was known for his bad temper. He knew better than to return the girl's advances, but to make a point, Javier grabbed Miguel by the hair and sliced his face open from the corner of his eye to his jaw, and then made the girl lap up the blood while he raped her from behind.

Before Miguel turned eighteen, he hunted Javier down and drove a hot poker through his eye, killing him instantly. A California politician witnessed Miguel's act of revenge from the backseat of his Town car and hired Miguel on the spot. He has been on the man's payroll for twelve years. Only once did he serve time for one of his dastardly deeds, and only for six months. He was loyal, dependable, and determined to get the job done, *at any cost.*

CHAPTER TWENTY-FOUR

Bassi Falls

Coffee tasted flat, mirroring Suzanne's mood. She poured another dollop of cream into her cup, added a dash of cinnamon and took another sip. Suddenly, the cup shattered in her hand. A shard of glass sliced through her right palm, the handle remained intact in her left. Hot liquid splashed everywhere. "How—" She stared at the floor in disbelief. When the room began to spin, she dropped the broken cup into the sink and hung onto the counter for dear life. The dizziness lasted a minute or two, accompanied by swirling images of fluorescent light fixtures suspended from a stained ceiling. The scream echoing in her head—had she heard it before? Dark shadows squeezed her peripheral vision into a telescopic dot. Her footing disappeared beneath her, and she collapsed on the floor.

**

Sam listened to ring after ring, waiting patiently for Suzanne to answer her phone. An APB had gone out on Miguel Guzman, and he wanted to be sure Suzanne was safe. When her message prompt came on, he squeezed his eyes shut, and unclenched his jaw. "Good morning, Suzanne, it's Sam—call me."

He tossed his phone on his desk, frustrated with the turn in their relationship. He was quick to retrieve his phone when it rang. "Sam Metzger—"

"Jake here, Sam. I think you need to see this."

"Can you be specific?"

"Yeah, sorry. We got an anonymous tip—six migrants murdered on the Bassi Falls Trail."

"Why am I just finding out about this?"

"The call was garbled. You know how the reception is up there—sketchy as hell. We just got here. Are you coming up?"

"Yes, I'm on my way."

"Call me when you get to Ice House Road and I'll meet you."

Sam's stomach churned acid. *What were migrants doing on Bassi Trail?* He was curious to know if the murders were linked to Guzman. He would comb the area for illegal grow houses with high hopes of finding Timarie and Paul Phillips.

**

Steven peeked through the sidelight window flanking Suzanne's front door and rang the bell a second time. When she didn't answer, he knocked. This time he pressed his cupped hands on the glass for a better view into the hallway leading into the kitchen. Next, he tried the latch on the front door. Locked. He went around to the back yard.

Suzanne wasn't out back, but the sliding glass door was cracked enough to let in the crisp morning air. "Suzanne?" He called. He let himself in. "Suz? Where are you?" He started walking towards the stairway, when he saw his sister lying on the kitchen floor in a puddle of blood. "Geezuz!" he cried.

He grabbed a dish towel off the sink, wrapped her hand, and checked her pulse. He lifted each eyelid, looking for a possible concussion. "Suz? Can you hear me?" He dialed 911.

**

Sam called Jake when he arrived at the fork leading to the Bassi Trail. "Be right there," Spence said. Sam looked at his phone, willing Suzanne's number to pop up and ease his pain. When it did, he laughed out loud.

"I was just thinking about you..."

"It's Steven, Sam. I'm on the way to the hospital. I found Suzanne lying on her kitchen floor, unconscious. Her hand is cut pretty bad. I found a broken cup in the sink—there was a lot of blood. Paramedic said she should be all right—but they want her to have a CAT scan to make sure—she sustained a concussion from the fall."

A chill ran the length of Sam's body. A lump formed in his throat. He held back something foreign, an emotion he felt once before...when she was missing...when Dixon had drugged her and left her to die. Before he could contain himself, the feeling erupted into a bellow.

"Sam! Sam—you okay?" Jake yelled, breaking into a run.

Sam doubled over, clutching the phone to his chest. A muffled voice could be heard between the folds of his shirt. Jake grabbed the phone.

"Officer Jake Walters here, who is this?"

"Steven Cash—is Sam all right?"

"Sam?" Jake wrapped an arm around Sam and helped him upright. "You okay? What's going on?"

"Suzanne's hurt."

"Oh shit." Jake handed Sam his phone. "Steven is still on the line."

"Steven—text me the details. I'll be there as soon as I can." Sam stuffed his phone in his pocket. "Take me to the bodies, then I need to get to the hospital."

The two men clipped along at a fast pace. Ahead, Sam could see the others circled around the crime scene. "How many?"

"Six. Youngest appears to be about thirteen."

The men cleared a path as Sam approached. He eased his way between them and squatted down. What he saw made his blood run cold again. The right palm on each of the bodies had been sliced open on what would be called the "line of life." Sam wondered if Suzanne bore the same wound, and if there was any connection.

"Pret-ty savage," Officer Grimes said, patting Sam on the back. "Jake said Suzanne's in the hospital. Go—we got this."

"Thanks. I'll check back in an hour."

Sam hiked back to his car. A single tear slipped down his cheek. He swore it was allergies.

**

Suzanne felt disoriented. "Is this necessary? I broke a cup—lost my balance, no big deal."

Steven's stare, incredulous, when he said, "You were out cold on the floor, lying in a puddle of blood. To me, that's a big deal." He leaned forward until they were eye to eye. "What happened?"

"I don't know. The cup shattered in my hand. Must've been defective or something—or maybe I squeezed too hard—I am becoming bionic you know."

"Cut the shit, Suz. You scared the crap out of me." He lifted her chin. "What would've happened if I hadn't stopped by? Ever think of that, Miss Smarty-pants?"

"Geez, Steven, you haven't called me that since I was ten."

He chuckled. "You think this is funny, don't you?"

Tears welled in her eyes. "No. Not one bit."

"I called Sam."

"Why did you do that?"

"What—he's not supposed to know? You're marrying the guy—why wouldn't I call him?"

Suzanne sighed. "F word. This really hurts." She held up her hand to relieve the throbbing. "I wish they'd hurry up and do the CT scan so we can leave." She closed her eyes and tilted her head back. Suddenly, the scarred face came into view. He looked right at her, then through her. She turned her head and saw six migrants lined up like ducks at the arcade. The scar-faced man ordered them to hold up their right hand. "Ladrones!" he shouted. "No one steals from me!" Then, one by one, he slashed their right hand open with his blade. Suzanne sat upright.

Steven's brow furrowed. "What the hell was that all about? You looked like you were possessed."

Suzanne shook off the images. "This was no accident," she said, waving her injured hand. "They're showing me what happened."

"Couldn't they have spared the blood—and the expense of this hospital visit?"

"I don't think spirits come with a handbook. They communicate the best way they know how. I was holding the cup in my right hand...I don't think it was a coincidence."

"Coincidence?" Sam stood in the doorway, his features shadowed with concern. "What happened?"

"I'm a klutz. What are you doing here?"

Steven placed his hand on her shoulder. "I called him, remember?" She flicked him away.

"Yes, I remember. You forgot to mention he was coming here." She shifted her weight on the narrow gurney. "I'm sorry, Sam...there was no reason for you to—"

"Behave like a man who cares?"

"I'm sure you were busy—I'm fine."

He stepped forward to examine her bandaged hand, repeating his question. "What happened?"

"A coffee cup shattered in my hand. Evidently, I don't know my own strength. Eighteen stitches."

Sam winced. "Is that all?"

"Think I should've held out for twenty?"

"Not funny. Were you having a vision when it happened?"

"How did you—?"

"Six migrants were found murdered at Bassi Falls—their right hands were sliced open."

Suzanne paled. "He accused them of stealing."

"Who?"

"The scar-faced man."

**

Sam left the hospital feeling relieved on one hand, in the dumps on the other. Suzanne suffered a concussion from her fall, but would be fine. However, her defensive demeanor required every ounce of patience he could muster. *I'm not the enemy.*

He tapped in Jake's number. "How's it going? Did the coroner get there?"

"They sent Dove, we requested forensics, like you said."

"Good. I'm on my way back up the hill. Ask Dove to wait, I'll be there within the hour."

"Will do. How's Suzanne? We've all been worried."

"She has a concussion—she'll be fine, thanks."

"What a relief. See you soon."

Sam disconnected the call, switched on his flashing red and blue lights, and increased his speed. The vehicles ahead moved over and he cut through traffic like a knife through butter, focusing on his driving rather than the twinge of heartbreak threatening to rear its ugly head. *She loves me,* he repeated to himself. He needed to believe it.

When he arrived on site, Dove greeted him with a handshake. "I've seen this kind of brutality in movies. There's a lot of sick fucks out there, Sam—this guy is sending a message."

"I agree, but to whom? We don't broadcast the details, and these people don't look like they watch the ten o'clock news—what am I missing?"

"You'd be surprised. I'm sure with today's technology, a selfie or two posing with the carnage would suffice as a warning to the next group brought in to pick up the slack."

Sam stood akimbo, shaking his head. "I'm not seeing a light at the end of this tunnel."

"Hang in there. How's Suzanne?"

Sam shrugged. "She'll be fine if her visions don't kill her."

Dove's wide-eyes narrowed to almost a squint. "That doesn't sound good."

"She had a doozy this morning—fell and hit her head. Sliced her hand pretty bad. Eighteen stitches. Fortunately, there doesn't seem to be any nerve or tendon damage."

"Damn—that's not cool."

"Tell me about it. A cup literally shattered in her hand. Sounds like the ghosties are trying to make a point of their own." He nodded toward the dead bodies. "Same hand as our victims. She says the spirits speak to her in Spanish. Some have been coming to her since the Phillips bought the Kenners place. And you know what we found there."

"Sounds like the cartel is using Goldorado County as a dumping ground for their illicit activity."

"And the hits keep on coming...ba-doom."

"Any more leads on the kid you suspected was dealing to the schools?"

"Nope. Disappeared. My guys have set their sights on a

replacement. No one has showed up thus far as we can tell. The good news is there haven't been any more drug induced deaths in the last week or two."

"Glad to hear it." Dove stretched out his hand again. "Let me get going so I can get my reports back to you."

Sam shook Dove's hand, bringing him in for a man-hug. "I'll be in touch."

"You do that—and give that beautiful fiancée of yours a hug from me."

"You got it."

Sam waved and turned back to the business at hand. Finding the slime-balls responsible for the six body bags lined up for transport to the morgue wasn't going to be an easy task.

CHAPTER TWENTY-FIVE

Desperation

Miguel sat on a bench, watching the sky change from inky blue to layers of powder blue and salmon, an AK47 perched between his knees. When the first sliver of light rose above the hill, he picked up his killing machine, aimed it at the sun, and fired. "Better than a fucking rooster," he mumbled. Two of his men appeared at his side in seconds flat, guns drawn, ready to do battle. "Bring me the gringos," he ordered.

The two men obeyed, and soon Timarie and Paul stood before him, barefoot, and groggy.

"The sun—it's a beautiful thing, don't you think?"

"It's actually a yellow dwarf star made up of hydrogen and helium. Scientists say it's been around for 4.5 billion years. I'd say it's pretty damn remarkable," Timarie said.

"How is your eye?" Miguel asked, without looking.

"Better—but my husband is experiencing dizziness. I think he has a concussion."

"I didn't ask about your husband—did I?"

"No, you didn't. But he can't—"

"Silence!"

A rooster crowed in the distance, making a mockery of the "Diablo's" order for silence. "I have work in the city today. Raphael will be in charge. Be advised that he is instructed to blow your heads off if you cause any trouble."

Timarie glanced at Paul. "Understood."

Miguel's henchmen escorted the couple back to the house.

**

Raphael overheard the conversation between the gringos and Diablo and wondered why Diablo trusted him. If he had the chance, he would bolt like a rabbit in a brush fire...but where would he go? He had no money. The police were looking for him...and if Diablo found him first, he would cut off his balls, and stuff them down his throat. Instead, he accepted his fate. He followed Miguel's orders and took charge.

"Ándale! Sit—there." Raphael pointed to a pile of tattered blankets in the corner. He turned his back, gritting his teeth. He liked the old couple. Especially the lady. She was smart, kind...like his abuelita. *Before she died.*

"Raphael—please. My husband needs a doctor."

"There is no doctor."

"But he'll die!"

"Not my problem."

**

Timarie sobbed softly against her husband's chest. His breathing was shallow, his pulse weak. Miguel had hit him hard —all because Paul wanted him to set her free. Diablo. *He's the devil all right.*

She could tell that Raphael was scared, even though he

acted otherwise. She could see it in his eyes. But what he did next assured her she had made a friend.

"Here," he said. Timarie took the wrapped cookie he pulled from his pocket. "He needs water." Raphael rinsed a plastic cup under the spigot right outside the door, filled it with water, and handed it to Timarie.

"Yes, we must keep him hydrated." Timarie brought the cup to Paul's lips and encouraged him to drink. After a few sips, she unwrapped the cookie. "Try and take a bite, honey. It will help your blood sugar." She twisted around to face Raphael. "Thank you, Raphael, you are very kind."

**

Raphael's eyes followed Miguel's truck down the road. Six men rode in the bed of the truck, the barrels of their guns gleaming in the morning sun. One man rode in the front seat with Miguel, which meant there were at least two in the house. He was hungry, but he didn't dare go to the kitchen. The cookie he was saving for moments like this, gone. Gone in a moment of weakness. He would be more careful in the future not to let his emotions get the best of him. Ser débil no es beuno. *Being weak gets you killed.*

CHAPTER TWENTY-SIX

Revelation

Steven hovered around Suzanne's bedside. "I can stay. I'm sure Karen would understand."

"Did you ever find out what was going on with her and her high school crush?"

"Or I could leave you here, alone, to suffer and die."

"That was uncalled for."

"You're right. No. I never confronted her. I did what you told me to do. I went home and tried to be nice."

"And?"

"I need to try harder. She was up texting at two in the morning. Obviously, she thought I was sleeping. The light from her phone must've woken me up. She had a big smile on her face."

"Ouch."

"Yeah. That's why I came over this morning. I wanted your advice on what to do."

"As if I'm the keeper to the answers...I'm sure you noticed that Sam and I aren't exactly copacetic."

"Yeah, what's up with that? You two aren't even married yet."

"It's me. All me. I met someone who has rocked my world, and I don't know what to do about it."

Steven threw up his hands, his brow furrowed. "Maybe you should talk to my wife. Seems you both are in a quandary about the same thing!"

Suzanne's head throbbed. The last thing she needed was a tiff with her brother. "I'm sorry. I don't think either one of us is out to cause harm." She patted her brother's hand. "Sam and I —if we're meant to be, we'll be okay...if not...better we know now, than later."

**

The clock struck 3 A.M. A dog barked somewhere in the distance, followed by another, and another. Barking turned to howling. The moon peeked inside Suzanne's window. Filmy curtains fluttered in the breeze. Suzanne struggled to stay in her rem state, but the energy invading her space demanded attention, and her eyes sprung open.

Her first reaction was to close the window, lower the shades, climb back into bed and return to her dream where she roamed white sugared shores, swam in aqua pools...where bare sun-kissed skin, covered in droplets, sparkled like diamonds in the sun...where she awaited his return...

But then her phone rang, the dogs barked louder, and the wind whipped her curtains into a frenzy. *Sam?* His smokey timbre brought the calamity to a halt.

"Hello?"

"Sam, it's 3 o'clock, what is it?"

"I have six dead migrants, two retired botanists missing, and my fiancée spent the day in the ER. I need to ask you one question."

"Oh Sam, can we have this conversation in the morning?"

"The scar-faced man...is he responsible?"

Suzanne fell back against her pillow. She thought for sure he was going to ask about Garian. She closed her eyes. The face loomed before her, his lips formed, a twisted, evil grin, his eyes, burning fires of hell. His closed fist opened and closed crushing tiny figures squirming in his palm. She opened her eyes. "Yes," she said. "I believe he is."

"I need your help Suzanne. I need to find this guy. I need to find Timarie and Paul. Will you help me?"

Suzanne looked across the room. One by one, Diablo's victims gathered, pleading. "Yes. Whatever it takes."

CHAPTER TWENTY-SEVEN

One Way Out

Raphael smelled the man even before his drunken weight settled onto the bed. One of the man's hands groped Raphael's still form, the other managed his pleasure, as he grunted and groaned softly in Raphael's ear.

Two men. If he killed this one, he might have a chance to get away. *But how?* He had no idea where he was, and the terrain in California could be every bit as unforgiving as the terrain he crossed to get to the border. Then again...what did he have to lose?

Raphael reached for the weapon hidden beneath his pillow. He held the lid from a can of beans he had found in the trash between his thumb and forefinger. When the man threw his head back in ecstasy, Raphael sliced his throat.

**

Timarie heard the thud. She heard gurgling, a wet cough, almost a whistling sound. She could hear shuffling, and heavy breathing. She didn't call out. She knew. She prayed Raphael broke free. She prayed he made it to safety. She prayed he wouldn't forget them. She prayed he'd send help.

**

Raphael crept past the man with the gun, his step so light, he made no sound. When he made it to the back of the house, he took off running, alerting the dogs. However, the gods were in his favor. A mountain lion appeared out of nowhere, sending the dogs chasing in another direction.

Once he was about two hundred yards from the house, he stopped running, and got his bearings. The wind picked up, and the moon slipped from behind a cloud, showing him the way.

**

Sam sat in the dark, still as the night. The conversation he had with Suzanne replayed in his head. Her tone was warm, sincere when she said she would help. *She understands.* They had been together long enough to know the connection between them was preordained. He had to trust that the love they felt for each other was also part of the plan. Lately, he wondered. He also wondered if he had the right to make her his own. Perhaps she was meant to provide the help he needed and nothing more. Maybe they were fated to catch the bad guys, serve as partners in crime, and not as partners in life.

Moonlight cast a shadow on the wall turning his coat rack into a menacing figure. Sam lifted his gun from the coffee table and pretended to shoot. "Bam. Take that, asshole."

**

After a short while, the spirits retreated, leaving Suzanne yearning for sleep. The pain pill she had taken for her hand had worn off. *Time for another.* She swallowed the pill, fluffed up her pillow and turned on her side. As her eyes grew heavy, Raphael appeared behind her lids. She saw him running. The moon mocked his efforts and his shadow morphed into a demon. The faster he ran, the larger the demon grew. Raphael kept running...until it consumed him.

CHAPTER TWENTY-EIGHT

Tempting Fate

After yet another fitful night's sleep, Suzanne was at her wits' end. "Linda, I need your advice."

"Of course. The answer is yes."

"How can you answer before I tell you what's bothering me?"

Linda chuckled. "It's what I do. It's what *you* do."

"I shouldn't have tempted fate. I should have let the images go. Chalked them up to fantasy, an attraction to a handsome man, and nothing more."

"And then what?"

Suzanne held up her injured hand. A spot of blood bloomed beneath the bandage. "I keep seeing this boy...he's in danger."

"Tell me about him."

I believe he has something to do with the spirits that are

hanging out with me, but I'm not sure of their connection. The boy may have come across the border with his family and somehow got separated. It's possible his family was murdered." She bowed her head. "I had a vision last night...the boy was running."

"Oh dear."

"Oh dear, is right. He was being chased by the devil."

"And what about Sam?"

"You're really good. He called me at three in the morning. He wanted to know if the scar-faced man I keep seeing is responsible for another group of illegals they found dead."

"I'm getting something with hands..."

"Yes. I cut my hand yesterday. And Sam said the victim's palms were sliced open."

"I am also seeing money."

"That's what I got too. They stole money from the killer."

"You know who it is, don't you?"

Suzanne cleared her throat. "I think so...at least I was able to identify the scar-faced man as Miguel Guzman. He's tied to the cartel.

**

Miguel drew a blue cheese stuffed olive into his mouth with his teeth and sipped his dirty martini. "No worries, my friend. It's all there."

The blue-eyed senator smiled, his tanned skin crinkling where his upper lid met the lower. His white teeth gleamed behind his politician's smile. "A little birdie told me you've been a bit harsh with your workers."

Miguel halted mid-sip. "Only the ones who steal from me—us."

The senator tapped bejeweled fingers on the glass table top. "You see the thing is, I shouldn't be hearing from little birdies...little birdies sing. And when they sing, people listen."

"I hate little birdies. They crap all over everything."

"Exactly. What do you intend to do?" The senator sipped his coffee.

"Clip their wings? Smash their beaks?"

"How's your martini?"

"Just the way I like it."

The senator rose. "If you paid your people, they wouldn't steal from you—*us*." He tossed his napkin on the table. "Handle it Miguel. Or I will."

**

Miguel staggered out of the hotel, his throat raw from swallowing the barbs he wanted to throw at the senator. *Fat fuck.* The man turned Miguel's stomach each time they met. The man's narcissistic demeanor rubbed him the wrong way. The senator was only interested in two things...*money and himself.*

How are you any different? He searched his mind for the answer. How many had he murdered in cold blood? *Survival.* If the immigrants talked? *Game over.* He was a survivalist, a numb, and desensitized survivalist. *Nothing more.*

His men pulled the truck up to the side entrance of the hotel, he jumped in, and they drove away. His next stop was to see Abolina, his favorite whore.

**

Raphael slid down the embankment to the creek. He wanted to take backroads, but was afraid to get too close to the highway. A sign he saw along the way gave him hope. *Goldorado 42 Miles.* If he could make it to town, he could turn himself in...seek asylum, maybe even get some protection. He knew the cartel would be merciless if they found him first. But at this point, he had nothing to lose. His goal was to save himself and the old couple he had grown fond of. He couldn't reverse his actions, take back the candy he had given to kids who had trusted him, but his redemption had to start somewhere.

He saw a car in the distance and jumped behind a bush. When the car passed, he returned to the gravel path along the creek the old woman had told him to follow. She said she knew very little about the area, but had researched farms in Northern California and said that most of the creeks led to the highway. She wasn't sure, but she thought heading north would be his best bet. Raphael was skilled when it came to following the sun, she told him Goldorado County was off of Highway 50.

**

Suzanne heard a knock at the door. To her delight, she saw Linda's sweet face smiling back at her. "Come in," she said warmly.

"Brought you some soup."

"Linda, you didn't have to do that—I'm fine."

"Cheddar broccoli. Full of protein and nutrients your brain needs to repair itself."

"How did you know cheddar-broccoli is my favorite?"

Linda chuckled. "My dog told me—she's psychic."

"That's right, I forgot. How is Daphne?"

"She sure enjoyed those shoes you brought over. Chewed up every one of them—except the pair that gave you sexy visions. I'm saving those for when she's a little older."

"I haven't seen Garian in a while. I'm hoping to see him this Thursday at class." Suzanne took the dish from Linda. "Let's go into the kitchen. I think the ghosts are gone for the day."

"I prayed about the boy. The boy you said is in trouble."

"And—"

"I keep hearing Charlton Heston's line from the movie, Ten Commandments when he played Moses and said, 'Let my people go.' Greed, deception. The boy is a victim of society's struggle to survive."

"That's what I told Sam."

"What did he say?"

"He blames him for the death of those kids...he's not inclined to change his mind."

"Such a shame. Meanwhile, the big guy sleeps like a baby."

"Big guy?"

"Deception. We the people trust elected officials to do right by the people. What if they are behind it all?"

Suzanne shivered. "You have a point."

**

"Where's my money?" Abolina cocked her hip, and held out her hand. She leaned forward brushing her breast against Miguel's cheek. He grabbed her waist and wrestled her to the bed.

"You get paid after. Not before."

She giggled, and thrust her pelvis to meet his groin. "It's been a while, my sweet, sweet, baby. I thought you forgot about me. Your friend on the other hand—"

"Never," he said, pulling her on top of him. "Show me how you earn your keep."

**

Hours later, Miguel's truck skidded in the dust, coming to a hard stop. The dogs attacked their pens with running jumps, their teeth gnashing, the barks intertwined with snarls and growls. Miguel jumped from the truck before the driver engaged the gearshift in park. He rushed to the man slumped against a wall near the front door. A rope looped around his neck held a shotgun propped beneath his chin. Blood and bone stuck to the bougainvillea vine behind him.

Miguel ran to the outbuilding, where Timarie and Paul huddled together. Miguel kicked the body lying near what had been Raphael's cot. His face burned in rage.

"Get up!" he called to Timarie and Paul.

Timarie shimmied out from beneath Paul's weight. Her face pale, her hair stringy and damp. "Your friend—" she nodded towards the dead body, "should've learned to keep his hands to himself."

"Where is the boy?"

"I have no idea. Everything happened in the dark. I just know what I heard. Your friend died with his pants down. What more do you need to know?"

Miguel glanced past Timarie, his voice void of emotion. "What about him?"

"My husband is barely breathing. He needs a hospital." Tears filled her eyes. "I beg you, please—let us go."

Miguel ordered his men to round up the dogs and the guns. Within minutes, they were gone.

Timarie went into the main house, rummaged through medicine cabinets, kitchen drawers, the pantry, and came up empty handed. A butter knife caught her eye and she grabbed it. *Just in case.* She looked around for a phone, any phone, perhaps a land-line. *No luck.* She filled a plastic container with water, grabbed a half-eaten package of graham crackers and a flashlight from the counter and returned to Paul.

She put the water to Paul's lips, and urged him to drink. "I'll be damned if I'm going to let you die, Paul Phillips."

❦

CHAPTER TWENTY-NINE

Lost and Found

Suzanne closed her eyes and let the message come through. Linda's words rang out in the back of her mind. *Let my people go.* Moses didn't ask permission. He took matters into his own hands. Suddenly, she saw Raphael walking along the side of the road. The sun was behind him, like a halo. *He's heading north.* Something about the area looked familiar.

**

Raphael knew he was close to a highway when he heard a long hauler blow his horn in the distance. He looked up at the cloudless sky, shielded his eyes from the sun. The morning had been cool, but now, the sun was directly overhead. He pulled his threadbare flannel closer to his chest. The chill he felt had nothing to do with the temperature. He heard gravel crunch behind him. He glanced to his left, then to his right, assessing the best direction to run. Neither way looked promising. *I can't outrun a bullet.*

"Ola." He heard the woman's voice, but kept on walking. He heard a car door slam. "Raphael—don't run. I can help you," she said. He stopped. Turned. He couldn't believe his eyes.

He stood frozen in place, his body yearning to collapse. He resisted with every ounce of energy he had left. How long had he been walking without rest, food, or water? Fourteen hours? Longer? Was he imagining the angel that stood before him? He couldn't tell—the sun was so bright.

"My name is Suzanne. I've seen you in my—your sister Trina told me about you."

"You know my sister? Where is she?"

"She is with the angels, but she told me where to find you. She told me about Diablo."

"No—you are trying to trick me. Go away!" Raphael spun around and started to run, but he tripped, and laid on the ground sobbing.

"Let me help you," she said, offering a hand. She crouched down, and slipped an arm around his shaking shoulders. "I'll bet you're hungry."

**

Sam paced the floor in his office. Suzanne had texted him, informing him of her find. He wanted to chastise her for going alone...after all, the boy was a criminal...but her words rang sweet in his ears...*he's just a boy.*

He glanced at the clock. She said she'd see him in an hour, two hours ago. *Where is she?* Should he call? Send out the troops? *Nah, if I know her, she's probably feeding and clothing him.* Just then, they walked through the door.

"Took you long enough." Sam tilted his head. "TJ MAXX?"

"His clothes were dirty and torn. I figured if he was going to sit in a jail cell, it may as well be in clean clothes with a full belly."

Sam circled Raphael. "Do you speak English?"

The boy positioned his index finger an inch over his thumb. "A little."

"How old are you?"

"Thirteen."

"How long have you been here?"

"I don't know, a while."

"Who do you work for?"

Raphael steered his focus toward Suzanne, her nod reassuring. "Diablo."

Sam held a photo in front of the boy's face. "Manuel Guzman?"

"Si."

"Where does he get his drugs from?"

Raphael shrugged. "How do I know?"

Sam's tone became sharp. "How did you get them? Were they delivered to you? Did you pick them up?"

"Sam—"

He returned Suzanne's reprimanding with a sheepish grin. "Have a seat, Raphael. Can I get you some water? This is going to take a while."

**

Suzanne's eyes followed Sam while he managed the boy's incarceration via phone calls, arranging for paperwork to be sent, chatting with his team in hushed tones, and finally, issuing an order to have the boy escorted to a holding cell on the second floor.

Elbows on the table, Suzanne rested her chin in her hands and closed her eyes. Images flickered behind her third eye...

The police station parking lot was well-lit, except for the area where her car was parked. The thought made her ears ring, her skin prickle, her mouth dry. *Being psychic doesn't make you indestructible.* She was about to turn around and go back inside the station when a large hand clamped over her mouth, and a sharp blade pressed against her throat.

"Where is he?" the deep voice pierced through her fear. She didn't need to see the face of her captor to know who he was. *Diablo.*

"No comprende."

He held onto her hair as he spun her around. The tip of his blade rested on her larynx, his eyes burned clear to her soul. "Where is the boy?" In the distance, she heard her name being called...

"Suzanne?" Sam's voice was clear, commanding. Miguel eased the knife back into its sheath. He stepped back, and disappeared into the darkness.

"Suzanne?" She opened her eyes. Doubled over, she gasped for air. When she rose, Sam was within inches from her body. She pulled him close.

"You're shaking—what is it?"

"Diablo. He knows we have the boy."

**

Raphael sat in his cell waiting for a Spanish speaking lawyer. He had watched Perry Mason episodes at his cousin Hector's house. He knew to remain silent until his *mouth piece* showed up.

Hector's mother, Joella, had a gringo boyfriend who lavished her with gifts when he came to visit. He bought her a 24" TV, complete with a satellite dish and an understanding that while he was in town, her "little shitkickers" take advantage of his generosity and ignore the various sounds coming from the bedroom. If they were lucky, he brought "snacks."

For the next three years. Hector, his siblings, Raphael, and his sister Trina, learned many things, how to make a soufflé, how to paint trees and mountains, how to win money by spelling words, and how to do the things Joella and her boyfriends were doing in the bedroom. One day, the gringo caught Joella in bed with another man. He smashed the TV against the wall, and never returned.

Raphael didn't know what to make of Suzanne. She was nice, but he didn't like that she knew about his sister, Trina, whom he hadn't seen since they crossed the border. He didn't believe Trina was in heaven, at least he didn't want to. And what about his mother? Was she there too? When he heard the door clank, he didn't expect to see Sam. *Está enojado.* Raphael knew all about anger. He gripped the cell bars tight.

**

Sam's clenched jaw emitted a deadly tone, "Who are you to Miguel Guzman?"

"I told you. He picked me up at the border."

"He wants you dead. Why?"

Raphael shrugged. "He's Diablo...he doesn't need a reason."

Sam's lips formed a smile. His eyes remained hard. "At the moment he doesn't know where to find you...but something tells me he's not going to stop until he does...and that doesn't bode well with me. Comprende?" Sam watched the color drain from the boy's face.

"Maybe it's the Gringos."

Sam couldn't contain the excitement in his voice. "What Gringo's? What did they look like?"

"They were old. The man was sick. I untied them. But I don't know if they got away." Raphael lowered his gaze. "She was nice to me."

Sam pulled out a county map and plastered it against the bars. "Suzanne said she picked you up here. Where were you coming from?"

Raphael studied the lines before him. "I don't read English."

"Do your best."

"Is this the river?"

"Yes. Did you follow the river?"

"Sí."

"Did you start by the river?"

"No. I followed it once I found it."

"How long were you walking before you found it?"

"I left before dawn. The sun was high when I saw the river," he said pointing to the ceiling.

"You were walking for about three hours?"

The boy shrugged. "Sí."

"Did you climb any hills? Or was it flat?"

"Hills."

Sam pointed at the map. "Did you come from this way?"

Raphael shook his head. "I think so."

"Make yourself comfortable," Sam said, and left.

**

Sam's touch lingered long after he left the room. It had been weeks since the last time they had been close. *Why am I so torn?* Suzanne's fingers danced across her clavicle. *What am I to do?* Garian's face loomed in the recess of her mind. Sam re-entered the room. Heat bloomed in her cheeks.

"Are we finished here?"

"No." Sam pulled up a chair, leveling his gaze to hers. "The boy may have given us a lead on Paul and Timarie Phillips." His fingertips brushed her arm. "Juvie will pick him up in the morning. In the meantime, he's safe. I'll have dinner brought in." He winked. "I'll even let him choose."

She felt lost in his hazel eyes. Almost dizzy. The moment was surreal. The man sitting before her was suddenly superimposed over another man's image, but with longer hair combed in a different style. His voice mimicked Sam's, only deeper, mesmerizing. Her vision doubled, her head felt light. "What are you doing?" she asked, jerking her arm away from him.

He rose, breaking the spell. "I'll have one of my men take you home."

She mustered a fake smile, embarrassed by her outburst. "There's no need. I'll be fine." The chill in the room dispelled the warmth she had been struggling to detach herself from. *How can I make him understand?*

"Let me know you're home safe," he said, and walked away.

CHAPTER THIRTY

Determination

Timarie knocked on the door, praying the person who answered would take her plea seriously, and not think her a lunatic. And even if they did, as long as they called the police and an ambulance, they could think what they wanted. When the door opened a crack, her heart raced and the adrenalin rush seized her composure.

"I desperately need your help," she said between gasps. Before the door closed, she heard a tiny voice.

"I'll go get my mommy."

A moment later, a heavy-set woman in a bathrobe appeared in the doorway. "Can I help you?"

Timarie fell to her knees, sobbing. "I need you to call the police."

**

Miguel counted $100 bills into stacks while his men loaded

the truck with the latest shipment of fentanyl. By sundown, the distributors would be lining up. By midnight, the lot would be gone. *By morning, the boy will be dead.*

He threw a stack of bills at one of his minions. "Paga a los hombres." The man smiled, stuffed the wad in his pocket and rushed out the door. Payday made his men happy. He sat back in his chair, and tapped the screen on his phone. "Call Jimmy," he commanded. The call connected.

"I need you to find the little fucker that brought candy to school in Goldorado. He killed two of my men." He paused to listen. "Sí. Raphael." Miguel ended the call, and bounced out of his chair. *Work to do.*

**

An Amador County Deputy pulled into the drive, kicking up a cloud of dust. Timarie flew off the porch to greet him. "My husband—he needs an ambulance!"

"Calm down, Ma'am. Tell me what's going on. Let's start with your name."

"Timarie Phillips. We were taken from our home."

The deputy squinted at the sun. "When did this happen?" he asked.

Timarie shook her head and shrugged her shoulders, her frustration mounting. "Please! Come with me, now! My husband!"

"Where is he?"

"I can't tell you how to get there, but I can show you."

The deputy opened the rear car door. "Get in," he said, his tone patronizing. "Which way?" He put the car in reverse.

Timarie glanced out the window at the woman and her little girl, standing like statues on the porch. Timarie nodded gratefully. The woman nodded back.

"Where you from?" The deputy inquired.

"Camino. We just moved here from Southern California."

"What made you move up north?"

"Turn left up here."

"Up there at the stop sign?"

"Yes! Please hurry!"

"We have speed limits here, Ma'am."

"He's going to fucking die if we don't hurry!"

The deputy put on his blinker, and rounded the curve.

**

The deputy grabbed the mic off the dashboard. "Debra, we got a 10-52 at the old Cody place. Sixty-five-year-old male. Yep, critical condition. We also have two dead bodies. Over?" Timarie heard the radio squawk. A woman's voice came back.

"Ambulance is on the way. Twelve minutes, over."

"Send me a couple of guys too, will ya Debra? Looks like we may have a 10-200 situation."

Timarie laid her head on her husband's chest. "Hang in there, my love. Help is on the way."

**

When the ambulance arrived, two paramedics lifted Paul onto a stretcher, working quickly to start an IV.

Timarie rode in the back of the vehicle, praying as they worked. Seeing the deputy's flashing lights following behind stirred conflicting emotions of gratitude, anger, relief. One half mile down the road, she saw at least six vehicles with flashing lights fly by heading toward the ranch. *Assholes.* Where were you when I needed you, she thought, trying to curb her bitterness. *If it hadn't been for the boy...*

CHAPTER THIRTY-ONE

Dream a Little Dream

S uzanne picked up the phone on the second ring. "Hey Linda." She sprang out of bed. "No, I'm up." She proceeded to give Linda the 411 on the boy and Sam while she ambled downstairs to the kitchen. "Before I left the station, I got this weird feeling when Sam touched me. It was as if I was looking at someone else from a *really* long time ago."

"Interesting. Do you think you've had a past life with Sam?"

Suzanne popped a pod into her coffee maker and pressed start. "I'm not sure. Whatever it was, the chemistry between us was remarkable."

"Well duh! Isn't that why you agreed to marry the guy?"

Suzanne sighed. "It's rather confusing when you're engaged to one man in this lifetime who means the world and another man from a previous life flips your switch."

"Have you heard from Garian?"

"Not since I broke our date. But there's a class tomorrow. I plan to be there."

Linda laughed. "I'd love to be a fly on the wall."

"I'm not counting on a warm reception, but I do want to learn from him."

"And Sam?"

"I can't marry him until I figure out my attraction to Garian."

Linda's tone transformed from light to serious. "Anything else you want to share?"

"Like what?"

"I'm seeing a murky grey aura flickering around you. Are you afraid of something?"

"I had a vision yesterday that wasn't too pleasant..."

"What happened?"

"I was in the parking lot outside of the jail. A man threatened to slice my throat if I didn't tell him where the boy was."

"Must be what I'm picking up on," Linda said. "Yes, I'm seeing a man who is out for blood."

Suzanne gasped. "Whose blood?"

"Whoever gets in his way."

**

Sam flew out of bed when he got the call from the Amador Sheriff's Department about the Phillips couple. A quick shower, and he was out the door in fifteen minutes. He felt a little fuzzy around the edges, but coffee would have to wait.

The polished hospital floors reflected his shadow as he hurried toward room 202. The deputy reported Paul Phillips was in critical condition, adding that it would be a miracle if he regained consciousness. Sam knocked lightly and stepped inside the room.

"Sam!" Timarie threw her arms around his neck and hugged him tight. "I'm so glad you came." She pulled him toward the bed. "They don't know if he'll come out of this. He's suffered severe head trauma." She smoothed her hand across Paul's bandaged forehead. "That bastard walloped him good." Tears rimmed her eyes. "He was only trying to protect me."

Sam settled his arm around Timarie's slender shoulders for a moment before steering her into a chair. "I'm going to need your help if we're going to arrest the man who did this."

"Seriously, Sam. I don't know why he let us live...He was so angry, I thought he'd implode...Especially after the boy killed two of his men and took off." She brought her hands up to her face. "I hope the boy's safe."

**

Raphael had never been in a jail cell before. The mattress smelled like puke. The pillow smelled like his uncle Padro after too many hours in the hot sun. But the food was good. Sam let him choose his first meal. He asked for an In-and-Out burger with no onions, an order of fries and a chocolate shake. The same meal Suzanne treated him to the day she found him.

Earlier that morning, one of the officers brought him an egg sandwich with bacon, a carton of milk and some kind of potato thing. After he ate it, his stomach bubbled. He felt sweaty. Were they trying to poison him? Just then, he heard Sam, barking orders at someone. Sometimes it was hard to tell the good guys from the bad guys.

Within seconds, Sam stood outside the bars, his hands on his hips, a 'this better be good' look on his face. "Is there something you want to tell me?"

"I don't feel so good, man."

"You're gonna feel a whole lot worse if you don't start talking."

Raphael doubled over. "I need a doctor."

"I spoke with Timarie Phillips, she told me what you did."

"Chingar, hombre, your friends are trying to poison me."

The boy spun around and bent over the metal bowl, just in time.

Sam threw his hands in the air. "Great!"

**

Suzanne arrived early to get a front row seat. Once the class got underway, she hung onto every word Garian said. "**Be open-minded.** Meditation might feel unfamiliar at first. Emotions and feelings may arise, but don't ignore them. Acknowledge your feelings. Welcome them, and return to your breathing. Feelings are a reminder that we are having a human experience."

She sensed heat emanating from his body as he passed by her. She was tempted to reach out and touch him. But why? What kind of cosmic spell was she under? She opened her eyes, and caught his stare. That's all it took to go back in time...

Garian had been out to sea for months. She was alone with the children, when there came a knock at the door...

"Who is it?"

"Captain Bishop, m'lady."

She unlatched the door, bracing herself for what she knew was her fate. "Come. You'll catch your death standing there."

"M'lady, I'm afraid I..."

"Tea? Or perhaps a cup of grog to warm your bones? Please, call me Alaina." She hurried to the cupboard to fetch a tankard from the shelf. "Winter has come early this year."

Captain Bishop stood fast near the door, his hat in his hands. "Yes, yes it has."

She served him a cup of grog, meeting his gaze. She knew by the look in his eyes that the news he was about to impart was not good. "He's dead, isn't he?" She blurted out, holding back tears. "My husband is dead—and he's left me alone to raise our children. The children he claimed were his heart and soul." Her two youngest children hid behind her skirts. The two oldest steadied her, one on each side like bookends. The baby cried in the other room. "Christian, fetch the baby, please." She wobbled at his release.

The captain set his cup on the table and stepped forward. "What can I do to ease your pain?" he asked. His hazel eyes reflected his sincerity, and his angst.

"The children and I will be fine," she replied, but her shaky words did not convince the man. He took another step forward.

"I took a room in town. I can help."

At that moment she wanted to rush into the Captain's arms, purge years of suffering from loving a man who only thought of himself. "He never loved me the way I loved him," she cried.

When she heard her name called, she was confused. *His voice.* Was Garian still alive? Had he returned to her after all? Suddenly, a tap on her shoulder ended the regression and she let go of her pent-up emotions. She opened her eyes returning to the present, her cheeks wet with tears.

Garian's words were warm, but his eyes were cold. "Hey, welcome back, it's okay, let it out. Release your pain."

"I'm fine. Sorry," she stammered, reaching for his hand. "I was definitely in a place I was not meant to be."

He took a step backwards, avoiding contact. "It happens. Let's move forward, shall we?"

**

Garian kept his voice so low as not to attract attention from the students exiting the room, but his tone was sharp. "What was that all about?"

"It's why I'm here. I'm seeking answers, just like everyone else." Her cheeks burned. Her heart raced. "Who the hell *are* you?"

"Listen...perhaps you've misinterpreted our connection. I like you, but what's important to me is teaching. I don't want the other students to get the wrong impression. It's little outbursts like yours that can cost a guy his job, nowadays."

"You're right. How foolish of me to think your class was what I needed." She gathered her notebook and purse. "As I said, I was in the wrong place."

Suzanne didn't wait for a response. She headed for the door, and didn't look back.

CHAPTER THIRTY-TWO

Caller ID

Receiving a call in the middle of the night was never good. "Metzger." A click on the other end. No Caller ID. "Asshole," Sam said, climbing back into bed. He adjusted his pillow and was about to resume his REM state when the phone rang again. "Damn it." He reached for his phone. This time the number really did spell trouble.

"Metzger."

"Hey Sam, it's Jake."

"I have caller ID, Jake. What'cha got?"

"A truck full of dead illegals."

Sam pinched the bridge of his nose. "Where."

"Ice House Campground. Site 36, Boulder Loop."

"Who's out there now?"

"Me, Shrimp, Vega, and Spence."

"I'm on my way."

Sam climbed into his jeans, a long sleeve T, and a pair of hiking boots. Following his bathroom routine, he grabbed a thermal vest, his gun, badge, and hit the road.

The hang-up bothered him. Taunted him. There was no way of tracing the number. Whoever was on the line knew that. His gut told him the caller was delivering a message.

**

When he arrived on the scene, Sam's men disbanded the cluster they shared with emergency personnel and bee-lined for the car. Sam pulled in next to the coroner and turned off the engine.

"How many?" Sam met his men half-way.

Jake fell into step beside him. "Thirty-two."

"How do you know they're illegals?"

"Can't be positive, but none of them have IDs. We found this," he said, handing Sam a photo. "The stamp on the back is in Spanish."

Sam clicked on his pen-light and studied the image of a young girl in a white dress, her face void of expression, her hands folded across her chest. Sam handed the photo back to Jake. "How did they die?"

"See for yourself. It's worse than the others."

Sam clamped his hand over his mouth. "Geezus!" The bodies were piled on top of one another making it difficult to tell which limb belonged to who. From what he could tell, each one of them had been shot in the heart. As if that weren't enough, their eyes had been gouged. *Another message?* At least a half dozen of the victims were children.

His phone vibrated in his pocket. "Metzger."

"It's Natalie, sir. Just got a call from a Mrs. Klein, she asked for you directly. She's a teacher at the high school, said she spoke with you about the fentanyl problem..."

"Yes, I remember her, what did she want?"

"She found her son dead in the backyard. She's pretty sure he jumped off the roof. She also said his lips were purple."

"I'm on my way to the station. I'll call her when I get there." Sam slipped behind the wheel. It was going to be one helluva night.

**

Spirits gathered around Suzanne's bed. The chill in the room made her stir in her sleep. As if their presence beckoned her awake, she tossed the covers aside and sat up. Raking a hand through her hair, she blinked several times. Her pupils adjusted to the dark. Their bloody eye sockets made her cringe, and she scrambled up against the headboard.

Trina stood at the back of the room next to a tall, thin teen who seemed out of place. The side of his head looked misshapen. "It happened when I fell," he said without moving his lips. Suzanne blinked again. *No.* She wasn't dreaming.

**

The knock on the door didn't register at first. Suzanne had spent most of the night negotiating with the spirit world. Sam's face on the other side of the glass pane in her backdoor was a pleasant sight.

When he saw her, his eyes lit up, his smile sheepish. "I brought donuts."

"Double chocolate with white icing?" She peeked inside the paper bag. "You remembered."

"I didn't bring coffee. I was hoping you wouldn't mind making a pot. I miss the aroma of brewing coffee while sitting in your sun dappled kitchen. Am I being presumptuous?"

"Come in. I'll start a pot, but I hope you don't mind, I just got up...haven't brushed or...you know."

"Of course." His smile grew into a chuckle. His warmth radiating into a bright aura. A weight lifted from her heart. She fixed a pot of coffee, and offered him a seat at her table.

"I'm so glad you stopped by...be right back."

**

She ran upstairs, washed her face, brushed her teeth and took care of business. She caught her reflection in her full-length mirror and decided to change into a strapless midi dress, white with a splash of purple flowers, and pull her hair back into a messy bun. Barefoot, she padded back downstairs. Seeing Sam sitting in her kitchen made her heart sing.

"I don't understand why I'm in such a glorious mood," she said, fetching two mugs from the cabinet. "I was up half the night with a room full of spirits...I need to brush up on my Spanish. It was unnerving."

Sam rose so fast, the chair tipped over, and he grabbed it mid-air. "What time did you see them?"

"Must've been around 2:30. I didn't look at the clock."

"Can you describe them to me?"

"Not sure, they came in and out...some of the faces were a blur, but the ones I saw clearly were missing their eyes."

"Geezuz, Suzanne." Sam buried his face in his hands.

"There's more." He looked up. "There was a boy–a teenager. The side of his head was smashed." She picked up a donut, reconsidered, and set it back on the plate. "You have no idea how much I appreciate your visit."

"I had the same kind of night...except I was there. The victims were shot, their eyes were extracted. I got the call at 2:30. The call for the boy came in shortly after."

It was Suzanne's turn to be shocked. Her head buzzed with activity. The voices all spoke at once. "Diablo."

∿

CHAPTER THIRTY-THREE

Respite

R aphael sipped water out of a plastic cup with a paper straw. A stranger stood by his bedside, her smile wide, and just as plastic as the cup.

"Raphael, I'm Catherine Alverez, I'm with Social Services. Servicios sociales. Comprende?"

Raphael nodded. "I'm dying, lady, what do you want?"

"No, you're not dying," she snickered. "You have appendicitis." She circled her belly with her forefinger. "It hurts here?"

"Yes."

"You were vomiting?" She gestured throwing up. He nodded. She continued. "I'm here to make sure you get treatment. The doctors are going to run some tests, do an ultrasound. My job is to make sure you understand what they are doing to you each step of the way. I will serve as your advocate. Do you know what that is?"

"Si. I think so."

"I can relay your questions or concerns to the doctors and staff." She smiled again, this time seeming more sincere. "We want you to feel better. What happens next will be determined after your recovery. Sound fair?"

Raphael lifted one hand as far as he could. "What about these?" He gestured toward the restraints circling his wrists.

"For now, those will stay. We may need a court order to have them removed." She checked her watch. "I'm not sure when the judge will receive your paperwork, but until then, relax, try and get some sleep. I will be right outside the door, checking on your status."

"I killed those men before they killed me," he confessed.

Catherine blinked a few times. Her brow gathered in the middle of her forehead. "Did you share that with Detective Metzger?"

"I tried. He's wasn't a good listener."
**

Sam entered Raphael's room hours later, carrying a bundle of comic books. "Thought you could use a little reprieve from looking at the ceiling."

His hands flapped up and down. "Who's gonna turn the pages?"

"Yeah, I see what you mean." Sam unfastened one of the boy's restraints. "I don't have the manpower to put someone outside your door. This is the next best thing. I can't have you running off on me."

Raphael turned away. Sam pulled up a chair.

"Miguel is looking for you. Do you understand?"

"Si."

"You never finished telling me what happened at the ranch."

The boy took a deep breath. "Like the lady told you. I killed two of Miguel's men."

Sam hit record on his phone. "Tell me what happened."

**

It was out of character for Sam to show empathy to a criminal, but the boy's story tugged at his heart. He had to wonder what kind of future Raphael would have had if Miguel hadn't snatched him up at the border.

"My mother, father, and sister...they must be looking for me." Raphael turned away. "That lady, Suzanne, she says she saw Trina." He faced Sam, teary-eyed. "You said she sees dead people..."

"Not always. She saw you–you're not dead."

Raphael wrapped his arms around Sam. His words came out in sobs. "I'm not a killer."

**

Sam called Jake and Spence into his office. "Anything on the Klein kid?"

Spence removed the toothpick dangling from his lips. "We questioned the teachers and kids at Kaleb's school. Same as the others, he was a good student, kind, well loved by his peers. Not a druggie."

"If you want my two cents," Jake added, "someone is giving these kids something that appears to be non-threatening, like the TicTacs we found laced with fentanyl."

"Check to see if there've been any new students in the past month. Talk to the yard duty people, see if they've seen anyone hanging around the school. I'll talk to the kid. I'm sure he hasn't told me everything."

Once the men were dismissed, Sam rummaged his brain, connecting any dots floating around in his grey matter. When he came up empty, he dialed Suzanne. "Do these ghosts, or spirits talk to you? Can you ask them questions?"

"They talk to me, sometimes...What do you want to know?"

"I want to know where Kaleb Klein got the fentanyl that killed him. If it wasn't Raphael, who was it?"

Suzanne chuckled. "I know the boy's death isn't funny. It's just that–well you have to admit, this conversation is a bit strange."

"You're my superpower. I'll be the first to admit *that*."

"I have roast in the oven...do you get any time off for good behavior?"

"I'm going back up to the hospital in a minute. Can I call you from there?"

"How are the Phillips doing?

"Timarie is as tough as nails. I think if Paul recovers it will be by her sheer will."

"What about Raphael?"

Sam chuckled. "Little shit is determined to win me over."

The line went silent for a few seconds before Suzanne replied, "I'll wait for your call."

**

Suzanne poured Sangiovese into a long-stemmed glass. Her emotions were in a tizzy. How could she be so torn? She sipped her wine on the way into the living room. The day was fading. She curled up in a chair, closed her eyes, and savored the vibrant, fruity taste on her tongue. It didn't take long for cerebral snippets of the past to steal her serenity...

She saw the cottage in the distance, heard violin music coming from within. She lifted her skirts, and bolted towards the door. She knocked. The music ceased. When Captain Bishop opened the door, his frown brightened, and he pulled her into his arms. Their passion continued into the back room, until their clothes were shed, and they lay naked on his feather bed. Captain Bishop pinned her arms above her head and tasted her sweet skin. Suzanne arched her back, welcoming his warm mouth.

"Marry me," he whispered. "I love you with all my heart."

"I have been a widow but a month."

"You have been a widow since your husband set to sea."

"And what about you, my dear captain? What will keep your feet planted on land?"

He looked deeply into her eyes. "All I need is you."

Suddenly, her phone rang, pulling her away from the vision. *Damn.* She took a swig of her wine and answered the call.

"Sam, hi."

"Sorry it took me so long to get back to you..."

"Your timing is perfect. I was about to become the talk of the town."

"Uh, oh. For all the right reasons I hope..."

"Nope. Verging on scandalous."

Sam laughed. "Thanks, I needed that."

Suzanne returned to her glass. "Did you still want to come for dinner? We can hang out, look for shooting stars..."

"I'm on my way. What can I bring?"

"I can't think of anything. Is roast beef and salad enough?"

His words triggered a frisson deep within her, "All I need is you."

Her heart and skin conspired against her, sending chills up and down her spine. "By any chance, do you play the violin?"

CHAPTER THIRTY-FOUR

The Score

Miguel leaned on the railing looking at the valley below. He sensed a presence behind him. "What did you find out, amigo?"

"La trulla—everywhere! Crawling around the ranch like *cucarachas*. Not much I could do."

Miguel slowly turned his head, his eyes burning with anger, his upper lip curled into a sneer. "What the fuck do I pay you for? Your pretty face?" He thrust an arm out, grabbed the man's throat and squeezed. "Encuéntralo o eres un hombre muerto!"

The man stumbled backwards, regained his footing and ran for the door. He knew Miguel made good on his threats. If he didn't find the kid, he *would be* dead.

As he ran to his car, he glanced up at Miguel looking down from the balcony. He swore his eyes glowed.

**

Raphael heard voices in the hallway and turned down the volume on the TV.

"You can't go in there, Ma'am."

"I just want to talk to him a minute, thank him for saving my life, and my husbands."

Raphael recognized the voice. It was the lady from the ranch. He felt for the remote, and arrowed down the volume. He could hear her arguing with the staff. When the voices faded, he turned off the TV and stared at the ceiling. If he let his eyes relax, the tiny holes in the ceiling tiles converged into strange creatures. He beckoned them to free him from his bondage. *No luck.*

Twenty-four hours on clear liquids was making him go crazy. His x-ray indicated he was in need of surgery. His advocate reminded him he was at the bottom of the rung, "Unless they suddenly burst." His pain was minimal for now. Sam had instructed the nurses he be notified if there were any changes.

He wondered if Sam actually cared? Or pitied him. He was embarrassed telling him about being beaten and raped. Sam listened, clenched his teeth, and his eyes filled with compassion. After he finished his story, Sam asked more questions about Miguel... "How many men does he have? Does he speak English? Does he make the drugs?"

Raphael wasn't much help. All he could say was that Diablo had eyes everywhere, and that his candy exchanged many hands. What Raphael didn't say was that even though he was restrained, he never felt safer.

**

The moon sat high in the sky. Miguel and his men were positioned at the border. A slight breeze carried the scent of desperation as the migrants crossed, unaware what lay in wait. Many fell to their knees, relieved, grateful, some just plain weary from their travels. The drug lord's henchmen were trained to cull the herd when given the signal. Soon, the border would be closed, and Miguel's work would be made more difficult. For now, he feasted on the possibilities before him. By morning, he would have what he needed to continue his operation.

CHAPTER THIRTY-FIVE

A Reason to Believe

S am made a quick stop at Buttercup Pantry for a slice of lemon meringue pie, Suzanne's favorite. Her invitation to dinner had his thoughts in a whirlwind. In the past months, her moods changed quicker than a five-year-old with a TV remote. Her unpredictability was one of the things he loved about her...*but this*...he found it difficult to gauge their conversations, let alone discuss his feelings toward her. *Patience.* If that's what she needed from him, so be it.

When he arrived at her house, he took a deep, calming breath. No one made his heart race like she did. No one tied his tongue or made him sweat like she did. No one had ever touched his heart, or made it bleed, like she did. He couldn't imagine life without her, nor did he want to. With each step he took towards her door, he relived a moment in love.

"You brought pie?" Suzanne took the bag from his hand and peeked inside. "Hmmmm, my favorite."

"Dinner smells divine. Haven't had a home-cooked meal since we had dinner at the Phillip's place." Sam followed Suzanne into the kitchen, admiring the way her hips moved, inhaling her sweet scent, restraining himself from pulling her into his arms and devouring her luscious lips.

"All quiet at the hospital? Everyone doing okay?"

"Yes. Paul Phillips is still in intensive care. No change. Timarie was released, and Raphael is behaving himself, thank god."

She closed her eyes, and pressed two fingers on her temple. "Something tells me the Phillips are going to adopt him."

Sam tilted his head. "Really? You think so?"

Suzanne nodded. "Yes, I do." She reached in the fridge and handed Sam a non-alcoholic beer. "He's having a hard time believing his parents are dead."

"Yeah, he told me you see his sister."

Suzanne plated two salads and set them on the table. "The important thing is to keep the boy safe."

"Once we get Guzman..."

"They don't call him diablo for nothing," she said, removing a casserole dish from the oven. She froze, holding the dish in her hands. "He's collecting an army."

Sam set his gun on the counter and washed his hands at the sink. "What does that mean?"

"I'm not sure, I'm just the messenger." She set the dish on the table. "This whole thing gives me an uneasy feeling, Sam. Miguel is no one to mess with. I not only fear for the boy, I fear he's out for retribution. An eye for an eye."

"At this moment I just want to enjoy this beautiful meal you've prepared. Can we do that?"

"Absolutely." Her smile brightened her face. She handed

him a knife. "Will you carve while I get the sides?" She went back into the oven for two small dishes.

"How are Steven and Karen doing?"

"I'm having lunch with Steven this week. He's having some issues. He thinks I have all the answers."

"That must be rough," he said, looking up from his carving task. "Everyone expecting you to know the answers..."

"It can be. And I don't. I only get what I get. And sometimes that's not enough. Like now. I can't tell you where Miguel is."

"Why did you ask me about playing the violin?"

Suzanne filled her plate, encouraging Sam to do the same. "I keep getting random thoughts about my past."

"With Garian?"

"Another man has entered the picture."

"You mentioned scandalous..."

"Yes! My husband, Garian, in this case, died at sea leaving me with five children. Another man offered to help take care of us."

"And this other man plays the violin?"

Suzanne nodded, her eyes twinkling. "I know it sounds insane—"

"Sounds very optimistic to me."

"Why is that?"

"I began playing violin when I was three."

**

Hearing Paul stir, Timarie glanced up from the novel she was reading. "Dear Lord, are you coming back to me, Paul?" His eyes fluttered. She grabbed the call button and alerted the desk.

A woman's voice responded. "Can I help you?"

"He's waking up! My husband is waking up!"

Three nurses rushed into the room surrounding the bed.

One spoke, "Mr. Phillips? Can you hear me?" Another checked his vitals, the third his drip line. Paul struggled to open his eyes. "That's it, Mr. Phillips. Time to wake up."

Tears trickled down Timarie's cheeks.

**

Sam helped Suzanne clear the dishes. It was late. Their evening together still held a hint of magic. He wasn't sure if a hug was in order, he didn't want to spoil it by taking the chance. He collected his gun, and started toward the door. Suzanne followed behind him, barefoot, quiet. When he reached the door, she put her hand on his shoulder. "Don't go," she said. He turned to face her. For the first time in months, he saw the woman he fell in love with, her eyes smoldering with passion, her touch warm, loving. He couldn't believe the words that came out of his mouth.

"I'd love to, but then what?"

She lowered her gaze. "You're right. I'm being selfish."

"No. I'm thrilled you asked—"

"But?"

"I need you to be sure I'm the one you want."

Sam kissed her forehead. "Thank you for dinner. Best night I've had in a long time. I hope you'll invite me again."

Suzanne reached out for a hug. "Thank you for loving me."

"Always," he whispered. "I'm not going anywhere."

∼

CHAPTER THIRTY-SIX

The Border

R aphael clicked through the channels searching for a program he could understand. When he landed on the nightly news, a shiver ran down his spine. A newscaster stood in the very spot he was abducted, talking about the border being closed. He turned up the volume.

"As of tomorrow, the president has declared that the border will be officially closed." The camera panned the area, disclosing hundreds of people waiting in line. "I'm Alyssa Graves, back to you Stan." As the camera went wide, Raphael recognized a face in the crowd. It was Diablo's minion, the one who drove the van. The one who first named him Carmelo. The one who raped him repeatedly the night he was captured. The one he wanted dead.

**

Sam got a call on his way home from Suzanne's. Raphael

said it was important. He scooted a chair next to Raphael's bed. "Where did you see Miguel?"

"On the TV. At the border."

Sam nodded and keyed a number into his cell. "Get me a sketch artist up here at Marshall ASAP."

"Did Miguel take you to the ranch right away? Or did you stop somewhere first?"

"There was a tunnel in the desert. They took me there first."

"Can you describe your surroundings? Were there trees? Cactus?"

"I just remember the bales of hay."

Sam thought for a moment. "Bales of hay in a tunnel in the desert. Were there horses?"

"I didn't see any."

"Guns?"

"Si."

"Do you remember how long you were traveling before you arrived at the tunnel?"

"Couple hours maybe. There was nothing around."

"Did you notice anything unusual about the tunnel?"

"It was dark when we got there. They put a sack over my head. One of the men pushed me, I hit something very hard, like rock or something."

"Anything else?"

"They were shooting their guns..."

"Like target practice? Or full discharge?"

"Both."

"Where else did Miguel take you?"

"Another place, but I don't know where it was. My eyes were still covered, but I smelled chemicals. I think it's where he makes the candy."

Sam googled Burro Schmitt Tunnel, enlarged the photo,

and turned the phone toward the boy. "Does this look like the tunnel they brought you to?"

"Si. Maybe. I'm not sure, I couldn't see much through the sack." He studied the image. "I don't see the hay bales."

"That's because it's a photograph, taken years ago. Not many people know about it."

"They should know the devil lives there."

Sam patted Raphael's arm. "I hope we can make that happen."

**

When Sam arrived at his office, Kelly, the dispatcher, presented him with a stack of messages. "This one sounded weird," she said, her lips momentarily disappearing between her teeth. "It sounded like a mechanical voice. It was creepy."

Sam held up the note and read it aloud. "You have something that belongs to me." He waved the paper in the air. "When did this come in?"

She grabbed the note from his hand and pointed to her chicken scratch. "This morning, 7:38."

"Was there a number on the caller ID?"

"Nope. Burner phone."

Sam dialed from his desk phone. "Nurses station, 4th floor." He waited to connect, his eyes boring holes in Kelly's face. "Tess, this is Sam Metzger at the Sheriff office. We have a patient in room 403. It's imperative that no one go in that room without having their credentials checked, do you understand me? No one. That means phlebotomist, food service, maintenance, Tom, Dick, or Harry. Even the doctors."

"Sir, you know I can't ask the doctors to–"

"The boy's life is at risk. I'm sure they will understand."

"At risk how?"

"I'll have a man outside the door. If you would kindly do as

I ask it may alleviate a lot of trouble. You know *who* belongs *where*, at this point, a badge means nothing."

"Yes, sir. I'll alert the rest of the staff."

"Only those you trust."

"This sounds very serious."

"Deadly serious."

**

The phone rang twice before Suzanne picked up. "Hey, Sam. I was just–"

"Can you stay with your brother for a few days?"

"Why? What's wrong?"

"Miguel is making threats. He knows we have Raphael."

"But how?"

"I wish I had the answer."

"I don't know. I'll have to call Steven and ask. We're supposed to have lunch tomorrow."

"I'd feel better if you left now. Today. I'll send one of my men in an unmarked car to make sure you're not followed."

"You're scaring me."

"I don't mean to...you're the only thing he has to barter with. He knows I won't give up the boy."

"I'll call my brother."

"Good. I'm on my way to the hospital to find Miguel's minion."

**

Consuela Martinez mopped around Paul Phillip's bed, humming softly. Timarie sat in a chair nearby, thumbing through a National Geographic. "Ez your son?" She nodded towards the door and cocked her head to the left.

Timarie lifted her gaze. "Son?"

"Down the hall."

"No, my children are grown."

"Oh, I thought you knew him."

"Well yes, I do, sort of, he's–"Timarie eyed the tattoo on the woman's brown skin. The pentagram, with the coiled snake in the center looked familiar.

"A friend?"

"No, not that either." Timarie pulled her phone out of her purse. "Speaking of friends–mine is texting me. Will you excuse me?" Timarie stepped into the hallway, wracking her brain as to where she had seen that tattoo before. When two officers whizzed by her, heading for Raphael's room, the memory came back quickly. It was the same tattoo she saw on the man's arm the night she and Paul were kidnapped.

**

Raphael was dozing when two officers burst into his room. "You get the restraints," one said to the other. "I'll get the wheelchair."

"Where am I going?" Raphael asked, his groggy voice a notch higher than normal.

"You don't need to concern yourself, son. We'll take good care of you."

"I'm not going anywhere with you," Raphael yelled at the top of his lungs.

The officer giving the orders slapped him hard. "Shut your fuckin' mouth or they'll be pulling your teeth out of your asshole."

Raphael doubled in pain. Before the officer could get him into the chair, Raphael threw up. "I'm sick," he cried.

"You're going to be dead if you don't cut the crap."

Raphael doubled up. Bile shot out of his mouth. "Oh God, it hurts so bad," he said, dry heaving.

The two officers conspired in hushed tones. "What do we do?"

"Call the boss."

"He's not going to be happy."

"No shit."

"Fuck it, get him in the chair." The man complied, tearing at the buckles on the restraints. Once Raphael's arms were freed, the man hoisted him into the wheelchair.

When the two officers passed by Timarie, she did a double-take. "HEY! Where are you taking him? STOP!" She scrambled toward the nurse's station screaming "stop" at the top of her lungs. A male nurse took off running after the men.

Sam stepped off the elevator, just missing the scuffle. By the time he realized what was happening, it was too late. The two men posing as cops were gone.

Raphael remained in the hallway, hunched over in his wheelchair, sobbing. "He found me. Diablo found me."

"I know, buddy, I know...but I'm here now...and in order to get to you, they are going to have to go through me."

A brunette nurse spoke up. "Raphael is scheduled for surgery at eleven tonight. I will be taking him down for an ultrasound as soon as I finish here."

Sam bristled. "No one takes him out of this room but me."

"Suit yourself." She shrugged. "I'll be gone by ten."****

Suzanne packed what she needed to get by for the next few days. Bag in one hand, phone in the other, she headed back downstairs. "I know Steven, it's not my choice either, but Sam insisted," she said, placing her brother on speaker phone. His tone was sharp.

"Did you even think to ask Karen if it was okay?"

"I did, Steven. She said she was happy I was coming."

"I'm sure she is."

"What's that supposed to mean? I thought you two kissed and made up."

"We did. Just me projecting."

"I'm not moving in, Steven. This is temporary."

"Fine. Bring some wine. I'll supply the music."

"How large of you. See you in a bit."

Suzanne set her lights on a timer and locked up. Sam's deputy, Jake Walters, waited in the driveway. She had an uneasy feeling in the pit of her stomach. Even felt a bit nauseous. She glanced over her shoulder and saw two entities near the kitchen. One of the men was missing half of his head, the other was missing his face. Both wore police uniforms.

CHAPTER THIRTY-SEVEN

Safe

Sam massaged the crick in his neck. Spending the night in the chair beside Raphael's bed was far from restful. As scheduled, Raphael went into surgery at eleven PM, but not before his appendix burst two hours prior. The antibiotics pushing through his veins staved off sepsis, but did little for the pain. Sam held the boy's hand during the worst of it, relieved when the time came to take him down to the O.R.

It was unusual to allow anyone other than staff in the surgery suite, but Sam insisted that the boy was at risk, and he needed to be protected by a law officer.

The surgery took seventy-two minutes from start to finish. Raphael was transferred to recovery, Sam shadowed him all the way.

Once the anesthesia wore off, Raphael was taken to a

locked unit where he could be monitored 24/7. Sam insisted he be there when the boy woke up.

**

It seemed like forever ago that Suzanne slept in her brother's guest room. She remembered how afraid she was...the visions...Jack hijacking her thoughts, her dreams...her toxic marriage to Ben...*You've come a long way baby.*

Her serenity was short-lived. It was as if the universe hit the send button, and loaded her brain with new information. *It's not over. He wants the boy dead.* She shivered. A holographic image of Miguel's face loomed before her.

Karen, always the observer, appeared in the doorway, holding two cups of coffee. "It's happening again, isn't it?"

"I'm not sure what you mean."

"I mean– the *visions.*" Her eyes narrowed. "What are you seeing *this* time?"

Suzanne accepted one of the coffees. "Oh, you know...the usual...a mean face with a big scar."

Karen's eyes widened. "Really?"

"What's going on with you and Steven?"

It was Karen's turn to baulk. "I wasn't aware there was anything going on with me and Steven."

"Exactly. Are you seeing someone?"

"What the hell kind of question is that?"

"Do you have the hots for Tage Betterman?"

"Is that what your brother thinks?" Karen covered her mouth. Her eyes twinkled. Her body shook. When she could no longer hold it in, she let loose, and laughed until she cried. "I can't believe he discussed Tage Betterman with you!"

"Is that a *no?*"

Karen set her cup down and collapsed into the chair next to Suzanne. "That's a 'hell no.'"

It was Suzanne's turn to giggle. "That bad?"

"Oh–I can see Steven's concern. Tage is as handsome as they come, but he's a narcissist, and not someone I would ever consider getting involved with, *and*, I'm pretty sure he has a boyfriend." Karen shrugged and picked up her coffee cup. "What about you? Rumor has it you and Sam are on the back burner."

"We're still engaged. I've just asked him for a little hiatus. I'm trying to figure myself out before I commit to forever. That's all."

"Who's the guy?"

Suzanne knew she couldn't lie. "A guy I met at a metaphysical store. He threw me for a loop. I've been taking his classes."

"And Sam's okay with you seeing him?"

"We've had coffee, a couple of drinks..."

"Yep. That's how it starts..."

"I haven't been unfaithful if that's what you're insinuating..." Silence had always been Karen clever way of getting her to come clean. "Except in my visions...we've had several lifetimes together."

Karen smiled, clearly intrigued. "Real-ly."

"Okay...Yes, in my visions the sex is incredible, and I sometimes wonder what it would be like if we were together in this lifetime...but I'm not willing to risk my relationship with Sam. Besides...I have a feeling that the guy broke my heart each time."

"That must make intimacy difficult with Sam."

"Sam and I may have had a past together as well. I just haven't figured it out yet."

"Wow. How did you attain this information?"

"I met with a past life regressionist, Diane Potter. She's one of the best around." Suzanne paused to sip. "It's been quite interesting."

"What does Sam think of all this?"

"He's being a good sport. I keep reminding myself there's a reason Sam and I were destined to be together."

"I doubt if Steven and I are soulmates. We keep growing further and further apart."

"I find it hard to believe. He worships the ground you walk on."

"Hah! He certainly doesn't treat me as such. He makes me feel stupid."

"I'll give you Diane's number. You may be able to gain some insight. My brother can be overbearing, but I know he means well."

"And you, my dear sister-in-law, need some sleep! Go back to bed. I'll finish my chores and maybe we can grab a bite in town later."

Suzanne rose. "How very kind of you not to mention my dark circles."

Karen hugged Suzanne tight. "I'm so glad you're here."
**

Miguel spent his morning sorting through his new captives. Nine-year-old twin girls would fetch top dollar for sex trafficking...Three young men, ages twenty-three to twenty-eight would be trained to replace the two men Raphael killed. The rest were disposable. He would send them to candy land, get his money's worth and dispose of them. *Like the others.*

His phone vibrated, interrupting his audit. "Si." The voice on the other line suggested he take the conversation away from listening ears. He obeyed, making his exit. "Hold on. I'm going to lose service for a bit."

"Let me know when you can hear me," the voice said.

Miguel walked quickly from the outdoor holding pen, to the other side of the tunnel, and ducked into an area he knew would receive a strong signal. "Okay. You have my attention."

"Excellent. You have a shipment coming in tonight

from–overseas. Be at the Ocean Beach pier at ten sharp. Look for fishermen wearing navy vests and matching beanies. Key word is Shanghai. Everyone has been taken care of, they're expecting you. Report back to me once you have the goods."

Miguel ended the call, feeling overwhelmed. Rounding up immigrants, making and dealing drugs were his jam. He knew who he was dealing with at all times. Collecting shipments made him uneasy. He never knew what to expect dealing with outsiders.

**

Suzanne took Karen's advice and laid back down for a bit. With her arm slung over her face to block the light, she saw a boat. Voices emanated from within. She couldn't understand their words, but their intention bled through the language barrier. Ten-gallon buckets of chemicals lined the bow. Automatic weapons rested on the knees of the crew. Their attire blended in with the night. *Why am I seeing this?* The universe didn't provide an answer. What it did provide was a flash of a man's' face. *Diablo.*

**

"Sam–I wanted to share my vision with you. It may be nothing...it may be huge."

"What'cha got?"

"You sound exhausted. Is this a bad time?"

"Your intuition is spot on. Both–two goons in police uniforms tried to kidnap the kid last night. Thank God Timarie Phillips was down the hall, keeping vigil over her husband. She saw them wheeling the boy out of his room and screamed bloody murder, scaring them off."

"How did they find out he was there?"

"Beats me, we're still looking into the matter. The good news is that the kid had his appendix removed last night, and he's doing well."

"You were up all night, weren't you?"

"Yes. I wanted to make sure–"

"Those men–they're not coming back, Sam."

"How can you be so sure?"

"I saw them in my dream. They're dead."

**

Sam didn't need a heavier load on his shoulders, but he was glad Suzanne was back in the game. When she started getting hits from the universe, he knew justice wasn't too far away. All he needed to do was keep putting the bricks together. Perhaps the boy was the keystone.

When Sam arrived at the hospital, he didn't go directly to see Raphael. He intended to thank Timarie for saving the boy's life, but when he reached Paul's room, he discovered the couple had been moved. His heart galloped in his chest. "Where were they taken?"

"Don't go fretting," the charge nurse said. "Mr. Phillips has improved extensively. We moved him to a room with more security, and a better view."

"Thank you for that..."

"Mrs. Phillips also had a word with Social Services. She insisted she be in the same proximity as the boy."

Sam smiled. He liked that someone besides Suzanne and himself saw another side of the boy.

He caught Timarie giving Paul a sponge bath. "I thought the nurses do the heavy lifting around here," he said.

"They offered. Gives me something to do. I miss our intimacy."

"I stopped by to thank you."

"No need. Once a mother hen, always a mother hen."

"You saved his life."

"Then I'd call us even."

Sam gave Timarie a hug and left the room. He had hoped

to have a marriage as strong as theirs one day, but as it stood, he and Suzanne were still failing at being engaged.

Raphael was asleep when Sam entered the room. The boy looked so young, so innocent. Sam knew better. So much had been stolen from him at an early age. Poverty had a tendency to rob the innocent.

Sam didn't need to be the one to rob him from his sleep, a nurse carrying a food tray with a clear liquid diet did the job for him. She placed the tray on an adjustable table, and grabbed a blood pressure cuff off of the wall. She wrapped it around the boy's arm, making him stir.

"Hey buddy, how ya feelin'?"

He looked at Sam, the nurse, then Sam. "Dónde estoy?"

The nurse replied. "El hospital. You had surgery last night." She rubbed her tummy. "No more tummy aches. Comprendes?"

"Si. I'm hungry."

"I brought you some broth and Jello. Let's see how you do before we up you to a soft diet."

When Raphael was settled, Sam leaned forward. "Did you know the men who came for you last night?"

"That was real? I thought it was a bad dream." He grimaced at the taste of the broth, but continued to sip.

"Any idea where the chemical shipments came in to make the drugs?"

Raphael shook his head. "No." He held up his cup of orange cubes, his expression perplexed. "What is this?"

Sam laughed. "Jello. You've never had it before?"

"No, man." He jiggled the cup. "Like my cousin, Lupe."

Once the laughter died down, Sam's eyes narrowed. "Suzanne thinks a big shipment is coming in. Miguel will be there to receive it. Be nice to catch him in the act–lock his ass up."

"All I know is he went to San Diego a lot."

"Did he make more drugs when he got back?"

"Si. More people got sick. He burned the bodies in the desert."

"Did you ever go with him?"

"No, but I heard the men talking when they thought I was asleep."

**

Sam phoned a guy he knew that worked vice on Coronado. After a few minutes of catch-up, Sam got to the point. "Any word on a big shipment coming in?"

Jim Barnes stuttered, "How–who–where'd you hear that?"

"I'm looking for Miguel Guzman."

"Guzman, eh? There's a name I haven't heard in a while."

"Probably because he's running his drug operation up here now."

"I haven't caught wind of anything going on...can you be more specific?"

"The chemicals are coming in by fishing boat–ten-gallon buckets."

"That's what I call specific. Any idea when?"

"Not sure, but I do know it will happen from one of your docks–at night."

"I don't have the manpower to cover every dock."

"How many fishermen stay out on the water after dark?"

"Too many."

**

Lunch at the Tower Café was just what Suzanne needed. She ordered the Pirate Salad with mixed greens, spinach, beets, feta, red onion, carrots and cinnamon-honey almonds, with the house blood orange-d'anjou pear vinaigrette. Karen ordered a California chicken salad that looked divine. They each had a glass of Chardonnay and shared a piece of salted caramel cheesecake.

Karen placed her napkin on the table. "Why don't we do this more often?"

"We've both been busy, I guess."

"Stephen told me what you said about him acting like an ass. Thank you for that. He's been working on his attitude. He actually thinks before he jumps in and tries to take control of everything."

"Ever since mom and dad died he's felt that taking control is his responsibility."

"He doesn't talk about them—your parents."

"Neither of us do. Maybe it's too painful."

"Do you still see your mom?"

"Sometimes. It's been awhile. Probably doesn't like the company I'm keeping."

"Oh?"

"Dead migrant workers, they've been hanging around lately."

Stunned into silence, Karen stared at Suzanne, her mouth partially open as if frozen. Suzanne smirked. "Yeah. Probably why I don't come around much."

Karen flinched. "I just can't imagine—that's all. I'd be scared out of my wits."

Suzanne pulled a strand of hair in front of her face and examined the color. "If I keep plucking out the gray hairs, I'm going to be bald before I'm forty."

"Are you still seeing a therapist?"

"No, not for a while..."

"How do you stay sane seeing dead people all the time?"

"I guess I'm their therapist. I can see them...that must be a comfort." Suzanne took a sip of her wine. "They're not malevolent, they want justice." She thought for a moment. "Except there is one–he's not dead. Not someone I'd want to meet in a dark alley. I keep seeing his face."

"Is that why you're staying with us? Is your life in danger?"

"Sam is being cautious. If it were up to me–"

"Is he dangerous?"

"I don't think it's anything to worry about..."

"Steven and I don't need any trouble..."

"Yeah, you're right. I should find another place to stay."

The chill between them rivaled the arctic. Suzanne pictured an elephant in the room, the size of the prehistoric Palaeoloxodon namadicus, the largest of the species.

Karen placed her hand over Suzanne's. "What's wrong? You're pale."

"I'm sorry. Can we go, please?"

Karen paid the check, and grabbed her purse. "Let's get you home."

**

Suzanne flipped through photos of elephants on her phone. *What does it mean?* The answer struck her between the eyes. Below the image of the Palaeoloxodon namadicus was a description, explaining its origin being Africa, and its migration to Asia. "That's it!" She dialed Sam. "Didn't you say one of the kids died from an overdose of carfentanil?"

"You're getting a hit?"

"I'm not sure...it feels like it. I'm seeing elephants migrating from Africa to Asia."

"And you are connecting the dots, how?"

"That's your job, Sam."

"What I can tell you is that the emergence of numerous synthetic fentanyl analogs, acetyl fentanyl, butyrylfentanyl, acrylfentanyl, furanylfentanyl and hydroxythiofentanyl, manufactured in China, have been made available on the internet. Carfentanil is the game changer. It's used to anesthetize elephants, rhinos, large animals...it's one of the most potent, and the deadliest opioids thus far."

Her voice rose a notch. "Aren't they regulated?"

"As soon as one of the analogs is regulated, another takes its place."

"I think the shipment Miguel is waiting for contains carfentanil."

"Where? There are many docks, vice can't cover them all."

Suzanne closed her eyes, conjuring the vision of men in wetsuits. "Is there a place where Navy Seals train?"

"Several, near Coronado."

"I'm seeing the Coronado Hotel to my right, there's a wall separating an area from the beach.

**

Sam called Jim Barnes in Coronado to relay the information he received from Suzanne. "You heard this from who?" was Jim's reaction.

"She's the real deal. We've been working together for a couple of years now. I trust the information she gives me one hundred percent."

The man hemmed and hawed, until, "Okay, Sam. I'll get my men on it."

**

That evening, Suzanne sat by the pool. The last of the sun's rays covered the water in a golden shroud. A warm hand touched her shoulder, and she covered the hand with her own. "It's beautiful, don't you think?" She turned to face Sam. Their eyes held, remembering.

"*You're* beautiful," he said, bringing her hand to his lips.

"What brings you here?" she said, rising. He released her hand.

"I picked up a couple of pizzas. Steven and Karen told me you were out here."

"That was sweet of you." She stepped into his arms and held him tight.

"You okay? You're shaking." He realized she was crying, and held her tighter. Moments passed without words. Until...

"I miss you. I miss us–"

"But–"

"I have to be sure."

"That you're not in love with that guy?"

"No, this is no longer about Garian. This is about me."

Sam kissed the top of her head and met her gaze. "I'm not going to pretend I understand what's going on, but I want you to know that my love for you doesn't have an expiration date. I'll be here." He gave her a squeeze. "Hungry?"

"Yes," she admitted. They walked arm in arm into the kitchen

CHAPTER THIRTY-EIGHT

Past, Present, Future

Miguel wasn't naive. The men bringing the carfentanil shipment into Coronado weren't either. It was as if they anticipated extra eyes on the water. Coincidentally, what sounded like gunshots and a sudden scuffle onboard a party boat drew the Coast Guard's attention away from the fishermen dropping the load. Of course, it was no coincidence that Miguel knew every dirty cop, Coast Guard, and border patrol agent in San Diego. Business was business. *Who says money can't buy you love?* Before the clock struck midnight, he had the shipment loaded on his truck and was on his way back to Northern California.

By dawn's light, Miguel met with his minions to distribute the chemicals to the various pop-up labs set up in the foothills. A fresh batch of immigrants had been rounded up at the border. It didn't take much to convince those who were down and out to seek a better life. With a promise of fair wages, room, board, and the chance to live the American Dream, they followed him like the Pied Piper.

**

Suzanne had planned to see Diane Potter last week, put an end to her quandary, but had ended up canceling. Sam needed her help. But now, she was eager to continue seeking answers as to why she was being thrown into the past with Garian and why she had distanced herself from Sam.

She settled herself in Diane's chair, making herself comfortable. "Relax," the hypnotherapist said. "Let's start with some deep breaths..." but before Diane finished counting down to one, Suzanne was already back in time.

She saw herself in the same once lavish house, surrounded by drawings and books. He was there. *Voltaire.* They were quarreling...

"Marquis de Saint-Lambert is a buffoon."

"You are jealous because we are in love."

"He is ten years young–" He swiped his face with his handkerchief and continued, his tone cynical. "The love he feels for you is beneath your skirts, and in your bed!"

"And your brother's spawn? Barely a woman–is she not warming *your* bed?"

"And if she were? Am I to remain lonely while you carry on with–"?

"I am with child. *His* child."

Voltaire's eyes filled with tears. An emotion she had not witnessed in all the years they were together. He turned and left the room, leaving her with the angst of knowing he truly loved her...

The transition was jarring. Past, present, future, swirled in her brain, as if someone was fast forwarding a movie with a remote. When the image stopped, she was still with child, but it belonged to another. *Captain Bishop.*

Captured by his gaze, she hummed softly, her youngest cuddled against her swollen belly. His bow gliding back and forth across his Leopold Widhalm violin, mesmerized them both. His eyes burned with desire as he played a melody, he knew she loved. Her heart was filled with joy for the first time in years, and she felt a twinge of guilt at how their relationship came to be. She didn't miss her late husband. In fact, she felt blessed, for her happiness came with his demise. She was grateful for the man who stepped in and showed her and her five children the true meaning of love.

As Captain Bishop ended the song, he bent down to kiss her on the forehead, and she smiled. "What is the name of that song, my love?"

"Heinrich Von Biber's "Rosary Sonata," I'm glad you enjoyed it."

"It resonates in my soul."

His hand rested on her belly, relishing the movement inside. "Our son or daughter agrees."

The images blurred, but the music remained as another lifetime wedged its way into Suzanne's altered state. She saw Voltaire, weeping...his arms wrapped around a newborn babe. The Marquis was behind him in the distance, flirting with an ingénue.

She tried to touch his cheek, dry his tears, but he did not see or hear her...it was if she were invisible."

Diane's voice beckoned... "Eight, you are coming back down the path, feeling restored. Seven, the information you were seeking remains intact. Six, your breathing is calmed by the knowing...Five, returning to the present...Four, your path is leading you back to now. Three. Whatever you experience in the past will be used to further your journey in this lifetime. Two...you are rested, and filled with joy. One. Open your eyes.

Suzanne blinked her eyes. "Voltaire was Émilie's one true love..."

"I'm glad you were able to get the information you were seeking."

"The last thing I remembered is that I died after my daughter was born. Voltaire was at my gravesite, while the Marquis, who was the father of my child, had already moved on to someone new."

"I find it interesting that heartache, even mistrust can follow us into the present."

"How does that work?"

"As a result of regressing hundreds of people, I have found that those who suffer in this lifetime generally have had something crucial happen in the past. For instance, a person who suddenly gets migraines at the age of thirty-five with no previous symptoms...once regressed, that person discovers at the age of thirty-five, they were kicked in the head by a horse."

"Basically, you're saying that my relationships in the past are screwing up my relationship in the present?"

Diane clasped her hands together. "That's not for me to determine. Think about what you've learned about your past and see if any of those discoveries apply to your situation today."

**

Out of curiosity, Suzanne drove to Planet Earth Rising. She needed to know if her new found knowledge changed the effect Garian had on her. She pulled into a parking space in front of the store and was about to get out of her car, when she glanced in her rear-view mirror. She saw Garian crossing the street, his arm around a beautiful blonde. They were laughing, kissing, enjoying the intimacy they shared.

Suzanne didn't need to witness anything further. The picture was clear. She pulled away from the curb.

Tumultuous feelings bombarded her soul. Images of the betrayal she had endured in her previous lives flashed through her mind. One question burned through the haze. *Why now?*

**

Stretching his legs beneath his desk, Sam stared at his computer monitor. He had received an email from Jim Barnes. *Nothing showed up last night. I had eyes on seven piers east of the military base, eight men on the water. No sign of Miguel. Jim*

"Where are you muthafucker?" Sam slammed his laptop shut and headed for the hospital.

**

Raphael sipped water through a bent straw, staring at the liquidy, pasty stuff in the insulated bowl. The nurse checking his vitals snickered. "It's cereal, we call it Cream of Wheat. Doesn't look like you're a fan."

He glanced at the nurse and wrinkled his nose. "No, gracias." He pushed the tray away.

"Would you prefer more broth? You need to eat." She rubbed her tummy. "Get things working again." She pointed to the bathroom. "Comprende?"

Raphael's eyes grew large. He took a spoonful of the cereal, held his nose and swallowed.

Sam arrived as the nurse was leaving. She lifted the lid on the cereal bowl so Sam could take a peek. "He said he didn't like it." She rolled her eyes. "Don't be too long, his doctor is on the way up."

Sam pulled up a chair. "How are you doing, my friend?"

"You like Cream of Wheat?"

Sam chuckled. "One of those foods you appreciate when you're older." Sam gestured to his stomach. "Hurt much?"

Raphael winced. "It's not too bad. I won't be able to run fast for a while."

"I had a talk with your Social Worker. We need to find a safe place for you to stay until we find Miguel."

Raphael paled. "You did not find him?"

"I'm afraid not." Sam stuffed his hands in his pockets. "That doesn't mean we won't. He's pretty elusive."

"Like a gopher."

"Gophers live underground."

"Si."

**

Steven joined Suzanne on the patio. "Like old times," he said, handing her a glass of wine.

"Two steps forward, three steps back."

"Your being here wasn't my idea. You could act a little more grateful."

"I *am* grateful. I'm also confused and a little scared. You and Karen are the only family I have. I feel safe here."

Steven scooted his chair closer to his sister. "What's scaring you? The drug lord? The dead bodies? Or getting married?"

"All of the above." She turned to face him. "That guy I told you I met, the one I have a past life with…turns out he's broken my heart more than once. I'm thinking that's where my mistrust comes from."

"I don't buy all of that bullshit, but I do know, losing your parents, your fiancé, being married to an asshole like Ben, and almost losing your life factors into the equation."

"Yeah, there is that…but this is different. I can't explain it."

"I would think your main focus would be on getting rid of your major threat. Who is this drug lord, and why isn't he behind bars?"

"Million-dollar question. He's as slippery as they get. And dangerous."

"You were able to track down a serial killer, human traffickers, psychopaths...how is this guy any different?"

Suzanne sipped her wine as the sun kissed the horizon. Shards of gold illuminated the clouds in shades of orange and pink, casting the grass in a deep emerald green. She longed to stay in this moment forever, away from stress, death, and heartbreak. But reality infringed on the magic, bringing her back to the present.

"Sam's here," Karen announced from the patio door. "Shall I send him out?"

Steven rose. "I'll let you two talk. Feel free to invite him for dinner. You know Karen, there's always plenty."

"Thanks, big brother." She reached out and squeezed his hand.

Suzanne stood when she heard Sam's voice. The sun's golden hue lit up his face and she couldn't help but marvel at how handsome he was. *He loves me, as Voltaire loved Emilie, and Captain Bishop loved Alaina.* But before she could speak...

"Miguel Guzman is still in operation. Not sure where, just yet. I imagine there will be more deaths."

"Are you here on business or pleasure?" Sam's shocked expression made her laugh.

"I–I," he stammered."

"It's okay. You're welcome to stay for dinner if you have time, that's all."

Her spontaneity caught him off guard. "I wasn't expecting–"

"It's okay, don't feel obligated." Disappointment gave her heart a pinch.

"I don't–I'd love to." He stepped forward and pulled her

into his arms. "Please don't push me away," he said, holding her close. "I miss—us."

Suzanne melted into his arms, breathing in his scent, feeling his muscular arms draw her against his heat. She was about to find his lips when she felt a piercing jab that started at the corner of her eye, down to the corner of her mouth. Her third eye saw red, and a scream stuck in her throat.

CHAPTER THIRTY-NINE

Big Mistake

Annabelle Dugan, Marci Roanoke, Madison Beecher, and Linaya Thompson followed I-5 from San Diego to Sacramento. Their week spent checking out SDU proved productive for Annabelle and Linaya, who planned to attend college in the fall, and fun for Marci and Madison who came along to party.

The foursome decided to veer off of their route to stop in Salinas, gas up and get a bite to eat, Marci gravitated towards a table of men in expensive suits. Her low-cut midriff top garnered her the attention she sought. Before long, the girls were invited to join the men.

"Where'd you get that scar on your face?" Marci asked the man sitting across from her while gulping down her second margarita.

Miguel's eyes narrowed. "I'll bet that big mouth of yours does more than ask stupid questions."

Marci grinned. "It would take more than a couple of margaritas to do anything *that* stupid."

Two of the men threw cash on the table and excused themselves. The other three girls were mortified. Linaya gave Marci a nudge. "We can't take this girl anywhere."

Miguel didn't react. His dark eyes bore holes in Marci's soul. She didn't back down. "It was just a question," she said. "I mean like, you're kinda handsome except for the scar."

"How would you girls like to spend the afternoon as my guest at mi casa? I have a lovely pool, an ocean view, and the best weed this side of the border."

The girls exchanged glances before Marci replied, "Annabelle's driving. It's up to her."

"Sounds like fun," Linaya said. She was the most adventurous out of the three. Annabelle, although very academic, was the biggest pothead of the four, Madison, the horniest. They all agreed, a couple hours max, and then back on the road.

CHAPTER FORTY

Somewhere Near Salinas

S am was vigilant to check reports coming from other counties during his first cup of coffee. One in particular caught his attention. Four missing girls. Last sighted in Salinas at a place called Hola Amigo. Further down the page, a young girl had been found along Interstate 5, not far from the restaurant, her face unrecognizable due to being dragged by a motor vehicle... *Barefoot, naked from the waist down, clutching a fistful of black hair in her right hand.*

"Jesus, Mary, and Joseph," he whispered. He didn't know anyone in Salinas. He dialed the central police station number. After a quick explanation of who he was, and why he was calling, he was transferred to Sergeant Patrick Foster.

"Help ya?" he said, his southern drawl, thick, his tone gruff. His sigh exuded an air of self-importance.

After identifying himself and repeating his credentials,

Sam got right to the point. "I'm interested in the unidentified girl, the one found on I-80."

"Can't stop thinkin' 'bout that one. Face split wide open on one side– the other side looked like hamburger meat." The sergeant paused. "Damn shame if ya ask me. What do ya want to know?"

"I'm looking for Miguel Guzman. Word has it he picked up a shipment of carfentanil in Coronado. Has the girl been tested yet?"

"Labs haven't come back yet. It's not like we're not catching a bus here, Sheriff. We take our time. Do the job right."

"If Guzman is in Salinas, I need to know."

"Duly noted."

"Do you think she's one of the missing girls?"

"You're right up in my business, now, aren't ya?"

"Guzman's one mean muthafucker, Sergeant. Believe me, you do not want him in your town."

"Give me a couple of days to get back to you. Our forensic specialist, Evan Stewart's out on maternity leave. The temp they have replacing him is a mudpuppy."

Sam hung up and continued scrolling, looking for any more clues that would lead him to Miguel. He came up empty.

His mind backtracked to the other evening, when he hugged Suzanne, and she freaked out. She said it felt as though a knife was slashing her face. Perhaps she was channeling the girl found dead on I-5. *Any excuse to hear her voice.*

"Hey Suzanne, about the other night..." He took a deep breath.

"I'm sorry if I came off as insensitive."

He exhaled, "No, no, no. You're fine, but you felt something on your face...can you elaborate?"

"I'm not sure what that was, Sam. Felt like–like my face was being sliced open."

**

It was late. Steven and Karen had retired early, the house was quiet. Suzanne sat outside, gazing at the stars, when suddenly she felt a chill. The temperature had been unusually warm, and had not dipped too far below the high once the sun went down. The cold spot circled her chair, enveloping her space. The vision came swift and clear, and she was pressed against the back of the chair. She saw four girls dancing poolside, the tiny scraps of clothing they wore looked more like undergarments than swim attire, with the exception of one girl who kept her T-shirt on. Each girl had a drink in their hand, they were toasting between sips, and gyrations. Beyond the group celebration sat a man. A straw hat covered his head. Sunglasses shielded his eyes, but there was no mistaking the scar on his face.

One by one, the girls dropped into the water. Except the girl in the T-shirt. She danced alone to a tune she couldn't hear. Her body kept moving. Gyrating.

The scar-faced man rose, walked to the edge of the pool to admire the floating bodies, and then turned to the last girl. Enjoying the fear in her eyes, he produced a switchblade from his boot and slashed her cheek open with one fell swoop. She grabbed at his hair trying to steady herself, but it was no use. "Tie her to the bumper and dump her body where the coyotes can feast."

Suzanne watched the scene play out, the men obeying, cleaning up after el jefe. She watched one man hoist the girl's body over the bed of the truck, watched him remove her panties and rape her. And when he finished, he invited the other men to take their turn. When no one stepped forward, the man looped a rope around the girl's ankles and lowered her to the ground head first. The other men jumped into the truck and took off down the road. Somewhere along the way, the girl died.

With tears streaming down her face, Suzanne cried out in pain. "Make it stop! I can't take anymore!"

**

Sam made haste when he got Steven's call. Barreling down Highway 50, he wondered what could've sent Suzanne over the brink. Steven said she was sobbing so hard she couldn't catch her breath.

When he arrived at Steven and Karen's place, he parked catawampus in the driveway and sprinted to the door.

"Where is she?" he asked, pushing past Steven.

Steven followed Sam down the hall towards Suzanne's bedroom. "Man, what did you do, fly here?"

"Do you know what happened?"

"No. She just started screaming. I went into her room and saw her curled up like a baby, bawling her eyes out."

Sam reached the doorway, stood outside, and tapped lightly on the door jam. "Suzanne, honey?" He sat down on the bed and began stroking her hair. "Baby, what's wrong? What happened?"

The haunted look in her eyes made him want to cry. The last time he saw her like this was when she had been abducted, drugged and God knows what else. He tried to put that image out of his mind. He scooped her up and cradled her in his arms. "It's okay. I'm here now."

**

Suzanne's head swam with images. She met Sam's gaze with confusion. "Who are you really?" she asked.

"It's just me, my love," he said, and for an instant she was in another place, another time. She melted into his arms, hugging him so tight, she could feel his heart beat against her chest. She didn't want to move, but she knew she had to tell him. He needed to know.

"Diablo...there's a girl...they..." she began to cry again, images of the brutality bestowed on her still fresh in her mind. "Diablo sliced her face open and had his men drag her body down the road."

"Can you see the highway?"

"The number 5. I see the number 5."

"They found the girl."

Suzanne hummed a few bars of the Janis Joplin song, *Bobby McGee*. "Salinas. That's where he killed them."

"Them? Only one girl has been found."

She closed her eyes. "There are others."

**

Miguel had his men distribute the shipment of chemicals he obtained in Coronado to several of the labs he had set up in Goldorado County. The men delivering the goods appeared to be landscapers, painters, construction workers. No one would suspect that many of them were hardcore killers. No one would care if any of them disappeared. To Miguel, no one was indispensable.

He pushed back in his leather recliner, a bottle of 1800 Coleccion Tequila on the table beside him. He admired the ornate pewter trimmed bottle. He swished the liquid around in the glass, took a whiff, and savored the Amaretto-like taste. Ten years in the barrel. At two thousand dollars a pop, it was guaranteed to be smooth. He liked smooth. His tequila, his life, his operation, his women...smooth was good. However, at the moment, before the alcohol clouded his brain, he thought about where the bottle came from. A gift from his boss. A small gesture for a job well done? Or a warning? A threat? An indication that things were not going as smoothly as he imagined? He took another sip. "Enjoy it while it lasts." There was a new sheriff in town, sniffing around, asking questions. Rocking his world.

**

Suzanne rolled up her window. The dry heat and long drive made her head hurt. She tried to focus on the lush green fields, crops of lettuce, cabbage, brussels sprouts. The land appeared fertile, despite rumors of a water shortage. But there was something else...a vibe. A sense of evil lurking beneath the picturesque countryside. She folded her arms across her chest, guarding herself against a sudden chill.

She dialed down the fan on the air conditioner. Sam glanced her way. "You all right?"

"Got a chill. Are we almost there?"

"Head still hurt?"

"Yes."

"Hope you're not coming down with something."

"Just a little hangover."

Sam squinted his eyes. "Say again?"

"They were drinking."

"Suzanne?"

"The girls. Margaritas. The men were laughing. Except one."

Sam took the next exit. "I could use a cup of coffee."

**

Suzanne sat in the car while Sam ran into the Quick Mart. He returned with two cups of coffee and a couple of pre-made sandwiches. "Eat something," he said, tenderly. After a long sigh, "I know this isn't easy for you."

"Feels like the first time, you know, when we went in search of those two missing girls. Except this time, I'm not feeling optimistic." She set her coffee on the console cup holder between the seats. "I can feel him close by." She closed her eyes. She saw three bodies floating face down in a pool. Tears rimmed her eyes. "The girls are dead."

"Describe what you see." Sam sipped his coffee and set it down beside Suzanne's.

Suzanne closed her eyes. "Each girl staggers toward the edge of the pool. I hear laughing. One by one, they fall in, sinking to the bottom, then floating to the top face down. The fourth girl watches in a stupor, until..." Suzanne looked to the heavens. "He slashed her face." She took a deep breath and exhaled. "The men picked her up and put her in the back of a pick-up after..." tears streamed down her cheeks. She opened her eyes. "After they raped her."

Sam dabbed her tears with the bottom of his T-shirt. "Honey, I hate to see you go through this, but I have to ask...can you tell me more about the truck? Color? Anything?"

"Grey."

"Can you tell what make?"

Suzanne squeezed her eyes shut. "I see a RAM logo."

"Good." He tucked a strand of hair behind her ear. "Can you see a license plate?"

Suzanne's brow gathered as she concentrated on the images behind her eyes. "It's covered in dust–looks like an 'N', a 'W', and either a zero or a six." She opened her eyes and shivered. "That's all I'm getting."

"There's more, I can tell–"

"Yes. You're not the only one who wants Miguel dead."

Sam placed his hands on her shoulders, "What do you mean?"

She shook her head. "I don't know, I have this feeling...it's like when you know someone is in the room but you can't see them...I've felt this before. Miguel works for someone. Someone big. Someone who is not what he seems. I see a mask. A smile on one side, a sneer on the other. And the image is fleeting, which gives me the impression that whoever he is, he is getting away with something."

"Miguel may not be acting on his own volition, but no one controls him either. He's a murdering son-of-a-bitch, and I want him behind bars."

Suzanne licked her lips then clicked her tongue between them. "I have a taste for–*tequila*."

"Tequila? You don't–or at least you didn't–are you serious?" Her expression remained the same. "Oh, I see, you're getting a hit."

"Smooth. I'm tasting tequila, and getting the word *smooth*."

Sam swiped his brow. "I'm not sure I'm on the same wavelength."

"He's near, Sam. I can feel him."

**

They drove around Salinas, scoping things out. When the sun set, Sam pulled into a Quality Inn. "I'll get us each a room," he said, opening the car door.

"Sam–" He stopped and twisted in his seat to face her. Her eyes felt glassy. Tired. She didn't want to be alone. "Can we share a room tonight?"

He raised his brow and shrugged. "Sure. I can see if they have two beds."

She bowed her head. "I deserved that."

"I figured you'd want your space, that's all."

She smiled, half- heartedly. "Thanks, that's sweet of you." He smiled, hit the door locks and moved on.

Her emotions wadded into a knot that stuck in her throat. She wanted to scream, she wanted to cry, she wanted to laugh out loud, yell at the top of her lungs. She glanced in the mirror to see if her face reflected the insanity she was feeling at that moment, but it wasn't her image that gave her pause. "Where've you been Mom?"

"Have you learned anything?"

"What are you referring to? A lot has happened."

"Just be careful. Coyotes can smell the weak ones"

"Are you talking about me? I'm the weak–" It was no use. Her mom was gone. A few minutes later, Sam returned with the key.

"All they had left were king size beds." He monitored her reaction. When she didn't object, he added, "We can grab a bite to eat. The desk clerk said there's quite a few places nearby, one he highly recommended. Coincidently, it's the last place the girl was seen."

**

Hola Amigo's dinner hour was in full swing. Patrons filled tables, booths, the bar, and the patio. Both Sam and Suzanne were on high alert, scanning the room facing the entrance, eavesdropping, making small talk. When they finished their meal, Sam perused the dessert menu. "I miss dessert," he said.

"Remember the wonderful desserts we had in Paris?" she replied, smiling like a Cheshire cat.

"I remember a lot of things about Paris." He reached for her hand, but thought better of it. "I knew it was too good to be true."

"Paris?"

"No. Us."

"Oh Sam," she sighed. "We can't go back...only forward."

"You went back–back to another time, another place, another man–"

"I'm not so sure he was the only one."

"What do you mean?" His wry smile faded.

"It's late. Another time."

Sam called for the check. "What about dessert?" she asked.

He didn't respond, she didn't push it.

**

When they got back to the room, each took turns getting undressed for bed. Sam turned on the TV and slipped under the covers, already regretting the situation. How could he be in the same bed as Suzanne and not touch her?

She came from the bathroom, freshly showered. He wanted her even more. Her scent drove him wild, the way her wet hair coiled around her neck in corkscrews. Her nightshirt was thin, accentuating her taut nipples, her full breasts. When she bent over to towel dry her hair, the fabric clung to her butt cheeks, causing his throat to go dry and his manhood to stir. "I can't do this," he said, and sprung from the bed.

"What did I do?"

"Nothing. You did nothing wrong." He grabbed his pants and shoes. "I'll sleep in the car."

"You can't do that–I don't understand–why?"

"This is why." He dropped his clothes and drew her to him, his kisses, hot, breathy. "All I can think of is how much I want you."

He expected rejection. Instead, she lifted her nightshirt over her head, and pulled him close. They tumbled into bed, kissing, touching, returning to a love they once shared.

"That's it," she cried, meeting his thrust. He kissed her harder, professing his love. When she was about to reach the pinnacle, she suddenly froze.

"What is it? What's wrong? Am I hurting you?"

Suzanne grabbed his face in her hands and demanded, "Who are you?"

"Baby, you know who I am–it's Sam." He rolled off of her and propped himself up on one elbow. He stroked her hair as he spoke. "It's me–Sam, the man who loves you so much I can't imagine life without you. It's me–the man who would walk through fire for you. You are my everything. It's as if my life wasn't complete before you, and never will be again if I can't have you, so please, if it's not me you want–"

Suzanne pressed two fingers against his lips. "When you're inside me, I feel like we've spanned the globe, made love in many lifetimes. How did I not see this before? How was I so blind?"

"Is that a good thing? Because you're scaring the crap out of me."

She snuggled close, feeling her heart beat in sync with his. "I want it to be."

**

Suzanne awoke in Sam's arms. His warm, strong body felt so good next to hers. She wanted to wake him, make love, feel him inside her once more before they continued their search for Miguel Guzman, but before she could entertain the thought further, Miguel's face appeared in her third eye, and killed her libido.

She rolled over and slipped out of bed. When she entered the bathroom, images of the dead girls appeared in the mirror. She gasped at the sight of them, their once beautiful faces bloated, and fixed in a scowl. She traced the open wound on one girl's reflection with her fingertip. "I'm so sorry this happened to you," she whispered. The girls vanished. Her own face stared back at her. The afterglow of last night's lovemaking erased by the spiritual intrusion.

A light knock in the door tore her away from her reflection.

"Good morning, beautiful. How did you sleep?"

She stepped into his arms. "Better than I have in a long time."

He tightened his embrace, kissed the top of her head. "Me too."

She lifted her gaze. "Let's go get that murdering son-of-a-bitch so we can go home."

CHAPTER FORTY-ONE

The Meeting

Miguel donned a pair of white linen trousers, a black silk shirt, slipped into a pair of Anderson Bean Rattlesnake skin boots, and grabbed his matching white linen jacket. He checked his teeth in a mirror near the foyer, and stepped into the morning sunshine. Duty called.

He had already surmised his meeting with the senator would begin as always...a lavish brunch, followed by cocktails served by scantily dressed females, and possibly a blowjob, depending on the senator's mood and before the daggers came out. Miquel knew he fucked up when he brought the kid, Raphael, into the picture. And the fact that the kid was still breathing made things worse. Miguel had considered grabbing some cash, a fake passport and heading to Switzerland, but *where's the fun in that?*

He parked in the rear of the hotel, brushed the wrinkles from his slacks and used the keycard the senator provided to let himself in. The elevator delivered him to the ninth floor, where he stepped into a life of luxury and a pair of steely grey eyes.

"You clean up well my friend." The senator gestured. "Have a seat. Chef has outdone himself. I'm famished." Miguel seated himself in a tan calfskin barrel chair across from his boss. "So, tell me, how was your drive up here? Traffic is getting unbearable, isn't it?"

"It wasn't bad, guess I caught it just right."

"Good. And how is your—oh, forgive my rudeness. I was about to ask about your family, but you don't have one, do you?" His lips stretched across his teeth. Was it Miguel's imagination? Or did they appear larger than usual? He ignored the senators intended mind fuck.

"You remembered, that's all that counts."

"Did you enjoy the tequila?"

"Very much. Thank you."

Two voluptuous women entered the room, one dressed in a long, rose gold fishnet dress. Her untethered breasts were perky behind the flimsy weave, her bare legs, long, and tan appeared through slits that parted as she approached the table. Cola brown hair hung loosely over squared shoulders. Her eyes sparkled like gems beneath thick black lashes. The other woman was more exotic looking, with large, dark brown eyes, and high cheekbones belonging to that of a high priestess, her full lips, moist, inviting. The white sarong she wore accentuated full breasts that floated more than bounced when she walked. Her platinum hair was wound into a tight chignon at the nape of her neck. Miguel sipped his mimosa made with fresh squeezed orange juice as he admired the view.

"How long have you been working for me, Miguel?"

"Ten, maybe twelve years."

"And in all that time, have you ever known me to be a spineless individual?"

Miguel was sorry that he didn't have a weapon handy to end the gringo's life. "Not at all."

The senator released his fixation on Miquel when the two beauties brought plates of eggs benedict topped with Chef's special hollandaise sauce, crab, and lobster. The blond returned with small baskets of fresh baked pastries, muffins, dry and buttered toast for each. The brunette placed platters of fresh fruit and thinly sliced meats in the middle of the table while the blonde filled china cups with an aromatic brew.

The perfect meal.

"Mmmm," the senator groaned, sliding one hand up the brunette's dress. "I don't know what I am enjoying more...this delicious food, or the anticipation of dessert."

The brunette smiled demurely, and brushed his hand away with her fingertips.

Miguel caught the disgust in her eyes when she thought no one was looking. "Where did you find such beauties?" he asked.

"Ukraine. Must be something in the water, our best stock comes from there."

Miguel glanced over his shoulder and turned back to the senator. "I think I'm herding from the wrong end of the border."

The senator stabbed a chunk of lobster and popped it in his mouth. "Think so, eh?"

When he was sure no one was in earshot Miguel added, "I'm sure there is just as much risk involved in trafficking humans as there is drugs," he replied between bites.

"Stick to what you know...that's what my daddy used to say. Less chance of fucking things up."

"Your father was a wise man."

"Yes, he was. He knew how to run a tight ship."

"As do you."

"Do I? Is that why the cops are sniffin' around?"

"Cops? You own most of them—how is that possible?"

The senator's beady eyes narrowed as he tucked a hunk of croissant between his cheek and gums like it was tobacco. "You tell me, amigo—how the fuck *is* that possible?" He chewed a few times and washed the pastry down with a swig of coffee. "Rumor has it he's from up your way. Goldorado County."

Miguel flicked away the thought with his hand. "Say no more. I'll take care of it."

"Music to my ears, amigo. Music to my ears."

The senator tossed his napkin on his plate and pushed away from the table. He leaned back in his chair, belched, unbuckled his belt, and unzipped his pants half-way. He crooked his index finger at the brunette. "Darlin'? Come on over here and show me what's for dessert."

**

Suzanne stood beside the car outside the hotel, staring out into the distance. A warm breeze blew her hair away from her face, allowing the sun to bathe her skin. Light permeated her third eye, and she found herself drifting into another astral plane, where a vision took shape. She saw a massive ranch home, surrounded by lush green landscaping. She could see a shimmering blue rectangle, butted up against deeper blue waters. Palm trees lined the property on two sides, a circular driveway featured a three-tiered fountain in the center.

She heard unbridled, shrilly laughter, bordering on hysteria. They were high. She sensed male energy. *Like a pack of wolves. Fresh meat.* There was no dignity in the hunt. The scene from her dream replayed once again...each of the three girls fell into the water, sunk to the bottom, and bobbed to the surface. *Why did he slash the last girl's face? Why was she singled out?*

Sam rested one hand on Suzanne's shoulder. "You okay?"

She placed her hand over his. "The girl they found on the highway...she was singled out. Why do you think that was?"

"I'm not sure we will ever know."

"Let's go back to Hola Amigo—maybe someone knows something."

Sam escorted Suzanne inside the restaurant where a lunch crowd had begun to gather. The hostess sat them on the patio. As she placed menus on the table, Sam held a photo at eye level. "Ever see any of these girls?"

"Last week maybe? I'm not positive though...there's a lot of college kids that stop here on the way up to Sacramento or the Bay." She looked puzzled. "Why? They in trouble or something?"

"Three of them are missing. One was found dead on the highway."

"God, mister, that's awful!" She covered her mouth. "If I remember correctly, they were sitting with a group of guys. Let me get Cassie. She might remember." She paused. "You're not the parents, are you?"

"No." Sam offered his badge. "Anything you can tell us will help."

"Be right back," she said, and headed back inside. A moment later she returned with a dark-haired woman in her early twenties. "Tell them what you told me."

The young woman looked nervous. "I see these girls in here. They were flirting with my customers. The men buy them drinks. The mean one, he got mad at one of them."

Sam glanced at Suzanne, and pulled up a photo of Miguel Guzman. "Cassie, is this the man?"

"Si."

"Do you know why he was mad?"

"I hear her ask him about his scar. He not like that."

Suzanne sucked in an audible breath. "That explains it."

Sam grabbed her hand and held it while he spoke. "Do you know who the men were? Are they regulars?"

"They come in every couple of months," the hostess said.

"Do you have credit card receipts?"

"They usually pay on one check. I'll check, but I highly doubt it. The owner comes in on Wednesdays to collect the receipts."

Sam returned his badge to his pocket. "There's still three girls missing. This may be the break we need."

Her chin dropped to her chest. She blinked away tears. "I'll go see if I can find the charge." She linked arms with the other waitress and steered her toward the door.

"You okay?" Sam brought Suzanne's hand to his lips.

"That's why he killed her so brutally...she embarrassed him in front of the others."

"If she can find the credit card transaction, we may be able to find out who's funding the operation."

"The clock is ticking."

"For who?"

"I haven't received that exact information yet..." She pressed two fingers on her temple. "We need to find that house. Maybe we can ask a realtor."

"Excellent idea."

Just then the hostess returned with a credit card slip. "Does this help?"

"Randolph J. Belfray?" He smiled. "Thank you, may I?" Sam snapped a photo of the receipt with his phone. "Thank you, young lady, you gave us one helluva gift."

Sam threw a twenty-dollar tip on the table and left. When

they were in the car, he pulled up the photo. "State Senator Randolph Belfray."

"Why does his name sound familiar?"

"He was being investigated for money laundering a couple of years ago. Somehow the charges were dropped. From what I hear, he's a real slimeball."

**

Miguel took the blond into another room not wanting to subject her to the senator's piggy noises while dessert was being served up by the brunette temptress.

"What is your name?"

"Oksana."

"Do you like my face?" he asked.

She touched his scar with her fingertips, then lifted her dress up to show him her scar. "Do you like?" She smiled, pulled her dress back down and sat beside him on the bed.

He grabbed her hand. "Let's get out of here."

"What about my work?"

He took ten one hundred-dollar bills from his wallet. "Will this take care of it?"

She wrinkled her nose and giggled. "We go."

On the way out, the senator hollered, "Hey? Where do you think you're going?"

"I want to show Oksana the sights." The brunette flashed an envious smirk and went back to work diverting the senator's attention. When the door closed behind them her job was done.**

Sam drove to the nearest real estate office. The place was empty, with the exception of a young man in a pink suit. "How can I help you?" he asked, slamming his laptop closed.

Suzanne spoke first. "We, my fiancé and I, are looking for a ranch home on acreage, on the water. We'd like a pool, and I'd love a circular driveway..."

"Please, have a seat. Not sure we have anything that fits your description, but one never knows...I'm Jerod, by the way."

"Sam and Suzanne," she said, grinning. "I have this picture in my head of what I–we want." She patted Sam's knee. "Sorry honey, I'm very excited."

Sam took Suzanne's lead. "You want that house you saw in that magazine, don't you?"

"It's perfect."

Jerod scratched his balding pate. "There's only one home I know of in this area that fits that description." He typed in a code, waited a few seconds and turned the screen toward Suzanne. "Something like this?"

Sam leaned closer to Suzanne and pointed. "That's it, isn't it?"

Suzanne clapped her hands. "Yes! It even has the palm trees. Do you have interior photos?"

"I'm sorry, it's not for sale. At least not at this time." He swiveled the screen toward him and scrolled down. Spinning it around again, he pointed to the spec sheet. "See, it sold two years ago."

Sam frowned. "Do you know who owns it? Perhaps we can make an offer."

"Let's see," Jerod said. "I don't know. It's owned by a corpo-ration. In other words, it's a party house."

Disappointment dripped from Suzanne's words. "Really, that beautiful home is used for *parties*?"

"Parties and political entertaining."

"Sam raised his brow. "Who owns it?"

Jerod pursed his lips. "Oh, I can't tell you that. Its owner is listed as a cooperation, that's all I can say."

"I love the area, don't you, Sam?" She directed her next question at Jerod. "Do you have anything nearby that we can look at?"

Jerod beamed. "Let's see!" While he typed away, Sam reached for Suzanne's hand and squeezed it. "How did I get so lucky?"

It was Suzanne's turn to beam. "One can only hope we are both lucky to find something nearby, my love."

Jerod typed in code after code, his brow cinched in concentration. Until suddenly, "Voila!" He faced the screen toward the couple. "What about this one? It's on the same stretch of beach as the other home, and it's a two-story, but you will have the same beautiful views, and the owner just dropped the price."

"What do you think honey? Want to take a look?"

"I'd love to. It's all about the view, isn't it?"

Jerod ushered Sam and Suzanne into his Cadillac SUV, and they were off. Jerod made small talk about the area's history while Sam and Suzanne spoke their own language to each other without a word. As they drove past the home with the palm trees and circular drive, Suzanne exclaimed, "Is that my dream house? Slow down, please, let me dream a moment longer."

As they slowed, a Dodge Ram pulled into the drive. The driver got out, directing his attention toward the SUV. Jerod, rolled down the window and waved. "Just admiring your home," he said, and rolled the window back up. "Shall we move on?"

Suzanne nodded. "Yes. It's everything I imagined and more."

**

Miguel didn't buy the "looky-loo" comment from the passerby. He had caught a glimpse of the man's passenger, and the other man in the back seat. He had seen them before...but where? Suddenly his sexual urge was squelched, and he no longer wanted to play. He squealed out of the drive.

"What is wrong?" the blond whined, "No swim?"

"Change of plans."

**

Sam watched the GMC peel out of the drive. Suzanne twisted in her seat. "Did you get a good look?"

Jerod flashed a smile in the rearview mirror. "Everything okay?"

Suzanne shook her head. You know, Jerod, unless you can find me that exact house, I'm not interested in looking at anything else."

Jerod's jaw dropped. "But–" he glanced at Sam in the back seat for support.

"Sorry, Jerod. When my fiancée makes up her mind, it's a done deal. Please take us back to our car."

Jerod's peppy demeanor fizzled into sullen disappointment in seconds flat. Silence ensued until they reached the office. Sam pulled a one-hundred-dollar bill from his wallet and handed it to the agent, "Thanks for your time, man." He shrugged, whispered, "Believe me, she's worth it," and gave him a wink.

Jerod nodded that he understood and grabbed the bill from Sam. "If you change your mind..." he thrust a business card at Sam.

Once the couple was back in the car, they compared notes. "I got the license plate number," Sam said. "Not sure calling it in will do me much good."

"I sense there is someone else involved. And the woman in the car...she's not from this country..."

"How can you tell?"

"I kept seeing bursts of light, smoke...people digging through rubble."

"I'd be happy with knowing which direction they went."

Suzanne cocked her head to one side. "That way," she said pointing to the left. Sam didn't question. He turned left.

**

Miguel checked his rearview mirror every thirty seconds. *Paranoid?* Wasn't like him to be el miedoso. *Scaredy cat.* That's what his friend called him when he wouldn't light a firecracker between his teeth. His friend José did it instead and burned the tip of his nose before the firecracker dropped out of his mouth and blew off his little toe.

He glanced at the girl beside him. Beneath the make-up and expensive clothes, she was just a kid. "I'm going to drop you off at the hotel, we can party another time."

"Please—not back there." She placed a hand on his thigh. "I will do anything."

"Suit yourself, but I have unfinished business there."

"I will wait?" Her expression brightened.

Miguel shook his head. *What am I getting myself into?* He pulled into a diner a block from the hotel, dug a wad of cash from his wallet and pressed it in her hand. "This should get you home."

He watched her walk away, turning once to blow him a kiss. Then she was gone.

**

Sam hung back, witnessing what seemed to be a tender exchange between Miguel and the girl...the way he tucked her hair behind her ear...caressed her cheek...the way she blew him a kiss before making a beeline for the café.

Suzanne sighed. "He's letting her go."

"Meaning?"

"His heart is changing."

Sam gasped. "Seriously? The guy's a cold-blooded killer!"

"He's tired."

"Too bad for him." Sam pulled out of seclusion, keeping his distance.

Sam shadowed Miguel to the hotel, careful not to be seen. He parked two rows behind him, and waited until he was inside before he said, "Wait here."

"Don't you think you should have back-up?"

"Nobody I can trust here..."

"Then I'm coming with you."

"Don't be redic–" Suzanne raised one brow, halting Sam's objection.

Once inside, Sam approached the front desk. "We'd like a room. Top floor if you have it."

The man peaked over the counter. His eyes slid toward Suzanne for a quick assessment. "Can I send someone to help with your bags?"

"No need. Our car broke down, won't be fixed until tomorrow morning. If there's somewhere we can grab dinner and a couple of toothbrushes, we'll be fine."

"I see. No problem." The man reached under the counter and handed Sam a vinyl bag with an assortment of toiletries. His tone remained dry. "Compliments of the house."

Once Sam produced his license and credit card, the exchange took only minutes. The man handed Sam a set of keys, rambled through the check-in jargon, casting a critical glance at Suzanne. "Enjoy your stay."

Suzanne couldn't contain her giggle. "He thinks we're going to go screw each other's brains out!"

Sam smirked. "Wish we had time." He backed her against the elevator's brass and mirrored wall and kissed her. Her body clung to his. The door opened too soon. "To be continued?"

Her fingertips brushed his lips, but she didn't reply. Her head felt like it was filled with bees, and she attempted to shake them off. "Do you think you should call someone? Let them know you're here?"

"What's wrong?"

"I have a bad feeling about this, Sam. At least call it in." She lifted her gaze to the ceiling and closed her eyes. "Diablo is up another two floors, and he's not alone."

**

Timarie helped Paul into the safe house. Raphael carried the bags, Spence led the way, checking each room, making sure it was clear. His phone buzzed in his pocket. *Metzger.* He picked up. "Ears burning? Just got to the safe house with the Phillips and the kid...what's up?"

"I'm in Salinas with Suzanne. We tracked down Miguel Guzman."

"Excellent! What can I do to help?"

"I need you to call Salinas P.D., tell them there's an officer down...I'll text you the address."

Spence gasped. "Have you been hit?"

"No, and I don't plan to if all goes well–it's a diversion."

**

Miguel barged into one of the penthouse bedrooms, his face twisted in anger. The senator glanced up from the bed, released the fistful of brunette hair he held between his knees and pushed the young woman to the ground. "What the fuck, Miguel," he yelled. "You don't fuckin' knock?"

"You had me followed?"

"I don't know what you're talking about–get the fuck out of here–can't you see I'm busy?" The brunette gathered her clothes on the floor and scurried to her feet. "Hey! Where do you think YOU'RE going?" he bellowed. She tossed him an apologetic smirk and ran out of the room. The senator slammed his fist on the pillow and rose, closing his robe on his way up. "Happy now?"

"Why are you having me followed?"

The senator lit a cigarette, took a swig of the amber liquid he had poured earlier, and glared at Miguel. "If I wanted you dead, I would have done it a long time ago."

"I don't believe you." Miguel paused, letting his tempered words settle. "I know how you operate–remember?"

The senator took another sip of his drink, his cool demeanor turning to ice. "I don't think you know the extent of my generosity, Miguel...because if you did, you would not be standing here right now, with your highbrow attitude and false accusations."

They heard the door slam.

**

All Sam needed was a break, and lo and behold...

He stood outside the elevator waiting for the down arrow to illuminate. When it did, he pressed the button. He figured anyone leaving the penthouse would have access to the upper floor. It was a gamble, but it paid off. The elevator stopped on his floor, the door opened, and what was inside was exactly what he needed...

He could tell by the way the brunette was underdressed that she had left in a hurry. Her perfume smelled expensive, despite the mingling scent of perspiration and sex, but it was her pallor and shaking hands that caught his attention. "Do you have a key to the penthouse?"

His polite tone threw her off guard, and she stammered, her accent thick. "No-no *speaka Engalise*."

Sam stepped closer. "Don't make me use my gun." Her eyes grew large and froze. Slowly, she reached inside her purse. Sam grabbed her hand. "Allow me."

He felt around inside the purse until the passkey appeared between two fingers. "Thanks," he said, with a wink. When the elevator stopped on the main floor, Sam blocked her way. "Not just yet." He pressed the *close* button, inserted the card, and rode the car to the top floor. When the door opened, he placed her in front of him, whispering in her ear. "Be a good girl and stay put until I'm inside." She nodded, tears pooling in her eyes. "How many are in there?" She held up one finger, hesitated and held up one more. Sam smiled. "Good girl."

He inched toward the door. He could hear men shouting. The voice that spoke the loudest he immediately recognized as the State Senator.

**

Miguel's rage simmered, manifesting in a voice so low it was almost a growl. "You're seriously telling me to my face that the man and woman following me have not been ordered by *you?*"

"That's the ticket, dumbshit." The senator crossed the room, flicking ashes on the carpet. He opened the sliding door, taking an exaggerated breath of fresh air. On the exhale he seethed, "If YOU'RE being followed. I'M being followed." He swung his body around to face Miguel, his cheeks pooling with crimson, his words sizzling into a fiery blaze. "Do you understand the magnitude of what will happen if we are caught? My life will be over! I cannot, *will not* go to jail!" He banged the glass on the table, shattering it in pieces. "Don't just stand there, asshole. Go find out who is following you and kill the sons of bitches before I knock your fucking head to the next planet!"

Miguel didn't heed the senator's warning. Instead, he closed the gap between them, grabbed the senator by the back of the neck, lifted him by the folds of his bathrobe and tossed him over the balcony. *Problem solved.*

**

The voices stopped. "Call to him, Sam whispered." The

brunette shook her head adamantly. "Call the senator and I will let you go."

"Randy?" she called out. "Baby, I forgot my bag. I'm leaving now."

Sam crept closer to the bedroom door, his ears straining to catch any sound. A sudden click broke the silence, and Sam's heart raced. "Hello, Miguel." Sam pressed the barrel of his gun to Miguel's temple. "Senator? Come out here, please." Sam swiftly circled Miguel's wrists in steel handcuffs and pushed him face-down on the floor. "Senator?" Sam called again, peeking around the corner. He checked both bedrooms, but they were empty.

The sliding door to the balcony stood wide open. Shards of glass glistened on the travertine tile like scattered diamonds. Gun drawn, Sam crept cautiously through the door, but the senator was nowhere to be seem.

"Where is he?" Sam demanded.

Miguel's lips curled into an evil grin. "How should I know? Maybe he jumped."

The sound of approaching sirens lent weight to Miguel's theory, but the sinister glint in his eyes told Sam he wasn't telling the whole truth.

**

Inside a hotel room two floors down Suzanne awaited news from Sam. Her skin prickled, and she felt cold. *Please keep Sam safe*, she prayed. When she heard sirens and screeching tires outside of the hotel she ran to the window. Facing the wrong direction, she saw nothing, but behind her lids, she saw a man fall to his death, and she shivered.

**

Two police officers pushed through the crowded lobby followed closely by two paramedics maneuvering a gurney. Sam stepped out of the elevator, his firm grip on his prisoner.

One of the officers rushed up to him. "Got word there's an officer down."

"Not sure where you got that idea. I'm fine." Sam produced his badge. "I'm taking this man to Goldorado County, where he's wanted for kidnapping and murder. I'll need an escort."

The older officer furrowed his brow. "This is our county. We can take it from here."

Sam produced a folded paper from his pocket. "It's all there," he said, leaving the two officers with their heads together. He glanced back while dialing Suzanne. "Meet me in the lobby. Time to head home."

**

Suzanne trailed behind the police vehicle transporting Miguel to the Goldorado County jail in solitude, her mind vacillating between the beautiful landscape and rehashing what had transpired in the last forty-eight hours with Sam. Snippets of their love-making tangled with recollections of her past lives with Garian Dodge, Captain Bishop, and the question at hand. Did she love Sam enough to marry him?

**

Sam glanced in the rear-view mirror at his prisoner's solemn mug. Miguel's face, etched with years of living on the edge, seemed relieved. Suzanne had mentioned his heart was softening when they witnessed him let the blond go earlier, before he went back to the hotel. Perhaps she was right. Sam knew what it felt like to be tired. So much had happened in the last few years, since he had met Suzanne...so many things he'd like to undo. He wasn't ready for marriage. He took a risk when he stepped into the elevator to the penthouse. He knew he was up against a monster and that his life was on the line. Yet, he didn't give it a second thought. *Suzanne deserves more.*

~

CHAPTER FORTY-TWO

Into the Light

Sam scrolled through the news on his laptop. The media was still having a field day with senators' death. *Senator Randolph J. Belfray jumps to his death...Senator commits suicide only months before the primaries...*Headlines screamed, but there was no mention that he had been in a hotel room with a notorious drug lord moments before his death.

Frustration bubbled within Sam. They were spinning the story, feeding the public the same sanitized version while ignoring the darker, grittier truth. He leaned back in his chair, staring at the scream, lost in thought. His gut told him there was more to uncover, something that tied Belfray to a deep-seated corruption that couldn't be ignored.

Closing his laptop with a sigh, Sam knew his work was far from over. The media's whitewashed story of Senator Belfray's death only fueled his determination. There lay the problem.

Would his vow to protect and serve supersede any vow he made to Suzanne? For now, Paul, Timarie, and Raphael were safe with Miguel behind bars. That had to count for something.

**

Paul and Timarie gathered the few items they had brought to the safe house. Raphael's fate was yet to be determined, but everyone was breathing easier since Miguel's arrest.

"Why don't you stay with us?" Timarie said, placing a hand on Raphael's shoulder.

Paul nodded in agreement. "We have the room and Timarie and I could use the help getting our business up and running."

Raphael took Timarie's hand and gave it a light squeeze. "Si. If they allow me to."

Sam piped in. "He still has a lot to account for, but under the circumstances..." He glanced at Suzanne. "I'll see what I can do."

**

After leaving the safe house, Sam dropped Suzanne off at home, explaining he needed to return to his office. "I'm going to be buried in paperwork for a while, so if you don't hear from me..."

Suzanne reached for his hand. She immediately sensed something was bothering him. "Everything okay?" He shrugged it off. But his eyes couldn't lie.

"Once the dust settles, we can talk about where we're going from here."

"Yes. A lot has happened."

"What's next for you?" He asked, his eyes now diverting hers.

"I want to have another session with Diane Potter, maybe find another group of weirdos like myself–"

His lips curved into a mischievous smile and they both laughed. "Just for the record, I've never considered you a weirdo."

"I have so much to learn, Sam. And it feels good. I know you and I–" She stopped herself from going further. "Call me when you lighten your load. We can have dinner."

Before Sam could respond, Suzanne slipped out of the car and headed for her front door.

Sam watched her go, his heart heavy, his eyes burning, a lump forming in his throat. He wanted so badly to jump out of the car, take her in his arms, tell her how much he loved her. *Do the right thing*. He put his car in gear, and drove away.

**

Suzanne walked from room to room, reacquainting herself with her space. She was happy to be home. Not that Steven and Karen weren't good hosts, but this was home, the place where she had grown up. Where she and her brother remained with their Aunt Noreen after their parents died. The house held so many wonderful memories, and the thought of moving into Sam's place made her sad. She had always hoped he's transfer to the Sacramento County Sheriff's Department, so she didn't have to uproot her past.

The house was quiet. Too quiet.

She relaxed in her wingback chair, inhaling deep breaths to help her transition into an altered state. She summoned the faces that had appeared to her many times over the last few months. One of them was the young girl, Raphael's sister, Trina. Suzanne wanted, needed, to know if Trina, and the others were at peace now that Miguel Guzman, Diablo, was in custody. Her answer came with a bright light, and a host of smiling faces. When the last spirit became one with the light, Suzanne started to retreat from her trance-like state.

"Not so fast." A familiar voice made her heart sing.

"Mom—where have you been? I've missed you," she said aloud.

"You don't need me sticking in my two cents. You've been doing fine on your own."

Suzanne's heart fluttered with joy. "I'll always need you around, Mom."

"I had planned to be there when you picked out your wedding dress..."

"Planned? I have a feeling you know something I don't."

"If we knew everything before it happened, what fun would that be? Good or bad, *thy* will be done. It's the way the universe works—only your soul is privy to that which has been charted in this lifetime. Your love is a gift from God, my darling. Nothing will change what is destined to be."

CHAPTER FORTY-THREE

Destiny

"Get comfortable." Diane eased into a chair across from Suzanne, pen and pad poised in her lap. "Take a deep breath, and slowly exhale."

Suzanne followed Diane's instructions, sinking into a relaxed state. Without coaxing, she found herself in the cabin she had become familiar with, her five children playing at her feet. A blustery wind blew through the open door, followed by a handsome face.

"My darlings, how I have missed you!"

Suzanne leapt to her feet, burying herself in Captain Bishop's arms. "We have missed you as well, my love."

Captain Bishop shed his heavy cloak, and settled near the fire. "Bring me my fiddle," he called to the oldest child. The boy fetched his violin and handed it over with the greatest of care. Soon, the children were clapping to the music, and the room swelled with love.

Diane's voice filtered through the gaiety, instructing

Suzanne to step away from the situation and become the observer. "What do you see?" she asked.

"Everyone is so happy," she replied.

Caption Bishop silenced the children and brought the instrument to rest beneath his chin. When the bow struck the first chord, Suzanne knew what was to come. Heinrich Von Biber's "Rosary Sonata."

As Diane took her deeper into her reverie, Suzanne learned the Captain's surname name was Simon. She also learned that they never wed because technically she was stilled married. Despite their disappointment of not being joined in holy matrimony, they lived their lives in bliss.

**

Sam's call came at the perfect time. Suzanne's spirits, lifted by the past life regression, soared higher as she anticipated jumping into Sam's arms. "I have so much to tell you," she said, her voice bubbling with excitement.

"I have something to tell you too," he said. The lack of enthusiasm in his voice was palpable, and her heart sank.

**

When she arrived at Sam's, she walked to the door, as if in a daze. The sound of music drifted from inside, and she melted with every step she took. She knocked lightly, not wanting to break the spell. The music stopped, and Sam appeared at the door.

"You got me thinking," he said, ushering her inside. "I had forgotten just how therapeutic playing my violin could be–it's been years."

"That song–how do you know it?" She sat on the edge of the sofa, poised to listen.

"Heinrich Von Biber's *Rosary Sonata*? My father made me learn it," he said, his voice tinged with nostalgia. "He told me, 'Son, one day you will meet a woman you love, and when you play this song for her, she will return your love tenfold.'" He rested the bow on his knee, his eyes distant. 'I never dreamed—"

Her mother's words surged back, flooding her with emotions, reigniting her recollection of her past lives with Captain Bishop, and Voltaire. In that instant, she knew. The sadness in Sam's eyes revealed what his words could not. "I understand," she said. "You're having doubts about marriage."

"You're the one who says everything happens for a reason. When I stepped into the elevator to go after Guzman, I didn't know if I would return or not. I know it's what I do, it's what I'm good at—and then I thought of you—And suddenly facing death for a living seemed unfair. I love you, I will until my dying day but—"

She pressed her finger to his lips. For the first time in months, clarity washed over her. She loved him with every fiber of her being. They were soulmates, destined to withstand the test of time. Smiling, she kissed him softly. "Play for me my love, like you have so many times before."

THE END

FACTS AND BACKGROUND

**This book is based on facts, half-truths, and mostly fiction.
Here are the facts:**

According to the DEA, nearly 22,000 pounds of fentanyl were seized at US borders during the 2024 fiscal year. Data from US Customs and Border Protection suggests that seizures of fentanyl, in both powder and pill form, are at record levels. Over the past two years, seizures of fentanyl powder nearly doubled, with the DEA seizing 13,176 kilograms (29,048 pounds) in 2023. Meanwhile, more than 79 million fentanyl pills were seized by the DEA in 2023, almost triple the amount seized in 2021. Last year, 30% of the fentanyl powder seized by the DEA contained xylazine, an increase from 25% in 2022. For more information, visit www.DEA.gov.

California is home to various criminal organizations, including several Mexican drug cartels. The most prominent are the Sinaloa Cartel and the Jalisco New Generation Cartel (CJNG), both of which have a significant presence in the state.

These cartels are involved in various illegal activities, including drug trafficking, arms trafficking, human trafficking, and money laundering. For more information, visit www.Ca.gov.

My story began with a question: Why are they here? You, the reader, can draw your own conclusions.

ACKNOWLEDGMENTS

First and foremost, I want to extend my deepest gratitude to my readers and fans. Your support, kind words, and reviews mean the world to me. You inspire me to keep writing. Additionally, I owe a heartfelt thank you to my childhood friend, Nancy St. Germain, for her unwavering anticipation of my next book. Words cannot express how much that means to me.

I would also like to extend my deepest appreciation to Linda Potter, an accomplished Past Life Regressionist and Certified Hypnotherapist, for providing a guided meditation that gave authenticity to Suzanne's situation. Linda not only helped me understand the process, she also graciously agreed to portray Diane Potter, a character in the story.

My deepest gratitude goes to Astrologer Barbara Ybarra for selecting a birth date for Suzanne Cash based on her character traits and for creating an astral chart that left me astounded. The reading fit perfectly with the plot—coincidence? I think not. Barbara had no idea where I was going with the story, and I had no idea what Suzanne's chart would reveal.

I cannot thank Psychic Linda Schooler enough for allowing me to write her into my stories. Although her character's words are mine, Linda's integrity, kindness, sense of humor, and intuition shine through, making her the real deal.

Thank you to my friends Beatrice Gregory and Kirk Colvin for their invaluable edits. Beatrice, fluent in Spanish, helped make my characters sound more authentic, and her feedback was gold. Kirk, a retired creative writing professor and leader of the El Dorado Writers Guild that I belong to, has been my guiding light for 25 years.

I would also like to thank my critique group, Michele, Linda, June, Tarra, Cathy, and Rick. Their comments and support keep me on task.

Not everyone is fortunate enough to have a friend like Terry Shepherd, who continually cheers me on, promotes my work, and remains my steadfast wingman through all my creative endeavors.

Lastly, I want to extend my deepest gratitude to my family —Don, Ashleigh, Erika, and Olivia. Your love and support are the foundation upon which I build my writing. I couldn't be the writer I am without you.

ABOUT THE AUTHOR

"The best secrets are the most twisted."

Sarah Shepard's quote from 'Twisted' best describes author Dänna Wilberg's quest to unravel life's mysteries with every keystroke, on every page. Her series, *The Red Chair, The Grey Door,* and *The Black Dress* featuring psychotherapist Grace Simms, pose the question: "What do we *really* know about a person?"

Dänna's paranormal *Borrowed Time* series, about a woman who acquires a psychic gift after a near-death experience, is filled with gems from Dänna's experience producing and hosting TV show "Paranormal Connection" for over fifteen years. Her background as an award-winning script-writer and film-maker further add to the magic of her storytelling.

Wilberg resides in Northern California with her family. She loves her children, grandchildren, traveling the world, and karaoke. She loves to dance, cook, make short films, dabble in her garden, and great music. Her mantra is reach for the stars.

Visit Dänna's website: dannawilberg.com

ALSO BY DÄNNA WILBERG

NOVELS

Borrowed Time Book 1 - Broken Promises

Borrowed Time Book 2 - Missing

Borrowed Time Book 3 -Mind Games

The Red Chair

The Grey Door

The Black Dress

ANTHOLOGIES

"Stood Up" in Reckless in Texas - Metroplex Mysteries Volume II
Anthology; Sisters In Crime(SINC)/North Dallas

"Surviving the 70's" (Memoir): Tales From The Golden State of Mind
Anthology.; El Dorado Writer's Guild

"Go Big or Go Home" in Malice in Dallas 2022 -Metroplex Mysteries,
Volume I; SINC/North Dallas.

"The Vow" in The Second Corona Book of Horror Stories 2018,
Corona Books UK

"Christmas Chronicles, SINC, Capitol Crimes Anthology, 2017

"Almost Thirteen" 2015, Our Dance With Words, NCPA Anthology.
Pretty Road Press

"Borrowed Time" short story, SINC Capitol Crimes Anthology, 2008

"Fork and Knife" Farm to Foul Play Anthology: Capitol Crimes

"Amarillo by Morning" Notorious in Dallas - Metroplex Mysteries
Volume II Anthology; Sisters In Crime(SINC)/NorthDallas

"A" Invasive Species - Anthology Sisters in Crime Northern California

COMING NEXT

Dreamscape

Psychic Suzanne Cash's visions have led her into treacherous situations before, but when she begins to question whether her nightly dreams are real or a glitch in her subconscious, she is catapulted into a new realm that not only taxes her sanity, but leads her into a multiverse she cannot control.

Fellow psychic, Linda Schooler, known to some as a dream weaver, is baffled by Suzanne's vivid recollections, and does a deep dive to interpret the symbolism behind what is being manifested in Suzanne's soul.

Detective Sam Metzger's frustration mounts when Suzanne confides she is being stalked by a madman in her dreams... After all, how can he arrest a man who doesn't exist?

Or does he?

www.ingramcontent.com/pod-product-compliance
Lightning Source LLC
Chambersburg PA
CBHW070638260626
47161CB00007B/2749